OUT OF THE DARK

By

Geri Foster

GERI FOSTER

Out Of The Dark
By Geri Foster

First Edition

Copyright 2013 by Geri Foster

ISBN 978-1482032512

Editor
Andrea Grimm

Cover Graphics
Kathleen Baldwin
Lilburn Smith

Author contact information: geri.foster@att.net

This is a work of fiction. Names, characters, places, and incidents are either the product of the author's imagination or are used fictitiously. Any resemblance to actual persons living or dead, businesses, events, or locales is purely coincidental.

Acknowledgments

This book is affectionately dedicated to the courageous women who lovingly pulled me through this story one word at a time. Caroline Clemmons, Brenda Chitwood and Carra Copelin. Without you, there would be no stories in my heart to write. Thanks to you, I believe.

CHAPTER ONE

Moscow

  Emily Richards opened her hotel room, stepped inside, and secured the lock. From behind, a calloused hand clamped over her mouth, threatening to shut off her much needed oxygen. Shocked screams crumbled into muffled murmurs.

  Her muscles tightened for action and cold sweat dotted her skin.

  The man's powerful arm wrapped around her chest and pulled her against a hard muscular body.

  Emily's purse and briefcase dropped to the floor. Clawing frantically, she desperately fought off her attacker by kicking and squirming. Her elbow jabbed his ribs, rewarding her with a grunt. Unwilling to let her attacker have his way, she twisted frantically to break free.

  "Be still," a male voice hissed against her ear. The terse command shot her determination to survive into terror. "Relax, it's me, Mac. I'm not here to hurt you."

  The hand fell away, and Emily stumbled forward before catching her balance. Fists balled, she turned to her assailant. "What the hell are you doing here?"

  A light clicked on, chasing away the darkness. He stood close to her, serious and unapologetic. "I need a ride."

  "How did you get in my room?" Brushing her hair out of her face, she noticed her hands trembled like a defendant waiting for sentencing.

  He shrugged. "Easy lock to pick."

  The nerve of the guy. "You can't just barge into my hotel room. I'm here on business."

  "I know."

  "A simple phone call and a request would have eliminated the whole macho scenario. I'd appreciate that in the future."

Dressed in black from head to toe, Falcon Securities agent, John 'Mac' McKinsey stared at her with a grim expression. He always looked grim. He *was* grim. She didn't think she'd ever seen him smile.

"I'm not asking." Mac soundlessly moved across the room to the window. Pulling back the heavy drape, he peered down at the Moscow streets below. "Frank is."

She threw down the hairbrush she'd snatched off the dresser during their struggle. "That makes it okay for you to scare the living crap out of me?" Emily ran her palms down her face to keep from breaking her cardinal rule to never use the F-word.

Annoyed at Mac for helping himself to her room, Emily picked her purse and briefcase off the floor and slung them onto a nearby chair.

The so-called suite she'd booked would hardly pass for a regular room. Hotel Katarina City might claim to be four stars, but that was a matter of opinion. It consisted of one large room, the bathroom and a tiny closet. The smell of cheap air freshener hung heavy in the room.

Mac moved away from the window and retrieved a black leather valise from the floor. Ignoring her, he put the bag on the suitcase rack. While the silence grew, he slid the zipper, pulled out a pair of jeans—black, of course—and tossed them onto the bed.

"I didn't mean to scare you. I had to make sure your neighbors didn't hear anything." He nodded toward the wall between her room and the next.

He had nothing to worry about. The guests in the next room kept their TV turned up loud, twenty four-seven.

"I finished a job in St. Petersburg," Mac continued with a shrug. "I have to get out of the country as quick as I can." He took his face out of the bag long enough to glance her way. "Frank found out you were here with access to a private plane."

A couple laughing in the hall walked past the closed door. Emily moved further into the room, careful to step around her unwanted guest.

Not sure what to do, she folded her arms and said, "I just settled a case for Stromberg Chemicals. I'm scheduled to fly out tomorrow. But that doesn't mean you can come. If you're on an assignment, as the Falcon attorney, I can't get involved. You know that."

"I do, but I didn't have a choice. I'm either on that plane or dead." His glance turned to a solemn glare. "Is that reason enough?"

She pinched the bridge of her nose. *This is crazy.* "You can't just show up at the airport in the morning and get on a private jet. You need papers."

He reached into his back pocket, pulled out a passport and tossed it on the nightstand.

Eying the permit, she swallowed. "Is that even legal?"

He looked at the blue book then tilted his head. "We'll find out tomorrow."

Mac kicked off his shoes, unbuttoned his jeans then slipped off his T-shirt as he headed for the bathroom.

Emily stepped back, her lips tight. Mac had a torso right out of a muscle-man magazine. He was ripped from shoulders to stomach. Talk about a six pack. This man's body was yummy, yummy delicious, dipped in fudge and covered with sprinkles.

She fought to gather her wits. "Where are you going?"

"Shower," he called over his shoulder then shut the bathroom door.

Looking at the ceiling, Emily murmured. "God, that man is so annoying." Amazed at Mac's audacity, she fell backward onto the king-sized bed, spread eagle. "Damn." The words swished on the air of a sigh. Closing her eyes, she wondered how in the hell she'd ever clean up this mess.

The sound of her cell phone ringing brought her upright. She reached for her purse. The caller ID came up. "Hey Brenda," Emily said, trying to sound normal in the midst of male testosterone overload.

"You about done there, girlfriend?"

"I fly out first thing in the morning."

"So you finished dealing with that bunch of Russians?"

Emily chewed her bottom lip as the sound of the shower running drifted from the bathroom. "Hmm, they are a stubborn bunch, and their court system is a nightmare. I've worked so hard my brain feels deep fried."

"You okay? You sound...nervous."

"No, no," Emily quickly chimed. "Everything is fine." If Brenda knew *any* Falcon agent was showering in her hotel room, the interrogation would go on for an eternity.

"Well, I hope they're paying you lots of money," Brenda replied.

"Not enough. Only the promise of a nice long vacation when I finish has kept me going."

"So you head out tomorrow?"

Emily had to get off the phone before Mac finished his shower. "That's right."

"I can't wait. Got my bathing suit rocking ready to go." Brenda laughed. "And I've lost five more pounds."

"That's wonderful." She eyed the bathroom door.

"Yes." Brenda screamed with joy. "I know, it isn't much, but I'm loving it. Thirty pounds lighter. Imagine, skinny, little me."

"Amazing," Emily pumped her fist. "Yay." Way too weak for her friend of twenty years to believe.

"You sure you're okay?"

"I'm great. Not thinner, but I'm fine. Just fine and dandy."

"When does your plane land?"

"I'm not sure with all the time changes." The thought of Mac completely naked anywhere in her proximity sent goose bumps running a marathon up and down her spine. "I'll call you from London. My corporate ride ends there."

"I'll be packed, waiting."

"Okay."

An uncomfortable silence stretched out like a poorly written deposition transcribed by a first year law student.

"Emily?" Brenda asked.

Oh God, here it comes.

Emily forced herself to sound perky, "Yes?"

"Are you okay with the whole Stanley thing?"

Deep sadness dug its sharp claws into Emily's heart. She squeezed her eyes tight to keep the tears at bay. Despite her efforts, the pain radiated like a festering sore, robbing her of happiness and normalcy. "I'm okay."

"I mean *really* okay. And don't BS me. I can tell when you're lying."

Hot tears scalded the back of Emily's eyes, causing her to blink them away. Not tonight. Not anymore. And not with Mac in her shower. "It's not like I was madly in love with the guy." She couldn't believe her own lie.

"Emily." Brenda's voice disputed her claim.

"Look." She walked over to the bay window and stared out across the Moskva River. The bright city lights glowed against a night black as a judge's robe. The sounds of honking horns, squealing tires and hordes of people traveled all the way to the fifth floor. Rain speckled the glass. "I'm doing the best I can to get over all this. I admit, thinking about him still hurts, but nothing I can't get past. I'll be completely back to normal by the time we hit the beach in Belize."

She needed that beach to heal her hurt and end the humiliation of the last four months. Maybe the sun would dry her salty tears completely and give her the courage to show her face to family and friends again. She only had three weeks until the wedding.

"You promise," her friend pried. "I can go over there and..."

Emily shook her head. "No, I'm good."

To her relief a call broke in and she looked at the caller ID screen.

"I have go. It's another client." She unbuttoned her jacket and kicked off her heels. "Get packed. I'm taking this vacation if it's the last thing I do."

Emily switched to the new call. Frank Hamilton, Director and CEO of Falcon Securities, waited on the other end.

Shrugging off her jacket, she tossed it on the bed. "Frank?"

"Emily?" Frank's voice always sounded like her father's scolding tone when she'd been caught sneaking in after curfew. "How's Russia?"

"The weather's a little chilly even for late June. But otherwise, fine." She waited for him to mention the fact he'd sent his agent to her hotel room in the middle of the night without bothering to let her know. "I just wrapped up a deal for Stromberg Chemicals. Why?"

The long silence signaled Frank might, for the first time, be at a loss for words.

"You leaving tomorrow?" he asked.

"Yes," Emily replied. "The company jet is scheduled to leave at eight."

9

"You need to do something for me," Frank said. Well, actually commanded. He didn't sugarcoat anything, and being nice had never been his forte. But she'd comply. That's why she stayed on his payroll, that and a dozen other reasons.

"What's on your mind?" Emily asked, waiting for the whole *Mac* thing to ease into the conversation. "It's been a grueling mediation."

Again with the silence. "Are you in your hotel room?"

"Yes."

"Uh, is Mac there?"

"He was waiting for me when I walked into my room. Do I need to tell you how pissed that made me? A simple phone call, an *earlier* phone call, would have been nice."

"Okay, okay." Frank chuckled dryly. "So he was waiting in your room?"

"He scared the living hell out of me. Think of it, Frank. I'm a single woman alone in Russia and you have one of your agents blindside me in my hotel room. Are you out of your mind?" Emily's voice rose, but she didn't care.

"Ah, he scares me sometimes too, but you get used it." Frank let out a tired breath. "Get Mac on the plane with you tomorrow."

The phone went dead. Emily looked at the darkened screen and wondered why that "gotcha" feeling hadn't kicked in yet.

"You're not getting away with this!" she yelled at the phone before tossing it on the bed next to her jacket.

She'd had some dealings with Mac before and wished he'd change careers. He had a way of getting himself and Falcon Securities in unimaginable trouble, and she meant *serious* trouble. Regardless of his methods, Frank swore Mac was one of the best agents he had, and he'd backed him a hundred percent. No matter the cost.

Speaking of the devil, Mac stepped out of the shower, wearing only a towel and carrying the fresh scent of hotel soap and her Aussie shampoo. Emily's knees grew weak.

"What's all the yelling about?" he asked.

God, his body should be considered a controlled substance.

"Frank called."

Mac stopped drying his hair and looked at her. "And?"

"He wants you to fly back with me tomorrow morning."

10

Shrugging shoulders that could belong to a dedicated bodybuilder, he stepped to the bed where his pants lay. His tapered back was as well defined as the front. For a guy, he had flawless skin. No tats, no moles, and no tan lines. However, the scars told a tale of a life lived on the edge.

Heat flared from her chest up her neck to her cheeks. Her imagination went on a wild safari.

But she still didn't like him.

From behind, his gluteus maximus moved in a rhythm that soaked up all the moisture in her mouth. Her nails dug into the palms of her hands as she watched the damp towel drape perfectly across his rear, the hollow of his lower back, and cling to the roundness of his butt cheeks.

Emily prayed she didn't have drool dripping out of her mouth.

The hotel suite shrunk to the size of a small single room at a pay-by-the-hour motel where the air conditioners didn't work.

No matter how annoying Mac could be, he had the hottest body she'd ever seen. With him wearing nothing but a towel, Emily grew more intoxicated than when she'd left the bar earlier after a couple of drinks. The hotel room spun like a carousel, and she fought to keep her breathing normal.

He turned and his amazing blue eyes pierced her paper thin armor. "So, what's the problem?"

Emily stopped and tried to remember what they were talking about. She could only stare…and imagine…and wish for…and…sigh.

He frowned and cocked his head. "You okay?

Emily licked her lips and slowly swam out of her daze. She crossed her arms again. "I'm pissed you showed up in my room without asking. At least you could have warned me."

Why doesn't he get dressed? Looking at his chest and the bulge between his legs was harder than not watching his rear. The man was physically perfect. His brown hair sported a cute cowlick right in the center of his forehead, but he wore it so short no one would notice whether it had been combed or not. The darker shadow on his lower face gave him a vaguely sinister look, but he couldn't totally pull off the bad boy guise. He was simply too damn good looking.

11

"I apologize for that, but I was in a jam."

"Yeah, sure."

"If you spend time in foreign countries, Emily, you need to learn some self-defense moves. They might come in handy."

Her brows squeezed closer together. "What?"

"Figure out ways to rig your door, so you know if anyone has entered since you left. Don't fumble with your keycard. Make sure no one is standing behind you." Again, he shrugged. "You know, stuff like that."

She grew speechless for a moment then put her hands on her hips. "Normally, I don't need to be a martial arts expert because usually, a spy isn't waiting for me inside my room. Besides, I have a can of mace somewhere."

"Best place for that is in your hand."

Emily shook her head. Did she hear him right? He breaks into her room, uses her shower then scolds her for being careless?

"A gal could get in trouble pretty easily around here," Mac said. "These Russians mean business. They don't care if you're a woman. And never, ever drink when you are in a strange environment. Too dangerous."

"Go to hell."

"Famous last words?"

She narrowed her eyes at the sarcasm in his voice. "I can take care of myself, thank you." How did he know she'd had a few drinks? Oh, so the spy had been spying. "You were watching me?"

He spread out his hands, hitched his hip, and wrinkled his forehead in a mocking manner she found insulting.

"You think I'd come into this room if I didn't have a handle on the situation. Hell, no. I saw you in the hotel bar with a couple of Russians who looked the lawyer types." He turned slightly. "I checked to make sure you didn't have a traveling companion. After that, I knew it was safe for me to make myself at home."

She smacked her lips and nodded. "And I see you have."

He removed a black T-shirt from the open bag, and slipped it over his head. As his arms came up, the towel slowly slid off his hips, down his well-defined legs and puddled on the floor at his feet.

Emily's knees wobbled and she grabbed the side of the dresser to keep from falling. She refused to acknowledge his penis

12

nestling in a soft pillow of dark hair. No, try as she might, she couldn't look away.

He shrugged the shirt into place then took his jeans off the bed and stuck one leg in, then the other. He bounced slightly to settle the pants in place then snapped the front closed. When he raised his head their eyes clashed, Emily tried to breathe normally so her heart would stop racing.

No underwear?

To hide her inability to stay upright, she leaned against the wall and tried her best to come up with something to say to break the embarrassing silence.

Luckily, he made the first move and knelt beside his bag. "Since the room is checked out to a woman, can you order room service?"

She moved toward the phone on the nightstand. "What do you want?"

"I don't care as long as it's food." He glanced at her across the king-sized bed. "I haven't eaten in two days."

She lifted the receiver. "I had a club sandwich the other night. It wasn't bad. Will that work?"

"Yeah, and a beer."

"Would you rather I order a full meal?" She studied his striking features, the tightness of his jaw and the perfection of his nose. "I don't mind."

"Just the sandwich." She started to ring for service when he instructed, "Nothing to drink for you."

She put down the receiver. "I had no intentions of ordering any alcohol. I'm a big girl, Mac. I decide when I've had enough to drink, not you." She sucked in a deep breath and hiked her chin. "If I want a gallon of vodka, that's my business."

"Once I get stateside, you can go on a three-day binge. But with my life on the line, we do things my way." He turned. "And my way is for you to stay sober. Maybe you should order coffee."

Emily stalked toward him. "I'll gladly order you a sandwich and a beer. But don't do that, Mac. I don't like it, and I find it insulting."

He glared up at her. "Then don't drink." Still squatted on the floor, he took out a gun.

Standing, he pulled back a lever and clicked a bullet out of the chamber. Moving to the bed, he turned his back to her, sat on the edge and began taking his weapon apart. "Please place the order, Emily. I'm hungry."

She picked up the phone. When a voice sounded at the other end, Emily said, "This is room 533, room service, please." After a brief wait, she continued, "Yes, I'd like two club sandwiches, fries, and a bottle of local beer. Yes, on toast please. I'd also like two bottles of vodka. Thank you."

Hanging up the phone, she turned to see his reaction. No way would she consume anything else to drink, but he needed to be put in his place. With his back to her, she couldn't tell if she'd struck a chord or not, and didn't care. Nobody bossed her around. Trying not to gloat, she walked across the room to get her smartphone. She intended to call Frank and tell him to get his damn agent out of her room.

Now.

Unfortunately, she only took two steps before Mac leaped up, grabbed her by the waist, and slung her on the bed. She bounced twice.

In an instant, Emily lay on her back beneath him, his mouth inches from hers. His breath carried the minty scented of her toothpaste, suddenly, inches from her lips. A smoldering hot look in his blue eyes reached out to the woman in her.

"Emily," he crooned. "You're a very bad girl."

"Let me go, McKinsey," she said between clenched teeth. "You touch me, and I'll end your career *and* your freedom."

Mac instantly held up his right hand and propped himself on his elbow. "I'm not holding on to anything. You're free to move. And who said anything about touching?"

Only a small amount of his hard body pinned her gently between him and the bed. The masculine scent of him turned her on like nothing else ever had. With a seductive smirk, he traced his finger lightly over her lips, across her chin and down to the hollow of her neck. He leaned closer, his mouth brushing her temple. Her whole body shook. "You thinking about sex, Emily?" he asked in a voice barely audible.

Despite the fact that a trail of heat scorched her flesh, she managed to speak. "Let me up."

He rolled off her and immediately came to his feet. "I meant what I said about drinking. No more booze."

Seated on the edge of the bed shaking, she shoved her hair back and said, "Don't tell me what to do. Don't get in my face. And don't ever do that again."

On her feet, Emily went into the bathroom and slammed the door. She slumped against the side of the sink. The fresh scent of the hotel's soap filled the steamy room, reminding her that Mac's body held the same fragrance.

Every nerve in her own body drew taut, and her heart hammered like an angry judge's gavel. She stared in the mirror. In the reflection, her cheeks were red and her face glowed unnaturally. Even her eyes appeared too big, and her mouth was wet, swollen and ready.

God help her, she'd never been so turned on and so frightened of her own feelings.

Knowing nothing could be more foolish or unprofessional than to have sex with Mac, Emily splashed water on her face and blotted with the small hand towel. Her nose was buried in the soft fabric when the door swung open, and Emily jumped.

His reflection stared back at her in the mirror.

"Room service is here," he whispered. No evidence of what just happened between them lingered on his face. Nothing gave his emotions away. "Best you answer the door."

That Frank and Mac would consider pulling something this dangerous, and against everything she believed in, made her absolutely livid. She knew exactly what had to be done.

Furiously, she tossed the towel in the sink then shoved her tousled hair back. Too angry to speak, Emily marched toward the door. Once there, she pressed her palms down the front of her silk blouse, straightened her tight skirt, and squared her shoulders.

"Tell them to leave it in the hall," he ordered.

Looking over her shoulder with her hand on the knob, Emily wondered how a man so handsome could be so rude. If she were a guy, she'd beat him up. But if she was a guy, she wouldn't be so turned on.

"Stay out of sight."

With the door chain secured, Emily instructed the uniformed bellman to leave the food cart in the hall. The food and drinks would be an extra "thank you" from Stromberg.

At the sound of retreating footsteps, Emily opened the door and stepped into the empty hall. The delicious aroma from the food tray made her tummy growl. She pushed the cart over the threshold just as Mac came out of the bathroom.

At one time, Emily had had a very normal mediation practice, until she'd accepted Falcon Securities as a client. Nothing had been normal since. She'd never fought so many legal battles in her whole career. And oh, the trouble those agents got into. It took every legal skill she possessed to keep them all from being locked up somewhere.

With the food in the room and the door locked, Emily snatched her cell phone off the bed and speed dialed Frank Hamilton.

After several failed attempts, she finally managed to hit the right buttons. Frank barked a greeting.

"This isn't working, " Emily said. "You have to find him another way out of the country. I could be arrested, disbarred, lose everything I have. I won't even go into the illegal issues this could turn into." She looked at Mac sitting on the bed eating his sandwich. "And of course you know he's the biggest jerk in God's creation, don't you?"

Frank's silence made Emily want to crawl through the phone and strangle the director for putting her and her career in this horrible situation.

"Yes, he's a pain in the ass, Emily." Frank sighed. "He took out a Russian informant, and his cover was blown. Mac has to get out of that hellhole ASAP. Look, it's not like I'm asking you to create world peace or anything."

Turning her back to Mac, Emily continued, "Frank, if I'm caught with him, it would be the end of everything for me. And I can't express how much I want to avoid a Russian jail." She glanced over her shoulder. Mac didn't seem concerned with the conversation. "I don't like him, Frank."

"He's a brave and noble man, Emily. All I'm asking you to do is get him out of there. If, and I mean if, *anything* should happen, I've got your back."

She let out a tired breath. "I can't."

"Emily, you live a perfectly normal life and never deal with terrorists, or human traffickers, or drug cartels. Mac and men like him are dedicated to making sure you never see the really, really bad guys. That man has risked his life for this country and your freedom so many times I can't keep up with the paperwork." While in full ex-CIA Director mode, Frank kept his voice calm and conciliatory, while leaving no doubt his was the final word. "Now, do what you can to help him get back safely."

Nervously, she swallowed. She knew better than anyone what these men risked on every mission. Their bravery and courage would never be displayed for the public to see. There was no applause or gratitude. Everything these agents did remained shrouded in darkness.

She held Mac's only way out of Russia, and she'd hate if anything happened to him or any of the agents.

Still...

Emily massaged the knot of nerves between her eyes. No matter what Frank said or how selfish she felt, Emily had to do the right thing. As calmly as she could collect herself, Emily said, "Frank, I resign as your company attorney. I will do my best to get your agent safely stateside. Once that's done, you won't see me again." She took a deep breath. "But you will see my final bill."

That said, she threw the phone at Mac. He caught it, his eyes wide with surprise.

"Yeah," Mac said, around bites of his sandwich. He took a swig of beer. "I haven't heard from Brody." Eyes narrowed, Mac pinned her with an annoyed glare. "I've said I'm sorry. Obviously, that's not enough. Should I cut my throat and bleed for her?"

Silence.

"I'm not the kind of guy who can pull that off, Frank. If circumstances were different. Maybe if it were Archuletta. But not me. I can't suck up to anyone. I'll walk back to Dallas first."

Emily turned and sat in the desk chair, not caring what the two men discussed. She was through. Her part done.

"Besides, she's the problem." Mac lowered his gaze then grumbled, "Don't worry."

Mac ended the call and placed Emily's phone on the nightstand.

The heater kicked on, and the hum of the fan was the only sound in the room. Emily looked at the two bottles of vodka and felt foolish. But not foolish enough to let Frank and Mac get away with their little stunt. This whole thing could blow up in her face. While Mac was allowed to operate under the radar, she wasn't, nor did she want to.

Exhaustion started at her bare feet and crawled all the way to her brain.

"Do you want your food?"

"I'm not hungry," she replied.

Mac reached over and took half her sandwich. When he finished the beer, she stood, went to the small fridge, and took out two cans of Diet Coke.

She put one on the food cart next to him then flipped the other open and took a deep swallow. The soft drink burned its way down her throat, but tasted delicious.

"Does the plane land in Heathrow?"

Emily took another sip. "Yes."

"When we get to London, you can go your way and I'll go mine."

"Frank said to get you stateside."

"Ah, he always says that." Mac opened his drink.

"You'll go to Dallas willingly, or I'll drag you."

Mac waved insignificantly at her threat. "We'll see."

"What's wrong with your hand?" she asked.

As if the injury were no more than a piece of lint on his clothes, Mac looked at the battered knuckles on his right hand. "I hit a guy." He leaned back on the pillow.

Another wound of valor.

"I haven't slept in a few days. Mind if I stretch out on the bed and snooze a little?"

He'd gone days without rest, another hit to her conscience.

"No, go ahead."

"I'll stay on this side if you want to come to bed." He motioned to the opposite side.

Come to bed.

18

That was the sexiest invitation she'd ever heard. To what? She didn't even want to imagine. Instead, she squeezed her legs together and tried to forget the mesmerizing warmth of being beneath Mac McKinsey. "I'll pass."

With the drink can empty, Emily leaned back in the chair and wondered if this night would ever end.

CHAPTER TWO

What a fucking nightmare.

Mac ran his hands over his face and would give anything to be somewhere else. Frank was pissed, and if Emily Richards had a weapon, she'd probably shoot him.

Yet, he had no one to blame but himself.

Only a stupid agent would jack with the company's attorney. Apparently, he fit the bill.

He'd thought his mission routine. Relieved, for once he'd pulled an easy assignment. But in a matter of seconds, it went from easy-peasy to a cluster fuck.

His assignment had been a classic intel recon. Get the data from his contact, create an exit for the CI then haul ass. Instead, after leaving the informant's apartment, Mac hit the stairwell and found three bad asses waiting at the landing.

In the end, Mac ran for his life. He managed to hitch a ride before finally ending up in Emily's hotel room. Mac shook his head at the irony.

Beneath lowered lids, he watched Emily move across the room. In his opinion, she was the most dangerous woman he knew. Hell, that just proved he was male.

Besides, all the agents at Falcon thought Emily was hot, beautiful too. But also, sophisticated, smart, and had a body that could make a man come in his pants. Few women came so nicely wrapped.

The problem with all that? Women like Emily had *forever* tattooed across their forehead, and men like him stayed far, far away.

Until tonight, he and Emily had exchanged few words. Usually Frank briefed Emily about the problem they were facing, and she'd ask the agents a few questions. They'd discuss strategy, but during mediation, agents rarely talked. And nobody celebrated afterwards.

Gracefully, Emily glided to the large window overlooking the city of Moscow. He remembered the mysterious scent of her perfume when he had her beneath him. Now, that essence drifted with her as she strolled around the room. Or had it been seared in his brain?

Mac's whole body trembled as he took a deep breath. No surprise, Emily rattled his primal need for sex and woke up his body's testosterone. He laid back and enjoyed the way she moved. Soft. Lithe. Effortlessly. A style all her own. Not fast, not slow, but lean and sexy as hell.

With her back to him, Mac admired the curve of her ass as he adjusted the front of his jeans and hoped she couldn't see the extent of his desire. Besides, Emily wasn't available…or was she?

Mac sat up. "Where's the rock?"

She turned, arms crossed, a look of surprise plastered on her pretty face. "What?"

He nodded toward her empty ring finger. "The engagement ring."

Emily hid her hand behind her. "I…I called it off.

"The wedding?"

Emily's gaze dropped to the floor, and she backed against the wall, chewing her bottom lip. "Yes." She looked up, daring him to interrogate her.

Mac cocked his head and leaned forward. Her long auburn hair fell gently against the sides of her face, making her appear small and *hurt*.

She'd also lied through her perfect, white teeth.

Something bad had happened, and he sensed Emily had come out the loser. That saddened Mac in a strange, unfamiliar way.

She turned back to the window. "Who's after you?"

Mac couldn't take his eyes off her ass.

"Are we in danger?" She glanced over her shoulder.

"Not sure. As far as I know, I covered my tracks pretty well."

She turned, her eyes widening. "But you're not sure?"

"In my line of work, few things are certain."

21

With a nod, she sat in the cushioned, straight-back chair facing him.

Closer now, Mac captured the scent of her spicy perfume again and sweat popped out on his forehead. God, he wanted her. Never good to want what you can't have.

Getting comfortable, Emily shifted slightly, smoothing the gray skirt over her shapely thighs. "I guess we'll find out tomorrow when we try to board the plane."

He gruffly cleared his throat. "If trouble is coming, it'll hit tonight."

Their gazes collided and her posture stiffened. "I see," she said, as if that were even remotely possible. She turned to where he'd placed his Glock on the nightstand and swallowed.

Mac prayed he wouldn't have to use the gun.

Trying to anticipate her reaction to a surprise attack, he mentally made plans to calm her if necessary. Weary from the last three days, Mac rolled over and bunched the pillows beneath his head. "I don't know the timetable, but I think we should be in London tomorrow afternoon."

With the private jet, they wouldn't have to go through Customs. Just a couple of clerks checking passports and stuff like that…until they landed.

"Look," he said, flopping on his back. "I know the risk you're taking, and I'm sure Frank will compensate you well." He searched her face. "Saving my ass goes beyond the scope of your job."

Her chuckle turned the inside of his chest warm. Her delicately arched brows rose. "Really?" As if unaware of her actions, she licked her lips.

Mac thought he'd never seen anything sexier. Her ex-fiancé was the dumbest bastard on earth to let this woman go. He knew he should look away, but couldn't.

"I'll be glad when we get back to Dallas," Emily said, rubbing her arms.

"You were drinking at the bar, Emily. What were you celebrating?" He looked at the bedside clock—nine-thirty Moscow time. When he glanced back to say something else, the look on her face stopped him.

She stalked toward him, mouth tight, eyes narrowed. Oh shit, what had he done now? She was pissed. "I'll do what I can."

"Okay," Mac said, knowing he'd gone one step too far, but not sure how he'd managed to get her so upset.

"Don't you ever spy on me again." Eyes flashing with anger, she rounded on him, her face inches from his. She put one knee on the bed and leaned forward. Apparently without a single thought for her well-being. She went further by jabbing him in the chest with an index finger.

Few people had the nerve to do that, and none before her had ever gotten away with it.

"You're an agent with no way out, but me." She thumbed her chest then cast him a nasty look. "Think about that, Mr. McKinsey. Without me, you're dead. So be nice." She waved her hand in the air. "Or else." Then she looked at him. "I have business connections in this country, and I have clients to consider. I'm not going to let you or Falcon interfere with that."

The glare she shot him would stop a watch. Her pretty blue eyes were a little glassy, and they dared him to open his mouth, but he wasn't that crazy.

Besides, how had they gone from "okay" to "I want to smack you", so fast? Evidently satisfied by his silence, she spun around and moved to the window.

After letting out a tired breath, Mac laid his head back. This was one screwed up day. Emily and her vodka shots weren't helping.

It troubled him that he needed her. He didn't like relying on anyone. But without that private plane, he didn't stand a chance in hell.

Now on top of everything else, Frank insisted he convince Emily not to resign. How was he going to accomplish that when he couldn't keep his mouth shut long enough to be civil? Much less talk her into something.

From day one, they had been like storm and calm, wine and beer, and high heels and combat boots. They simply didn't mix. Also from the beginning, she'd made his heart race and his libido stand up and salute.

"I apologize," he said and meant it. "I didn't mean to be such an ass." He sat up. "That's the second time I've said I'm sorry. You know I had no choice coming here. If I had, I would be someplace else. I don't have to tell you how Frank feels about messing with civilians."

She sniffed a little, but appeared reluctant to reply. "I accept your apology. Let's try to make the best of this situation until we get to Dallas."

"Deal." He pointed to her laptop. "Can I borrow that?"

Emily opened the computer, powered it up then typed in her password. She handed it to him without protest.

He pulled up the secure Falcon website. After typing in his password, Mac took the thumb drive from his pocket and uploaded the intel he'd managed to get out of St. Petersburg.

"No porn sights," she instructed.

"There you go again, Emily." He grinned, shaking his head. "Always thinking about sex."

She glared at him and straightened her spine. "I do not."

He smirked, put the thumb drive back in his pocket and shutdown the computer. Thankful she wasn't asking too many questions, Mac put the laptop on the nightstand next to his weapon. "Maybe it's just the booze."

Emily stomped her foot. "I am not drunk. I had two drinks. Now stop saying that."

Swallowing a chuckle, Mac held up his hands in surrender and closed his eyes.

"Mac…"

With a playful attitude, he ran his pinched thumb and forefinger along his mouth. "My lips are sealed."

"Ha, what's the likelihood of that?"

"Bad, mean Emily," he said, squinting his eyes and smiling.

She put her hands on her hips and tossed her long hair over her shoulder. "See, less than ten seconds."

The ringing cell phone stopped their banter. After he swallowed, they exchanged guarded glances. "Answer it," Mac said.

"Hello." Holding the phone out to him, she said, "It's Tony Archuletta."

"Yeah," Mac said into the receiver, still warm from her touch.

"Hey, Mac, I wanted to bring you current with Ramón Marino. I've searched every inch of Venezuela. He's nowhere to be found. I spoke to a couple of the locals. They said he might have lit out for his hometown in Columbia."

"My gut tells me Marino is behind my cover being blown here. It's too damn convenient for those three goons to show up out of the blue."

"What about Viktor Pertinolf? He's always on the prowl for Falcon agents."

"Yeah, but it's you he wants. And I think Brody had Viktor pretty well locked down before my mission started."

"Could be bad karma."

Mac ran his fingers through his hair. "It could, or there is some shit going on we don't know about yet."

"That's more like it." Tony chuckled. "I understand you're hitching a ride with Emily Richards."

"Only because she's here on business and has access to a private plane."

Tony whistled. "Lucky guy." Mac heard another chuckle.

"You're as bad as Frank. You both think you know so much."

"It's all part of the job, buddy," Tony said. "Back to the subject, how'd you get the agency's attorney to let your bad ass on a plane with her?"

Mac tossed Emily a taunting smile and winked. "Tony, you crush me, bro. You know how charming I am." Mac laughed. "She's decided to share."

Emily glared then turned away.

"Okay, good luck," Archuletta replied. "I need to ditch this phone. Catch you on the other side."

After disconnecting the call, Mac handed Emily the phone. "How is he?"

"On his way out of Venezuela."

"You guys get around."

"Worldwide."

Ready to relax a little, Mac leaned back. Since he'd showered and eaten, he felt better. His life may still be on the line, but no one had a gun pointed at him right now. Relief loosened his shoulders. After this job, Mac thought he might take a little R&R. It'd been a long time since he'd just kicked back and watched the waves roll in.

Stretched out, he propped his hands behind his head and closed his eyes.

"Are you going to sleep there?" Emily asked.

"I might take a quick nap." Knowing there was no way in hell she'd fall for it, Mac patted the other side of the king-sized bed. "Like I said earlier, there's plenty of room for both of us." He opened his eyes. "I promise to behave myself, no matter how much you think about sex."

Arms locked, she stood in the middle of the room tapping her right foot. "Stop that. You're doing your best to make me uncomfortable, and it's just pissing me off. Since I'm your ticket out of Russia, I suggest you find a way to control that mouth of yours."

"I'm going to sleep. Do you have a wakeup call in?"

"Yes, I put one in this morning."

"Okay, then…" Mac started to say.

Suddenly, the door to their room crashed open and two guys rushed in. They were armed and ready to kill.

Glock in hand, Mac fired twice and took out the men before the intruders' eyes could adjust to the dim light.

When Emily didn't respond quick enough, Mac jumped off the bed and grabbed her arm. "We have to leave now. It's going to get real ugly."

"What?" she screamed. "This isn't ugly?"

"I've seen worse." He released her.

Obviously, she hadn't. No doubt, nothing like this ever happened in the normal world, especially hers. With her nice orderly life, Mac figured she'd probably never witnessed anything firsthand worse than maybe a car accident.

"What's going on?" Emily had her hands to her mouth, her eyes the size of saucers.

"Nothing. Get the pilot on the phone. We leave now." Grabbing what he could, Mac snatched up his bag and threw in an assault rifle that had belonged to one of the Russians then Emily's briefcase, laptop, and purse, while she slid on her shoes and grabbed her jacket.

Shouldering the bag, he jammed his Glock in the back of his waistband and pulled his shirt down to conceal the weapon. He took her cell phone off the dresser, handed it to her and repeated, "Get the pilot on the phone while we move."

Mac inched around the corner where the door used to be and checked the well-lit, carpeted hall. Clear.

Taking Emily by the hand, he led her out behind him. They darted for the stairwell. Security would investigate the sound of gunfire, and Mac didn't want to be anywhere around when that happened.

Down two flights of concrete stairs, Mac stopped and leaned Emily against the cinderblock wall in the narrow shaft. He took her chin in his hand. "Listen, we don't have time for you to go screwy on me. Call the pilot now."

"I don't know...I don't know."

"Emily." He shook her gently. "Call him and tell him to ready the fucking plane. You're going to get us both killed."

With shaking fingers, Emily punched several numbers before she actually got anyone on the line. "Mr. Malloy," she gasped. "There is an emergency and we need to leave tonight."

Listening for any sounds that they were being chased, Mac hugged the wall and kept an eye on the doorway. Nothing so far.

"I understand," Emily said. "You have certain papers to file and all that, but we'll be at the airfield in an hour. And you'd better fucking be ready to leave!"

She disconnected the call and looked at him for approval then her eyes widened and her hand covered her mouth. "God, I dropped the F-bomb."

"You did good. Now stay close to me. When we go through the door to the lobby, we need to act as calm as possible."

"Mac, I'm scared."

"Nothing to it, Em. Stay close. I won't let anything happen to you." He looked into her eyes then brushed his lips against hers. "Not ever."

The kiss sent a spark of something strange and wonderful through his body, and the shadows in her eyes relayed she'd felt something as well.

They made their way to the ground floor. Mac forced a smile. "This will be the easiest thing you've done all evening."

Arm and arm, Mac felt her body trembling. "You're okay, Em," he said calmly. "Don't fall apart on me now."

They entered the wide lobby with its tall white columns and comfortable seating areas then headed for the door. Her body crushed against his side.

Just as the front desk came into view, Mac turned away and looked down at Em as they continued toward the revolving door.

The uniformed doorman tipped his hat when they walked out into the misting rain. The sidewalk and streets were wet and black.

A police car, with piercing sirens, pulled up in front of the hotel. Two armed men jumped out of the Volvo and darted inside. Mac turned in time to keep them from getting a look at his face.

Careful not to draw attention, Mac pressed Emily's head to his shoulder and steered her down the sidewalk to the corner. They turned and melted into the darkness.

CHAPTER THREE

Grasping Mac's hand, Emily swallowed a scream. While recalling the scene in the hotel, Emily's lips trembled and her knees wobbled. She longed to run like a demon chased her, but valiantly reined in that impulse as they strolled toward the exit. The fear of losing control and turning into a hysterical maniac tugged at her mind.

More than anything, she wanted to curl into a ball until the horror passed. But she knew one wrong move on her part could get them killed. Unable to do anything but follow Mac's lead, she shivered like a dog left out in the cold and stayed close.

When they had exited the hotel, cool night air slapped her in the face. The chilly temperature revitalized her briefly and braced her against the terror, but did little to calm her nerves.

As if in a daze, Emily marched stiffly beside Mac and prayed no one followed. With every step, she had to fight the urge to glance back because to do so could call unwanted attention to them and prove fatal.

A breath caught in her throat when Emily realized she'd never seen Mac like this. Fast, cunning, deadly…and totally in control. Not a hint of concern or worry wrinkled his brow or affected his outward demeanor. It scared the hell out of her in one sense and yet eased her traumatized mind in another.

After a block, Emily no longer resisted the urge and looked back. She turned at the scream of more sirens and saw emergency vehicles with flashing red lights, speeding toward the hotel.

Again, she wanted to break into a run, but Mac gripped her hand and gave the appearance they were doing nothing more than taking a stroll in the night air. That he carried his duffel bag meant nothing in this area of hotels and tourists.

As the hotel faded into the mistiness, they turned east toward Gorky Park. Mac hailed the only cab in sight. When the small yellow vehicle stopped, Emily gladly jumped inside to get out of the elements and away from the scene that fueled her fear. She hoped the metal surrounding the vehicle would somehow shield her from harm.

After the door shut, she wrinkled her nose. The interior reeked of sweat, booze, and vomit. Her stomach rebelled violently, but she knew she had to control herself. She swallowed hard and rolled down the window to take a gulp of fresh air.

Finally, her heart rate slowed.

"Where is the plane?" Mac asked.

"It's at the private section of Sheremetyevo Airport." She pointed to the sign stretched above the highway. "Exit here. This will take us to the right terminal."

While her brain refused to work fast enough to translate, Mac repeated what she'd said in Russian as smoothly and calmly as a judge rendering a verdict.

As they headed in the right direction, Mac slumped back in the seat and pulled her against him. She hated being weak and frightened. Yet, she clutched Mac's shirt in her fists and buried her face in his chest. Nothing had felt better or more reassuring in her whole life. The strong, steady beat of his heart melted her fear like warm sunlight on snow. At the moment, his hands gently rubbing her back soothed her more than any professional massage.

"It's okay, Em," Mac said. "It'll all work out."

She looked up as the driver maneuvered one of Moscow's busier streets and mingled with the usual airport traffic. To add to her stress, the slow drizzle hindered their progress, but at least they were moving in the direction that would get them safely out of the country.

Moments later, they arrived at their destination. Rain had turned the private airport's tarmac black, and fog flirted with the horizon. Hopefully, they'd get out before the weather crippled their escape.

Recognizing the pilot, Emily exhaled and found the courage to release Mac from her death grip and get out of the cab. Sam Malloy stood with the airport officials, signing the necessary papers for them to leave. Ed Myers, the co-pilot, hadn't arrived yet. Taking her purse from Mac's bag, Emily found her wallet and paid the cabdriver. Then she and Mac moved toward the small terminal

She smiled at the customs agent and presented her papers. It shouldn't have surprised her that Mac's documents were in order. Falcon worked wonders when it came to protecting their agents.

"Welcome, Miss Richards and Mr. Finch," said the clerk. She gave Mac a questioning glare. He winked. She wanted to smack him.

As they left customs, Emily leaned closer. "Finch?"

"Tony is our resident passport guy. At the moment, I'm Atticus Finch." He looked at her and smiled. "To Kill a Mockingbird…?"

"I guess that's better than Elmer Fudd."

"Oh, I've been him before." Mac laughed. "Tony has a bitch of a sense of humor."

"Sounds like it."

They moved quickly through all the necessary channels and were waiting for the final okay to leave.

With a nod of approval, Mac and Emily departed the terminal and walked a hundred feet to the waiting plane. She looked up the portable stairs to the entrance of the plane. "I think that open door is the best thing I've seen all day."

"Hey," Mac teased. "I'm offended by that remark."

Before they could take the first step, Sam Malloy, the pilot walked over to them. "Who is he?" he asked, flipping his pen against the clipboard. "I need to give the authorities the names of all passengers."

"He's Atticus Finch. We've been through customs already. Where is Ed?" she asked, hoping to distract Sam before he questioned Mac's fake name. She peered toward the parking lot. "I made it clear we leave tonight…now."

"He couldn't be reached, but we'll be fine." Sam nodded toward the plane. "It's a Cessna 500," he explained, as he studied the overhead clouds. "There's no problem flying solo, as long as the weather doesn't become a hazard."

Sam handed the ground crew the clipboard then walked up the stairs to the plane. Emily made sure she and Mac were right behind him. With the engines revving, Emily couldn't help taking one last look back at Moscow.

What if there were more bad guys?

What if the authorities found out Mac was a special agent?

What if they didn't make it into the air?

At the entrance of the plane, Sam turned and stopped them. "Am I to assume you have cleared this with Stromberg?"

"I'm sure it will be fine," Emily managed. "I'll settle everything with the CEO when we land."

"You seem awfully nervous, Miss Richards," Sam said, his eyes narrowed with suspicion. "Is anything wrong?"

Emily took a deep breath and inhaled the damp air deep into her lungs. Slowly, she exhaled through her mouth. She released her clenched fists and smiled a grimace.

"No, nothing," she replied, mentally forcing her voice to remain calm. "I just finished my business early and decided to leave tonight. I have a briefing in Dallas, and I'd like to get there in time to prepare."

Sam looked at Mac then walked back down the stairs. "I'll be right back."

Emily watched with dread as he practically ran toward the customs office, cell phone pressed to his ear.

"I think he knows you're not legitimate. He's probably calling the police."

"Don't worry. We're okay."

"How can you say that?"

Mac shrugged. "Take it easy, Frank and the CEO of Stromberg are close. Do you think I would have been sent to you if Frank didn't have everything planned out?"

The pilot returned and instructed Mac and her to make themselves comfortable.

Stunned, Emily could only stare. "What just happened?" she turned and asked Mac.

"My guess is he called his boss."

Emily shook her head. "So everything must have been in order."

"I told you."

Inside the plane, Mac flung his bag in the captain's chair in front of him then dropped into the large two-seater in the middle aisle.

Emily reached up and took several pillows from the overhead bin and handed two to Mac before taking her seat. It would just be the three of them. Sam would fly them to Heathrow, and they'd catch a commercial flight from there.

After they were in the air, she'd make arrangements to get them home. Also, Brenda needed to know where she was, as well as her office staff, and her sister, of course.

For now, Emily couldn't keep her eyes off Mac. The last time she'd seen him he had been knock down gorgeous—decked out in a sharp gray pin-striped suit with a red power tie and a crisp white shirt, Rolex and all. By all outward appearances, he'd looked every bit the well-tailored businessman. Certainly not a man accused of punching Mexico's ambassador and holding him at gunpoint until he secured a team member's release.

No, not Mac.

Of course, she knew Mac didn't wear a suit and tie every day. Not in his line of work. She guessed camouflage, black T-shirts, and combat boots.

The things these elite warriors managed to accomplish would astound the American public. But again, they kept the country safe and constantly battled evil forces.

Sam came to see that they were secure. "I talked to Stromberg and everything is fine. We'll be leaving any minute. We're waiting for the okay from the control tower."

Emily looked out the window at the wet tarmac and wondered what had happened back at the hotel and why. Who wanted to kill Mac? And why put all those innocent people in harm's way?

Needing a drink, Emily stood and went to the fridge in the galley. She brought back two bottles of water and handed one to Mac. He took several gulps before looking at her with a smile on his lips.

The luxurious interior of the plane was top of the line. Oversized, beige leather recliners, an eating area, a lounge, a fridge full of food, and cupboards stocked with liquor. There was even a nice warming oven for hot towels.

No galley, but there was a great sound system and pillows. Lights everywhere, but you could darken the cabin for sleep with the touch of a button.

A scent of clean vanilla and expensive leather drew her into a nice quiet zone.

Even with all the comforts of home, she was still wet and dirty.

The radioed voice from the cockpit announced they were to taxi to runway number two. It had seemed they'd waited an eternity. The plane crept backwards from the terminal, and Sam lined them up perfectly for takeoff. Soon, they'd be on their way home.

"What the hell?" Sam shouted.

Emily released her seatbelt and moved to the cockpit. Two vehicles raced toward them from the right. Sirens blared, red lights flashed. In the lead car, a man hung out the window with a huge weapon pointed at them.

Sam hit the brakes as a loud boom shook the aircraft. Unable to tear her gaze away, Emily watched as a large projectile with a fiery tail streaked toward them.

CHAPTER FOUR

Outside the window of the Cessna, Mac spotted two cars speeding across the tarmac toward their aircraft. An RPG hung out the side window of one vehicle with the business end pointed right at them.

Cold sweat popped out of every pore on his body, and his heart pounded like a jackhammer. How in the hell were they followed? By who? And why? After years of being an agent, Mac had an instinct about these things, and right now, nothing added up.

Fearing their chances were slim to zero, Mac shot from his seat and darted to the small cockpit. Taking the co-pilot's seat, he grabbed the throttle and slammed it forward, accelerating the aircraft's speed toward takeoff.

The engines roared as the plane raced down the runway close to 180 mph, body-slamming everyone backwards. A missile whizzed past the windshield and crashed into a cargo hanger. The smell of jet fuel filled the cabin of the small plane. Smoke and fire shot skyward and made him cover his eyes against the flare. Before the shooter could reload, Mac revved the engines again.

"Are you bloody insane?" Sam demanded.

Pulling the yoke toward his chest, the nose of the jet lifted, taking them airborne. Mac secured his seat belt, praying whoever was in the tower radioed for other aircraft to get the hell out of the way. The plane bucked as another RPG whizzed over the left wing. Between Emily's screams and Sam's blustering, Mac kept climbing for altitude.

Sam struggled to pry Mac's fingers off the throttle.

"What in God's name are you doing?" Emily screamed.

"Getting us out of here."

"Sir!" the pilot shouted as he wrestled to gain control of the plane. "I don't know who you are, but I'm responsible for this aircraft," he argued in his clipped British accent. "I insist you return to the airfield this instant."

"No fucking way," Mac said, stiff arming the pilot away from the controls. "Em, put your phone on speaker and dial Frank."

When he heard no response, Mac glanced at Emily. Judging by her wide-eyed expression and rapid breathing, she appeared to be stunned speechless and on the verge of hyperventilating.

"Any day now, Em," Mac bit out between clenched teeth.

Visibly trembling, she nodded then proceeded to drop her cell phone...twice.

"Now, Em!"

"I'm trying!" she screamed as the call connected.

"What the hell is going on there?" Frank's voice demanded through the tiny speaker, getting their attention like the deafening blast from a canon.

"Frank, it's Mac."

"So, I gathered. Where are you?"

"We've been chased out of Russia. We're in the air, but the pilot wants to return back to the airport. We can't do that and live to fill out all the damn paperwork."

"Okay," Frank said. "What's your name, pilot?"

Smashed against his side of the cockpit, the older man replied, "I'm Sam Malloy. I work for Stromberg Chemicals. Sir, I can't allow this aircraft to be hijacked. I demand you instruct whoever this person is to release the controls immediately."

"Sam, I've spoken with Walter Metcalf, the CEO of Stromberg, and he's assured me of his company's complete cooperation with getting my man out of there." Frank paused. "Now, I'm sure you have to check this out, if you haven't already. But I'd advise you to go ahead and fly the plane because last I checked, Mac isn't a pilot."

"What!" Em and Sam screamed at the same time.

"He's a damn good swimmer," Frank added. "But he's no pilot."

Mac snorted at the revelation. Maybe he couldn't fly, but he'd gotten their asses out of there before someone managed to kill them.

Releasing his grip on Sam, Mac hoped the pilot wouldn't have a heart attack before getting his seat back.

"We all good?" Frank asked.

Securely back in control of the plane, Sam clutched the controls like a sixteen-year-old with his first lover.

"Yeah," Mac replied.

Holding him hostage with her mean mediator glare, Em grabbed his arm. "That was a stupid thing to do," she said through tight lips. "We could have been killed." She released him only to squeeze the bridge of her nose. A very perfect nose.

He leaned down and looked out the window. "We're not out of the woods yet. The only reason another missile isn't heading our way is the guy's probably out of ammo."

"Still, you don't know how to fly a plane, Mac."

"I don't know how to do a lot of things, but that doesn't keep me from doing what I have to do to stay alive until help arrives."

Arms crossed beneath her breasts, Emily turned and stomped to her seat. "You're insane."

Mac scrubbed his face and rubbed his eyes. *Maybe she's right, but when I find out who's behind this mess, somebody's going to die.*

Damn, his heart hadn't settled down yet. Out of adrenaline, the nice leather recliner looked tempting as hell. On his way out, he closed the door between the cockpit and the cabin. "I'm tired."

"I'm sure you are after that harrying ride you just gave us."

Smiling, he looked over at her. "Least I sobered up your sweet ass."

Opening her mouth to obviously correct him, she stopped, closed her lips tight and shook her head instead. Nostrils flaring, she savagely yanked on the hem of her soiled, silk blouse, pressed her hands down the front of her linen skirt then turned away like she'd smelled something foul.

"I had two drinks." The glare she threw at him over her shoulder double dared him to challenge her.

He only noticed how the light reflected off the softer shades of red in her hair, how her gorgeous eyes sparkled, and how her fresh complexion glowed.

No. He changed his mind. Gorgeous didn't come close to describing those eyes. He couldn't think of a word that would. Up went the tempo of his heart rate again.

37

He chuckled at the thought of Em stepping out into the unknown, tight laced and politically correct. Mac enjoyed this other side of her. Em was one smart lady. And he kind of liked that she didn't take his shit.

Damn, he wanted her. While he'd never admit a thing…he almost liked her.

Mac dropped into the comfortable recliner beside Emily, laid his head back, and took a deep breath. If she ever suspected how damn scared he'd been, she'd faint. Nothing in his arsenal of good ideas had assured him he'd get off the ground. He hated to think what would have happened if he'd failed, worse…if the other guys had succeeded.

After being up for three days, his head banged hard as a rapper's boom box. Stomach wasn't much better. It turned somersaults like a gymnast at the Olympics. His tongue stuck to the roof of his mouth, and energy seeped from his body as the events of the last three days finally caught up with him.

"I can't believe you tried to fly a plane with two innocent lives aboard."

He opened his eyes. "I could have let the RPG take us out."

"You could have stayed out of my hotel room."

"Then I'd be dead."

Her cheeks reddened from his insult. She didn't reply, and he knew why. Unintentionally, he'd pushed a button. Obviously, Emily didn't like being responsible for harming anyone. A do-gooder, and those people usually got people like him killed.

However…

Leaning closer and propping up on his elbow, he looked at her. Her shoulders sagged and the sadness in her eyes pulled Mac in a way he didn't like.

As a man who'd fought most of his adult life, Mac recognized innocence no matter how it came packaged, and that's what Emily's whole demeanor reeked of. No doubt she lived a completely blameless life. He felt that in his chest and knew it in his heart.

You could preach till you ran out of breath, but Mac knew there was no God in what he did. He killed bad guys and had learned to live with that choice years ago. If he hadn't, he'd either be an alcoholic or a manic depressive. Everyone knew people like that couldn't help anyone. No, killing never came easy, but it was a necessary evil, and oftentimes, he played the boogieman.

There was nothing he'd like more than to take Em into his arms and make her feel better. But his job didn't work that way. You either dealt with the carnage on your own, or you let it envelop and consume you.

He wasn't sure what he'd said, but her sobs kept him from falling asleep or passing out, but not in a bad way. There was something healing and cleansing about a woman's tears. Especially when whatever had happened wasn't entirely his fault.

Letting go of all restraint, Mac lowered his head and pressed his lips to hers. She didn't resist or lean in to him. She simply allowed. A kiss was a kiss, but this proved to be something special. She tasted delicious, open and so damn soft he wanted to melt into her and stay there. Salty tears flirted with the corners of his lips and touched his soul. Nothing existed, except her and him.

He pulled her closer, waiting for a protest. When none came, he deepened the kiss. His sensory organs went into overdrive. His breathing hitched, his heart rate accelerated again, and his dick immediately came to attention. He smelled her. The scent of a woman consumed by want.

Hands on her back, he pulled her closer. In a haze of desire, he heard her let out a sleepy little moan, and Mac almost lost it. His tongue went on surveillance and what he found shocked and delighted him in a gentle and endearing way. In his whole life, Mac had never kissed a woman like Emily. While in the back of his mind he kept reminding himself that he didn't particularly like her, his body betrayed him and made its own assessment.

Heat swallowed him when she wrapped her arms around his neck. Mac stood at heaven's gates, and they were wide open. Slowly, he ran his fingers through her silky hair. Craving more, he opened his mouth wider and covered hers completely. Refusing to release her, his head started to spin.

Man, this could go on forever.

He wasn't sure how it happened, but her skirt came up around her waist, and Mac stroked her long smooth legs as they wrapped around his hips.

Turbulence bounced the airplane, but he didn't care. He had more urgent matters to be concerned with. Like sex with the prettiest woman he'd ever seen in his life.

They broke apart only long enough for Em to open his jeans. He shoved aside the thong she wore and as smooth as silk he slipped inside her and found her wet and tight. The lights were dim, but Mac looked up to see her eyes smoldering dark with desire and need.

He softly cupped her breasts and moaned when they fit perfectly into his palms. Even through her bra and silk shirt, her stiff nipples raked his hands, and he gently squeezed them with his fingers. Em rose up only to slowly lower herself on to him, driving him deeper into her sex. A gasp escaped her lips as she struggled to breathe.

Her perfume intoxicated him quicker than a double shot of whiskey. The delicate touch of her skin against him drove desire further and ignited a fire deep in his chest.

Mac thought he'd explode any minute, but not until he'd heard Em reach her release. She tossed her hair back and ground against him. Mac took her hips and set a perfect rhythm for both of them. In and out, up and down. He couldn't take much more before he'd embarrass himself by coming too soon. She pulsed around him, making Mac grit his teeth and inwardly beg for mercy.

She cried out, and her warm juices flushed around his cock and Mac's release crashed through him. Sensation ran the length of his spine and back to his scrotum. His cum vaulted out of the tip, spilling inside her in a rush of heat.

While they both gasped, Mac kissed her swollen lips before enclosing her in his embrace.

***

When Mac woke, Em lay curled against him sound asleep. They were still alive, still on the plane, and still in the recliner when his ears popped. Then Sam's voice came over the intercom.

"Please secure your seatbelts. We will be landing in twenty minutes."

Mac pushed up and tried to clear his head. Em had her back to him with her arms curled beneath her cheek for a pillow. Her nice round butt was velcroed to his crotch. Gently, Mac put his hand on her hip and shook her awake.

"Where are we?"

"Ready to land. You need to buckle up."

Sleepy-eyed, she slowly traveled back to the present. As she sat up, she shoved her hair out of her face and smacked her lips. Yawning, she raised her arms above her head and stretched. He knew he shouldn't stare, but Mac loved the way her shirt's silk fabric molded around her firm breasts.

Getting to her feet, she moved across the aisle and sat staring straight ahead. The silence bugged him. Had she forgotten they'd just had sex? He sure the hell hadn't.

Tongue tracing her lips, Emily pressed her hands down her skirt then pulled at her blouse. Without looking at him, she quietly slipped back into her high heels.

He asked, "You okay?"

She pressed her lips together and blinked. "I'm fine." For some unknown reason, she went all stiff and formal. Back to being a lawyer and in control. If his guess was right…she had one hell of a headache.

"We're ten minutes away from landing," Sam announced. "We'll be arriving at terminal one, gate six." The cockpit door stood open, so Sam could see them. "Have you made the necessary arrangements, Miss Richards?" the pilot asked over his shoulder.

"Yes," she replied. "We have a four-hour layover, so I'm sure we can easily go through customs and get to our gate on time."

"Very well."

"Once we land," Mac said, "I'll need to use your cell phone to get in touch with Frank again."

Emily nodded. "I told him about our plans, but he said to keep him posted."

"Did you tell him about the guys blowing up the hotel?"

"No." She shook her head. "I thought you might want to give him that news."

"Okay, when we land, I'll take care of it."

Soberly, she asked, "Do you think the killers at the hotel are connected to the same ones who chased us to the airport?"

"Damned if I know." Mac rubbed the back of his neck. "I pretty much took care of the Russians. And anything left behind, Jake cleaned up. So, I'm not sure what's going on. I can't think of anyone who'd want to kill me. At least not right now."

"Eight hours ago, I wanted to kill you," she said lightheartedly.

He squinted and flashed a knowing grin. "You sure about that? Not long ago you were Saran Wrap, and I was a leftover casserole."

An impish grin pulled back the corners of her lips as she blushed then slumped back in her seat. "I just want this over. I'd love to get back to my nice boring life."

He chuckled. "What the hell is that like?"

"Boring." Then she sat up. "And very predictable."

"Oh, you like predictable?" Mac stretched out his legs where their feet were side by side. "Or do you like spontaneity?"

She leaned over, giving him a nice view of her cleavage, and whispered, "Both."

Strange, Mac couldn't remember the last time he openly flirted with a woman. Emily had a way of making him feel things he'd buried long ago. Things that came in the middle of the night and forced him to care. Who would have thought Em, the tight-assed company attorney, was secretly sweet, funny, and unique? It surprised and reminded him of all the shortcomings in his personal life.

"Well, we're safe now," said Emily, crossing her legs. "We'll leave London and be in the States before nightfall. The adventure comes to an end."

Mac hoped she was right, but he doubted it. Instinct told him an inevitable collision was about to take place. Could he protect Em? The last thing he wanted was her to become collateral damage.

The plane taxied to the gate, and Sam killed the engines. Mac stood and helped Emily to her feet. Releasing his hand, she went to Sam and thanked him for all his help before departing the plane.

When Mac passed the cockpit, Sam crossed his arms and gave Mac a "dumbass American" glare, but Mac didn't care what that "rod up the ass" thought. "Keep the skies friendly," he said.

As they entered the terminal, customs awaited. Since he'd left all his weapons on the plane, Mac had nothing to claim. Em only had her laptop, briefcase, and purse.

When his turn came, Mac pulled out the papers prepared for him. Knowing Tony, those papers were good as gold. They'd stand up to the highest standards in any country.

The noise in the busy terminal gave Mac a headache. As he glanced at the milling crowd, he wished for a deserted island somewhere in the tropics with nothing, but coconut trees and soft waves lapping at the beach. And Em.

A mixture of different cultures of food traveled up his nostrils and made his stomach growl. Once through security, they learned their plane would be departing three gates away. Thank God. Nothing he hated more than running through airports, hoping to catch a flight.

When they finished with customs, Em looked down at her clothing. "I need to make a stop at one of the stores and find something to wear."

Two corridors down was a small clothing store situated between a souvenir shop and a coffeehouse. Once inside, the only thing Mac picked up was a toothbrush and toothpaste kit. That was all he needed.

On the other hand, Emily picked up a change of clothes, and they met at the cash register. She pulled out her credit card and paid for the purchase. Who knew a woman could shop so fast? He'd expected to spend at least an hour waiting while she browsed for something to wear.

Another surprise. The woman could make up her mind.

In the men's restroom, Mac splashed his face with water and gargled. He took out the toothbrush and cleaned his teeth. While he didn't look better, he felt pretty good. Now he wanted to get back to Dallas and figure out this mess.

Closing his eyes, he thought back to him and Em making love. It had been amazing, but not something he would dare hang on to. As the company's attorney, Mac knew she was off limits. He'd have to let all that go. He knew better than to dream of a different life. That didn't exist for guys like him.

When he emerged from the men's room, Em waited nearby. She'd purchased a clip to bunch up her hair and that disappointed him. He liked her curls down, but she didn't look like she was in the mood to hear his opinion.

Damn, his heart sped up from just looking at her. How could he get across the ocean without making love to her again? In a flash, Mac thought of the hot sex they'd had earlier and wondered if she thought of them as well. Her face looked like she'd spent all afternoon in the August Texas heat. Without speaking, he nodded his approval of her new outfit. A white pullover, a pair of tight, faded jeans, and flip-flops.

As Mac fell in beside her, she waved two sheets of paper in front of him. "I have our boarding passes. We'll be home before you know it."

"I'm ready for that."

Slyly, she glanced sideways at him. "You look a little better."

"You don't look so bad yourself."

Em didn't reply as they made their way toward their designated gate. In the boarding area, she looked around. "There's a restaurant." She pointed to a small, franchised shop. "Let's eat before we board. I don't know about you, but I'm starving."

"Sounds good. I could eat something."

The waiter led them to a table near the main walkway and took their drink order. From where they sat, they could see the plane parked outside that would take them to Dallas. With a little time to kill, they placed their food order and relaxed. Mac sipped a Heineken, and Em had a small glass of white wine.

Rolling his shoulders, Mac leaned back in the leather chair and relaxed. Their food came and the delicious aroma had Mac picking up his fork, ready to eat. With his utensil inches from his lips, he felt the hard barrel of a gun pressed against his side.

One wrong move and he was a goner.

CHAPTER FIVE

The salad Emily ordered looked delicious. While she poured dressing on top of the lettuce, three strange men approached their table. Emily stilled. These guys didn't look friendly, ready to have dinner, or likely there to welcome them to London.

No, definitely not a hospitality committee. As a matter of fact, their mean snarls didn't look good at all.

She dropped her fork and tried to stand.

"Not so fast there, young lady," the largest man said with a strong British accent.

Emily looked into the meanest eyes she'd ever seen. Her leg muscles tightened, ready to run.

The redheaded man with the gun whispered against Mac's ear, but she clearly heard him. "Hello there, you little fucker." Then he twisted his face into a brutal sneer. "Long time no see, ay?"

"What do you want?" Mac asked. Tension straightened his body. "And get that damn gun out of my ribs, or I'll scream like a girl being raped."

"You do that and I'll blow ye head off in a hurry, I will."

The shortest of the three said, "Bruno sent us."

Mac paled and swore under his breath. "What the hell does he want?"

"Ain't what he wants. It's what Ramón Marino wants. And he always gets what he wants. Y'know what I mean?"

"Go to hell."

"You first, mate."

"I keep askin' meself how this fucker's still alive," the redhead said. "He killed two of our best men, didn't he, Charlie?"

In response, Charlie smiled, showing rotted teeth. "Yeah, and he's still walking around." He cracked his knuckles and Emily's heart slammed against her ribs with the impact of a sledgehammer. "I'm gonna mess him up real good before we kill him."

Mac tried to stand, but the man who told her not to move placed his hand on the chair, and the other guy jabbed harder with the gun.

Mac raised his hands. "Okay, gentlemen, let's go." He forced the chair backwards and rose.

The bigger man latched on to Mac's biceps.

Looking around, Emily noticed no one in the airport paid them a token of attention. Even their server disappeared. Emily wondered how these men managed to get into the airport armed, let alone past security.

Mac glanced at her with a sadness that practically broke her heart. They planned to kill him. The bigger guy grabbed her arm and pulled her out of the chair. She struggled against his strength, but it was useless.

Yanking free, Mac stopped. "I'll go with you, but leave the girl alone. She stays here."

"No deal, bloke," the redhead said. "We got our own plans for her. Cute little chit, she is." He stroked Emily's cheek and she jerked away. "Sides, she's got what we're after." He grabbed at her purse, but she refused to relinquish it. "Where's the flipping camera, Emily?"

Three sets of hungry eyes turned and stared. Emily felt like flesh eating Piranhas were consuming her, and she had no escape. The hair on her arms rose, her body tightened, and she feared she might vomit at any moment. After looking at the three villains, Emily vowed she'd find a way to kill herself before she'd allow these animals to touch her.

Still, hordes of people traversed the corridor, yet none noticed the danger surrounding her and Mac.

"I'm not going anywhere." Emily grabbed the edge of the table, flipped it over, and screamed until her lungs burned. "Terrorists!" She sucked in a gulp of air. "There's a bomb!"

People within hearing range shrieked and ran for the nearest exit in a panic.

The flying table and its contents forced the man holding Mac at gunpoint to jump back. When he did, Mac moved in the opposite direction. In a blur of action, Mac punched *Charlie* in the jaw, twisted his arm behind him and rammed his head into a nearby wall. Then he turned his attention to the redhead. Mac beat him with both fists, kneed him in the groin then slammed his face against a table.

Two armed British soldiers patrolling the airport turned and charged toward them. Two other security guards came from the other side of the terminal.

Emily kicked the short guy in the shins. "That man has a gun," she screamed.

As police and military personnel reached the area, Emily and Mac backed away.

Apparently not wanting to stand around and be dragged into hours of interrogation, Mac took her hand and they headed for their gate as if nothing had happened. When she dared a look back, chaos ruled the moment until the three men were handcuffed and led out of the airport by a security patrol.

"You're pretty handy to have around, Em," Mac said.

Shaking, Emily couldn't think of a reply. A quick dose of fear drenched her to the core, making her hands tremble. "What were those men after?" she demanded. "They were going to kidnap us...kill us. Why?"

Glancing at the tile floor before looking at her, Emily saw Mac's sadness. His eyes searched her face. Taking her arms, he said, "Em, I have enemies all over the world. Those bullies work for a guy I had a run-in with four years ago." Letting out a sigh, he released her and combed his fingers through his hair. He glanced out the large window toward the waiting planes. "Short story, there are people who want me dead. It comes with the job."

She pointed behind them. "But back in the plane, you told me no one was trying to kill you right now."

Lie.

He'd lied to her. For what? So she'd feel better?

"What's the deal, Mac? Obviously, people are always trying to kill you." She backed away. "It comes with the job. How insane is that?" She bit back tears. "How can you stand it?"

Nothing prepared Emily for the wrenching in her chest. Yes, she'd suffered a broken heart, but what she felt now was a different emotion altogether. What a sacrifice Mac made for his country. To constantly be hunted, forever on the lookout, never able to relax and live a normal life.

"I'm sorry." She reached up and patted him on the shoulder when she wanted to pull him into her arms and not let go.

"None of this is your fault," he said. "I chose this life a long time ago and I'm resigned to my fate. I just plan to do as much damage to the bad guys as I can before they take me out. Then we'll be even."

The PA system announced it was time to board. As a gesture of kindness and feeling it was the least she could do, Emily left Mac and went to the counter to ask if they could upgrade their tickets. After what they'd been through, Frank could pay the extra money. If he dared complain, she'd punch him.

Being part of the first group to board, Emily and Mac passed through the jet way and entered the plane. Maybe they'd get a nice meal and a good movie. Home sounded better by the minute.

As other passengers settled around them, Emily handed Mac her briefcase and laptop to put in the overhead bin. After all the pushing and shoving, Emily scooted to the window seat while Mac took the aisle.

Ready to leave England, Emily buckled her seatbelt, closed the window blind then leaned back and took a deep breath. The rich aroma of coffee and canned air lifted her spirits. The engine purred like a love song.

After adjusting his seat, Mac settled in.

Smugly, Emily said, "Frank is going to have a fit when he sees how much this flight cost him."

"No, he won't." Mac chuckled. "Money doesn't mean anything to Frank. It's all about justice to him. After what you went through, he'd gladly buy you your own private plane."

She tapped her index finger to her lip. "Hmm, wish I'd known that earlier."

The passengers settled, the "Fasten Seat Belt" sign came on, and the door closed. Another sigh escaped when the pilot slowly steered the plane away from the terminal. She felt safe for the first time since Mac had entered her hotel room.

While traveling to Heathrow, Mac had fallen asleep right after their lovemaking. It didn't hurt her feelings because she knew he must have been exhausted. While he rested, Emily had moved to the other seat and called Brenda to assure her they were going to Belize regardless. Nothing, absolutely nothing, could keep that vacation from happening.

She'd made their flight arrangements and contacted her office. Then she relived every second they'd spent making love so wildly she'd nearly passed out from pleasure. No man had ever made her feel so whole and completely satisfied. Chills ran a race up and down her spine just thinking about her body connected to his.

Once the plane leveled out, the flight attendant offered them a delicious meal and wine. Afterwards, Mac turned to Emily. "What was that goon in Heathrow talking about when he said he wanted the *camera?*"

She'd hoped Mac had forgotten about that. Guess she couldn't get that lucky. "Hmm, I'm not sure." As a distraction, she opened the window shade and stared at feathery white clouds.

"I am." Mac wore that "tell me the truth" stare. "I heard it clearly. Now tell me what's going on. And how are you involved?"

"Nothing."

"Do you have a camera?"

No way. She refused to discuss that with Mac. It wasn't any of his business. And she had no idea how the guy at the airport knew she'd taken pictures. She'd made sure no one saw her. "I might have a camera."

"Did you take pictures in Moscow of something confidential?"

"No."

"Okay, why did that guy want the camera? And Em, I want the truth. If you're tied up in anything…"

Angry that he'd even insinuated she'd done something wrong, she twisted in her seat to face him. "How dare you accuse me after all I've been through?" Her voice shook.

"I'm not accusing you. I'm asking a simple question." He leaned a pulse away from her lips. "Now, where the hell is the camera?"

Insecurity made her hesitate. Did he have to know everything? If he knew the entire story, she wouldn't be able to stand the humiliation. Not after being as intimate as they'd been. Unable to face him, she looked away.

Before she could react, Mac reached down, grabbed her purse and started rummaging through the contents. Furious at his boldness, she snatched her bag back. "Don't you dare pry through my things."

He gripped her chin. "Tell me or I'll strip search you right here, right now." He narrowed his eyes. "And I'll enjoy every minute of it."

Her breath caught in her chest, and she struggled to swallow. "You wouldn't dare."

He raised a brow, his cobalt blue eyes burned hot as a poker. "I think by now you know what I'm capable of doing, Emily." That said, he released her and held out his hand. "Give it up."

Not able to trust herself to speak, Emily reached into her purse and removed a contact lens case. She slapped it into his palm. "There." He gazed at her with a puzzled look on his face. "Well, you wanted it." She nodded toward his hand. "There it is."

"You wear contacts?"

"No, I don't wear contacts. But one of those lenses is a camera."

Mac popped open the case to reveal two lenses soaking in a clear liquid. "Which one?" he asked.

"The right one."

"It looks like a normal lens."

"Of course, it does. That's the whole idea."

Mac stared from the contents in his hand to her and back again. His brow wrinkled.

Ha! Let's see the great spy figure that out.

"What the hell are you up to, Em?"

"I'm not up to anything."

"The hell you're not. This is some serious confidential shit."

"No kidding."

"What's it doing in your possession?"

Emily stared at the back of the seat in front of her and folded her arms. "It's a long story."

"Yeah, well, we have hours with nothing to do, except you telling me what the hell's going on." Mac leaned closer, took her arm, and pulled her toward him.

She captured his scent, felt his heat, and sensed his anger.

"Now." The word slipped out of his mouth as smooth as water off glass.

There was so much she didn't want to tell him, things she didn't want him to know. But somehow, someway, someone had found out about her taking pictures, and now, she had to come clean. It would hurt, but she had to own up to her part in this crazy game. "It's an invention."

Mac closed the case and placed his elbows on the arms of his seat. "Whose invention?"

Emily held up her hands. "Let me finish then you can ask questions."

"Okay."

"A *friend* of mine is an inventor. He creates gadgets for the government, the military, and stuff like that. After years of research, he developed that lens camera, and I agreed to try it out for him. I went to Red Square one evening and snapped several pictures. It was sort of dark, and I honestly wasn't paying attention to whom or what I shot."

The flight attendant came by and asked if they needed anything. When Emily asked for another glass of wine, Mac gave her a warning look. Oh yeah, if she ever needed to get drunk, now was the time.

"Lay off the sauce until I get the whole story."

Accepting her wine, Emily shrugged. "That's the whole story."

"Why at night?" he asked.

Emily took a sip of wine then replied, "That was one of the problems. The elimination of a flash. That and certain images."

"A camera without a flash, in the dark?" Mac shook his head.

"It wasn't about the flash. My assignment...I mean *favor*, was to test the trigger device." She pulled a small plastic stick out of her purse, about the size of a pair of tweezers. "You wear the lens, look at something, and click the lever like this."

She pushed its top like a ballpoint pen. "It takes a snapshot of whatever you're looking at. Stanley...I mean, my *friend*, asked me if I'd try it out while I was in Moscow since he'd been having trouble with the timing of the clicker thingy."

51

"Stanley?" Mac asked. "Who's Stanley?"

Emily shrugged and took a sip of wine. "Just a guy I know."

"So, how do we find out what you took pictures of?"

"Only Stanley can do that."

"Why?"

"It's his creation. He developed the lens, and the flash, and the clicker, and the software that develops the pictures."

"Where is Stanley?"

Discussing Stanley made her uncomfortable. Even the sound of his name on her lips hurt. And explaining what a genius he was only intensified her loss. What she'd never have and what she'd live with the rest of her life.

Besides, she hadn't intended to test the stupid thing until her sister Victoria called Moscow and practically begged her to do Stanley the favor. The only reason Emily had to be the one to experiment with the prototype was because months ago the lens had been designed to fit Emily's eye.

"He lives in the Dallas/Ft Worth area," she said.

"Okay, so when we land, let's pay Stanley a little visit."

"No!" she shouted, earning the attention of nearby passengers. Covering her mouth, she looked around at staring eyes. "I can't go there."

Mac's eyebrows drew together. "Why not? He gave you this thing, didn't he?"

"Yes, but I haven't seen him since and have no desire to."

"Then how were you going to deliver it to him, so he could see if his invention really worked?"

Emily gulped her wine. "Mail it."

Mac slumped back in his seat and finger combed his hair. "No fucking way."

Those were the last words they shared until the plane landed because Emily refused to tell any more than necessary. Besides, she was going home and being with a Falcon agent for the past twenty hours had proven too much. She needed to escape back to normality. Mac had already managed to open old wounds she'd hoped were healed.

As they walked into the terminal, Emily looked around at all the things that made Texas home. The busy terminal, the greenery, and the glaring sun were all wonderful signs of home. Nothing would be better than to add a frozen margarita and an order of chips and salsa.

As she turned to say goodbye and wish Mac luck, he grabbed her around the waist and kissed her. It took a moment, but she melted as fast as an ice cube on a hot sidewalk. She dropped her laptop and briefcase to cup his face.

She never wanted the kiss to end. The awesome taste of male testosterone kicked her hormones into gear and made her hungry— no, starving—for more.

He finally broke the kiss, leaving her dizzy and disoriented. Their eyes met. "Thank you so much for all you've done. Without your help, I'd be dead."

Had he kissed her as a way of saying "thanks"?

Well, that sucked!

Trying her best to appear unfazed, Emily forced a smile past her disappointment. "Always ready to help a client." She blinked back any hint of tears and added, "Oh, that's ex-client."

"Listen," Mac said, taking her hand. "Don't give up on Falcon Securities. We need people like you, so we can do what we have to do to keep this country safe. Frank's an ass sometimes, but he's the best person I know."

Emily forced a smile, withdrew her hand, and said, "I'll think about it."

"Brody is waiting outside," he said. They'd texted Frank and he'd replied that an agent would be there to pick them up. "Do you need a lift?"

"Oh no, I'm fine." Brushing back her hair, she said, "I have a friend on the way." No way was she going to tell him she planned to take a cab home.

"It won't be a problem to drop you off. Then I'll come back later, and we'll go visit Stanley."

A client knowing where she lived was another professional no-no. She believed she was happy and successful because she managed to keep her social life and her professional career completely separate.

But she'd managed to blow that to hell.

They walked together only because they were going in the same direction. When the doors to the outside opened automatically, Emily took a deep breath of good old Texas air and immediately felt better.

She turned to say her second good-bye when two men stepped forward, grabbed them both, and shoved them into a dark SUV. Emily didn't think this was the ride Mac had been expecting.

CHAPTER SIX

Mac struggled to get to Em, but two guys, one on each side, caught him off guard. The dark, tall one with the goatee had Em's arms behind her back, propelling her toward the open door of the Lincoln SUV. It pissed him off that some guy would manhandle her like that. When this ended, that son of a bitch had a smack down coming.

Mac tried to spit out the dirty rag they'd stuffed into his mouth to keep him from screaming. Em swung and kicked like a woman gone wild. Inside the SUV, she punched the skinny guy in the jaw, and after she freed one arm, out came her sharp claws.

Where in hell had this version of Em come from? She certainly hadn't fought him off like this.

The burly one couldn't stop her. Mac guessed Em didn't weigh more than a hundred and ten pounds, but she fought like a heavyweight. Quick and furious, nothing was off limits. She kneed one guy in the groin, and he doubled over. Then she smacked him in the face, grabbed his stringy hair, and shook his head like can of soda. As Mac watched Em the Wonder Woman, he struggled with his own release.

Somehow, she'd managed to rip the gag from her mouth then screamed loud enough to gain the attention of the gate attendant as they pulled out of the airport.

When the SUV hit the 183 freeway and headed toward Ft Worth, Mac and Em were both doing their best to get free. Mac knew the men were armed, but they'd be dumb ass stupid to fire a weapon in a moving vehicle. Way too dangerous.

The bigger man managed to clip Em on the chin, and she went down hard on the floorboard. Mac didn't like any man who hit a woman, no matter what the circumstances. He especially hated that the asshole had hit Em. Mac head-butted the guy in front of him then leaned against the door and kicked the attacker in the face with both feet.

Mac yanked his hands free, and the fight was on. With his arm cocked, his hand fisted, he slammed into the guy that had decked Em. A right jab and a left hook and the jerk with the kinky hair went down for the count, slumping against the back seat. The fat boy pointed a gun at Mac, but he knocked it out of the man's hand, and a bullet zinged through the roof.

That got the driver nervous, and he shouted for the kidnappers to end the struggle or start killing. With the gun on the floorboard, that was going to be hard.

Mac jackhammered the goateed guy with a punch packed with two hundred and twenty pounds behind it right to the throat. The asshole flipped backwards and landed on top of Em. Mac dove for the gun and got lucky.

He rose and leveled the weapon at the only conscious person besides himself. Placing the barrel against the back of his head, Mac shouted to the driver, "Stop the fucking vehicle, now!"

From the glint in his eyes in the rearview mirror, Mac knew the driver was packing. "You even think of using a weapon, and I'll blow a hole in your head so big you could drive a semi through it."

The driver took his foot off the accelerator and hit the shoulder. Traffic sped by at a frightening rate. With the gun still on the driver, Mac grabbed Em's arm and pulled her free. "Get up, baby girl."

Her head lolled sideways and her eyes fluttered. He grabbed her by the waist and pulled her against him. Pride pulsed through his body. Em had put up one helluva fight. Most women would have fainted. Goddamn, she'd make a good agent.

With the SUV stopped and out of traffic, Mac asked, "Who sent you?"

"I don't know. I'm just the driver."

"Okay, who sent them?" He pointed to the three out cold.

"Look man, I don't know nothin'. These guys came to my crib and asked me if I'd like to make a couple hundred bucks. Told me all I had to do was drive." He turned to face Mac. "I ain't got time for this shit. You get me, man? I'm just out for the ride. That's all."

"You weren't out for the ride when you told them to kill us." Mac pulled back the trigger. "Look man," he mocked. "I'm about to blow your fucking head off if I don't get some information."

"I don't know nothin'." He held up his hand. "Honest to God."

A black Cadillac Escalade pulled up behind them, and Brody Hawke jumped out, sporting cowboy boots and a fine looking gray Stetson. Another Falcon agent moved cautiously to the passenger's side.

Brody tapped the driver's side of the car with the barrel of his gun. "Open the door."

With three guns pointed in his direction, the driver complied then covered his head with his palms.

"How you doing, partner?" Brody asked.

Brody was Falcon's token cowboy. A real Old West kind of guy. Fast on the trigger and always looking for a fight. And he rarely had to go far. With the finesse of a bull rider, Brody grabbed the three hundred pound driver by the collar and slung him to the ground. He kept him there by stomping his cowboy boot against the back of the man's neck.

Concerned for Emily, Mac opened the back passenger door and helped her stand. She had a nice size bruise on the left side of her chin and blood stained the corner of her mouth. "You okay?"

Shoving her hair back, she glanced up at him. She'd never looked more beautiful. She leaned into him, and he cradled her against him. "Are we safe yet?"

"I'm working on it." He took Em and put her in the backseat of the Cadillac. She immediately leaned against the headrest. He shut her in the air-conditioned car and turned back to Brody. "Guess you know what hell we've been through?"

"We've been getting it piece by piece. When I saw you nabbed at the airport, I called Frank. Decided I'd better follow and see what was going on." Brody looked at the Falcon vehicle. "How'd she get involved in all this? Frank only wanted her to get you out of Russia. That's where it should've ended."

"Well, it kept getting more and more complicated. The scary part is one of those goons called her by name. They know who she is."

Brody spit then shook his head. "That's not good."

Another car pulled up, and three Falcon agents got out, put the kidnappers in the car, and took off. An agent drove the kidnapper's vehicle to Falcon.

Brody watched the car pull into traffic. "Frank wants to question them at headquarters."

"So the hell do I."

"Let's head back to the ranch, partner."

Smiling, Mac climbed in the passenger side and Brody drove toward Dallas. They'd be at the office in less than thirty minutes, depending on traffic. There was a small fridge in the back of the vehicle. Mac leaned over and retrieved a bottle of water. After unscrewing the cap, he handed it to Em. She tipped it to her mouth.

For some reason, Mac had more questions than answers, and by God, somebody sure the hell had better come up with the right shit.

Looking down at his wrist, Mac knew one thing was certain. Someone had compromised his GPS. He had a tracer on his ass.

When the vehicle stopped and the engine turned off, Mac helped Em out of the car in the underground parking garage. It ripped at his conscience that she looked so shaken—the wrinkled clothes, tangled hair, and all the bruises. Any make-up she might have been wearing was long gone.

"You okay?" he asked again.

"No, I'm not okay." The growl in her voice affirmed she definitely wasn't in a good mood. Who could blame her? She'd been fighting for her life since Moscow. And he knew she had to be exhausted. Dead tired and ready for this entire trip to be over.

They entered the building directly from the parking garage then shoved open the door to Falcon Securities.

The receptionist, Zoe, jumped from her chair. "My goodness, what happened to you?"

"Can you take Ms. Richards to the ladies room and let her freshen up a little?" Mac asked. Emily couldn't be in more loving arms. God help them all, but Zoe Ross adored everyone and everything. There was no kinder person on earth.

Zoe wrapped her arm around Em and pulled her tightly against her side. "Come with me, sweetheart. We'll have you back to normal in no time." As they walked away, Zoe gave the two agents a concerned glance.

After exchanging looks, Mac and Brody entered Frank's office. Behind the large oak desk sat the leader and commander of Falcon Securities. An ex-CIA Director with a Marine attitude and a mouth like a Boatswain's Mate.

"What the hell is going on, Mac?" Frank pointed to the door. "Why in the hell did you drag her into this mess?" His face brightened, and Mac guessed his blood pressure soared. "And just what in the holy hell have you gotten into?"

Weary, Mac slumped into a large chair across from Frank and dragged his fingers through his hair. "I don't know. I wrapped up that mess in St. Petersburg. When I was finished, there wasn't anything we'd have to go back and clean up. Jake made sure of that."

Frank said, "Tony is on his way back to the States now. If I can keep from it, I'm not sending him out for a while. It's getting too hot."

"It's getting too hot for all of us. You know the Russian mob is getting more powerful by the day. Used to be the military was all we had to worry about. I heard rumors they're dealing in nuclear shit."

"I've heard that too, but unless we're called in on an assignment, we'll leave it be," Frank said.

"Em…Ms. Richards and I were attacked at Heathrow. Ugly guy said something about Bruno and Ramón Marino. That's never good."

"No, it's not," Frank agreed. "Don't you have a handler on him?"

"We lost him in Columbia," Mac said. "Last I heard, Marino and his drug cartel were setting up business in Bogotá. But I spoke to Tony and he said Marino wasn't there. If Tony can't sniff him out, he's gone way underground."

"Tony's due in soon. You hear any shit, Brody, you call in Jake. I mean the slightest noise."

Brody nodded.

Concerned deepened the lines on Frank's face. That didn't fare well for the agents.

"You got it, boss," Brody said. His brows wrinkled as he looked at Mac. "I always figured, as much as Marino hated you, when he wanted you dead, he'd do it himself."

Frank slapped his desk. "We don't know that's not his plan. Guys in London might have just been following an order to deliver you to Marino."

"Could be," Mac said. "But after all this time?"

"Grudges last forever, son, and in his mind, you're the reason his sister is dead."

"I didn't kill her. A Mexican sniper took her out, not me."

"No matter, you kidnapped her out of that convent."

Mac didn't like being reminded of that. He hadn't meant for it to go down that way. But when the shooting started, there was no stopping. Angelina Marino was in the crossfire. "I didn't mean for her to be killed."

"I know that, but Marino doesn't care. It's a matter of family honor."

"He doesn't have any fucking honor."

"Tell him about you being tagged," Brody said.

Mac leaned back and propped his elbows on the chair, his palms clasped. "I went to the snitch in St. Petersburg like we arranged. He gave me the thumb drive I sent to the NSA. When I walked out of the apartment, I looked down, and three guys were waiting on the bottom landing for me. I took out two, cleared a window, and started running."

"That assignment came straight from the DOD," Frank said. "That snitch had valuable information that the President wanted kept out of enemy hands."

"I called Tony and he found me a ride to Moscow. When I hit the city limits, you directed me to Em's…Ms. Richards' hotel."

"I'm with you so far," Frank said.

"Okay, I'm there less than a couple hours, and two guys bust in the door with killing on their minds and loaded guns in their hands."

"You get caught on the hotel surveillance camera?" Brody asked.

"They didn't see my face," Mac said. "Then Ms. Richards and I get to her fancy private plane and a goddamn RPG comes flying at us out of nowhere."

"I got that phone call," Frank grumbled.

"Then we get to London, and there are three of Marino's guys waiting for us. Said Bruno sent them." Mac stood and started pacing the office. "This is where it gets interesting." He looks back at Frank and Brody. "The guys wanting to kill us knew Em's name. And that she was in possession of a high level camera she'd been testing for a friend."

"What?" Brody whistled softly. "Damn, this would make a good movie."

"What the hell is this about a camera?" Frank asked then looked at Brody. "And every mission we take could be a movie."

Mac waved him off. "I'll let her tell you about that. But back to what I was saying. We make it out of Heathrow alive only to land at DFW and find more men waiting for us. I don't know what's going on, but someone has hacked my signal."

Frank rubbed his chin. "I'm the only person who knows where you guys are all the time."

"Who tells you?" Brody asked.

Silence grew like a balloon filling with water. Frank picked up the phone. "Get Josh Bozeman on the line."

Frank put his hand over the receiver. "They can't."

"Bozeman!" Frank shouted. "One of my guys has been compromised. Mac McKinsey. Don't bother to ask me how I know. I just do. You find out how this happened, who the son of a bitch is, and I want him hung out to dry. I want Mac's signal changed immediately. You fix this mess. You got twelve hours, or I'm coming to Washington to tear somebody apart." Frank slammed the phone down, leaned back in his chair, and studied Mac.

"Should we have my chip removed?" Mac asked.

Frank shook his head. "No, that won't be necessary. It's all going to work out. Trust me."

That scared Mac more than anything he'd been thrown lately. "You get those three guys from the airport locked up?" he asked.

"Yeah." Frank smiled. "You and Brody go pay them a visit."

"Em's cleaning up. She'll only be a minute."

"I'll see to Ms. Richards," Frank replied, shooing them out of the room.

Mac followed Brody as he made his way to the stairwell and down one floor. They came out into a hallway that had four rooms, two on each side. Turning a corner, a stark white wall revealed a two-way mirror. Behind it, a ten-by-ten interrogation room.

"Don't bother with the driver. I want the one that had the gun," Mac said. He was the one who'd slugged Em.

Outside the three doors, a single armed guard stood watch. Mac entered the room on the left. Brody waited outside and would observe from the corridor.

The guard followed Mac inside.

The empty room had no windows, one door, a small table and two wooden chairs. Mac pulled out a chair, flipped it around and straddled the seat. He propped his arms on the back and looked at one scared, shackled son of a bitch. His face looked like it'd run into a brick wall.

"What's your name," Mac demanded.

"I ain't sayin' nothin' without a lawyer. I know my rights."

Mac leaned over and slapped the SOB on the head. "You have no rights. You kidnapped two people at the airport. We have you on the surveillance cameras."

He looked around. "What is this place, man? This ain't no jail."

"You're right, it's not. And you know what else? Not another living soul knows you're here. I could cut your throat, dump your body in the Trinity, and none would be the wiser." Mac propped his chin on his folded arms. The suspect twitched and his eyes grew larger. "You'll tell me what I want to know or you're a dead man. But before that happens, I can make you wish you'd never taken your first breath."

With a confident smirk, the guy leaned forward. "I ain't scared of nothin', man."

"Then you're as dumb as you look. I'd guess you never been waterboarded? Held up by your thumbs?" Employing his best sadistic smile, Mac opened a small drawer and pulled out a long handled Zippo. He motioned for the agent to grab the prisoner's head and pull it back. Mac walked behind him and flicked the trigger; a flame shot out.

"Ever had your eyeballs burned?" Leaning in, Mac moved the fire closer. The guy screamed in horror. His eyes darted around like pinballs.

"I don't know nothin', 'cept this guy came over and asked if I wanted to do a job for him."

"You see him before?"

"No."

The flame moved closer. Mac smelled the kidnapper's fear. "You sure about that?"

"This other guy hooked us up."

Heat scorched the hostage's cheek.

"That guy got a name?"

Fire singed his eyelashes, and the bastard screamed like a girl.

Mac grabbed his hair and moved closer. "You think I'm shitting you, pal?"

"Name is Castro, Mick Castro."

"Where does Mick live?"

"243 Park. In Oak Cliff." He talked so fast Mac could barely make out what he said.

Mac clipped the lighter closed, and the prisoner was released. "I'm going to pay your friend a call. If you're jacking with me, I'm coming back, and I'm going to give you a fire enema."

The culprit held his shaking, shackled palms against his eyes as sweat rolled off his face.

Mac and Brody went back upstairs. "Waterboarding, my ass." Brody said. "You've never done that to anyone."

"I would to someone who's hurt Em."

"Em?" Brody asked. "When did she go from Ms. Richards, to Emily, to Em?" Brody laughed. "Exactly what have you two been up to?"

Mac grunted. "Don't go getting any ideas, Brody."

"I'm not. Just asking, that's all."

"Em's a brave woman. Considering what we've been through in the last twenty-four hours, a lesser woman would be completely scared out of her mind."

"Don't want to make you sore, but she didn't look too good back there."

Mac stopped. "What the hell does that mean? She fought off two thugs the size of linebackers."

"Yeah, but…" Brody started.

"*But*, my ass." Mac poked him in the chest.

"Whoa, there now. You're acting like a stallion in a pasture full of mares."

"All I'm saying is she's been through a lot."

Brody held his hands up in surrender. "Okay, partner."

They went into Frank's office to find Em sitting down, clutching a mug of tea, and Frank with his drink in a paper cup from the local coffeehouse.

Em glanced at Mac and his gut tightened. She had a black eye and a big blue lump on the side of her chin. She'd pulled her hair back and held it secure with a rubber band. Compliments, no doubt, of Zoe. When this was over, Zoe would probably scold him like a schoolboy.

"Did you find out anything?" Frank asked. "Something we can use to learn who's behind all this?"

"Got an address in Oak Cliff."

"Brody, you'll go check it out." Frank turned to him. "Mac, I want you to take Ms. Richards to a safe house for the night." When Em started to interrupt, Frank silenced her with a raised palm. "We don't know what's going on, and I'm not taking any chances with a civilian."

"I don't think that's necessary," Em spoke up. "I'd love to go home, take a shower, and sleep."

"I'm sure you would. However, we dragged you into this. And until we know who wants you and Mac dead, I'm playing it safe."

Em stood. "Oh no, they don't want me dead." She pointed at Mac. "They want him dead." She forced a smile. "I'm just along for the ride."

The room fell silent. Not even Frank wanted to burst her bubble. Everyone in the room, except Em, suspected that whoever was behind all this knew about her. They wanted them both dead.

"I'm leaving for Belize in a couple of days. A friend and I are going out of town."

So, why hadn't she mentioned she had a vacation planned before? Maybe a little romantic getaway? Mac's mood soured. Evidently, the sex they'd shared didn't mean much.

Belize.

"I'm sorry, Emily," Frank said then cleared his throat. "Those men in Heathrow called you by name."

She whirled around. "They must've heard Mac. Maybe they checked the flight manifest...or..."

"No, ma'am," Brody said with his deep Texas accent. "They knew who you were. For whatever reason, that bunch wants you both."

Thoughts of the camera and pictures she'd taken flashed through his mind, but he wanted to wait before saying anything to Frank. This could all still be a big mistake. Stranger things had happened.

"But I didn't do anything."

"We know that," Frank said. For the first time, Mac heard sorrow in his boss's voice.

"But surely..." Em stuttered.

"It's for your best interest."

"It will probably only be for a day or two. You can rest up real good before your vacation. Sometimes those trips can wear a body out." Brody poured that Texas drawl on a little too thick and smiled like a damn choirboy.

"Can I at least go to my house first? Pick up a few personal belongings."

"'Fraid not," Brody said, his face sad as a weaning calf. "We only want to keep you safe."

Her shoulders slumped, and she dropped back down into the chair. "Fine."

"Okay. Mac, you take Ms. Richards to one of our safe houses. Brody, you head to Oak Cliff."

"Ah, I can do the address search, and Brody can see to Ms. Richards."

Frank studied him for a hard moment, and Brody's brows lifted to his hairline. Mac didn't care. If they were alone, his boss would be cussing him up one side and down the other for even questioning his judgment. But with Em in the room, Frank was being rather polite.

"You could." He smiled and Mac knew he'd get an ass chewing sometime in the future. Frank didn't forget anything "But I want *you* guarding Ms. Richards. Understood?"

Mac nodded as Brody left the room. He slapped Mac's shoulder on the way out, following it with a chuckle. Mac knew Brody would find out all he could and report back to him. It wasn't that Mac didn't think Brody could do a good job. It was that he felt it was time to put a little distance between him and the company attorney. *If* she decided to stay on.

She stood and looked at him, a deep scowl on her face. Must be concerned her friend might be disappointed they wouldn't be lying on the beach, catching some rays.

Mac let out a deep breath. *Oh well, life sucks.*

"Zoe has everything lined up. Check with her on your way out," Frank said. "I want you out of town for now. Get to the outskirts tonight. Tomorrow morning, you can hit the safe house. That *tracer* problem has been solved. Operator error."

What the hell did that mean? "Got it."

Mac waved Emily ahead of him as they left Frank's office. He stopped at the reception desk, and Zoe had a manila envelope for him and a set of car keys.

When they got to the underground garage, Mac turned to Emily. She was rummaging through her purse. "Look, I'm sorry about your vacation."

She lifted her head. "What?"

"Your vacation. I'm sorry you're going to miss it."

"I still plan to make that trip, no matter what. Especially after all I've been through."

"Hopefully, we won't be too long, and you and your boyfriend can be off to Belize."

"I can't wait."

He opened the door for her, and she crawled into the front seat of the SUV. "Yeah."

Emily grinned. "My friend and I have been planning this for months."

66

"Your friend, *Stanley?*"

"Do not mention his name," she insisted.

After closing her door, Mac moved around to the driver's side and slid behind the wheel. "If you and your sweetheart want to spend some naked time together in the tropics, that's fine with me."

She arched a brow and smiled. "Oh, I can see how *fine* it is with you."

"See what you want, but I've never been jealous in my life." He turned, put his arm behind her seat, and backed up the vehicle. Before shifting into drive, he looked at her. "I've never cared enough for anyone to be jealous."

"Everyone cares."

"Not me. I'm thirty-two, and I've never had a serious relationship." He sped out of the dark garage. "And I don't intend to." Love meant too much to lose, too much pain. If he avoided getting serious, he didn't have to worry about letting anyone down. That included Emily.

He couldn't deny she was the most beautiful woman he'd ever seen, and the sex blew his mind, but he simply wasn't the serious kind. He'd keep her safe, and if necessary, he'd give his life. But not love her the way she deserved.

"You're really an ass," she said. "You know that though, right?"

"Yeah, I do."

"No one cares if you have a serious relationship or not. And I certainly don't care if you ever love anyone," she snarled and pointed her finger at him. "Besides, we all know how hard it would be to love someone like you."

"That's the way I want to keep it."

"Then you're in good shape."

CHAPTER SEVEN

They left the underground garage and headed north. Emily wanted to go home, pick up some personal items, and check on her dog, but that had to wait. Falcon had different plans for her, and anything she suggested went unheeded.

Emily yanked open her purse, fished out her cell phone, and dialed Brenda. Sitting so close to Mac drove her insane. Even with his callous behavior, his sheer presence sent her body into unwanted arousal. He had somehow managed to kiss her the way she'd always dreamed, with unbridled passion and sinful purpose.

She still smoldered on the inside from their lovemaking on the plane. Never had she wanted a man so much, so emotionally and so desperately.

She turned and studied the sharp dips and curves of his face. His silvery blue eyes were in deep contrast to his dark brown hair. A strong jaw and remarkable cheekbones gave him a carved, sinister look. The lips that tossed her into the depths of desire were well defined and amazingly outlined with a viable ridge.

She had to stop staring. Didn't he just say he wasn't a forever kind of guy?

"Don't say anything," Mac reminded her as she brought the phone to her ear.

"I won't. But people need to know I'm okay." She waited, hoping Brenda would be off-duty and they could talk. The sound of a friendly voice would lift her spirits and remind her that somewhere out there people were going about their normal lives. With all the macho crap around, she needed to hear a female voice.

Evening had crept over Dallas as the city readied itself for nighttime. Fewer people swarmed the sidewalks, and the five o'clock traffic converged into a steady stream of headlights moving away from downtown.

"Maybe your boyfriend is busy tonight." Mac stared out the windshield. With both hands on the wheel, he maneuvered around the one-way streets "Might have other plans."

"Hi," Emily said at the sound of Brenda's voice. "I called to let you know I'm a little behind schedule, but we should be able to leave Saturday. Can you switch the flights?"

"Yeah, sure. But where the heck are you?"

"I'm wrapping up some unexpected business with a client." It did no good to cast him a nasty glare because he didn't take his eyes off the road. "As soon as I'm free, I'll get back with you."

"Okay. You sure we can leave Saturday? I only have so much time off, and I don't want to waste it."

"I'm sure. We've both waited a long time for this. See you on Saturday."

"Okay, Saturday. I have to run. I picked up an extra shift."

"No problem. I'll see you soon."

Exhausted, Emily disconnected, leaned back against the leather headrest and closed her eyes. The clean smell of the vehicle made her want to doze, but she'd developed a blinding headache and a throbbing jaw from the punch she'd taken in the SUV when they were kidnapped.

The thought of all they'd been through made Emily want to cry. Not simply tears of frustration, but a downpour of overwhelming rage, frustrating loss of control over her life, and utter defeat.

"You okay?" For the first time, Mac took his gaze from the freeway.

Blinking, she turned away.

They'd just passed the airport exit off 183. As she looked toward the DFW airport, memories of their abduction slammed into her with the force of a call of contempt from a judge's bench.

The vehicle slowed and he asked, "What's wrong?"

The dash lights illuminated lines of concern on his face or was it fear? Mr. Neanderthal didn't know what to say.

"Everything is wrong. I am as far from okay as a person can get." She abhorred screaming women, but right now, she didn't care. "I am an honorable woman, Mac. I play by the rules. I don't do foolish or stupid things. My life is structured around doing the right thing at the proper time with decent people. Understand?"

69

He paled.

"I've never run from anything or anyone in my whole life. I've never been shot at. I've never flown through an airport to escape people trying to kill me. I've never in all my twenty-eight years been kidnapped."

"Yeah, ah, well…"

"But ever since you put your big toe in my hotel room, my life has been a living hell. And I'm sick of it!"

"Okay…Ah…I'm bad."

"Why can't I go home? Nobody's after me."

"Whoa, whoa, whoa." His face etched with denial, Mac waved his hand, shunning her hysteria. "I'm not going against Frank. He's smart not to take any chances. Besides, Brody is following a lead coughed up by the guy we took into custody. Maybe he'll turn up something."

"And if he doesn't?"

"Then we wait until we know beyond any doubt that it's safe for you and your sweetheart to go to Belize and enjoy your vacation."

"Really, Mac?" Pulling back her fist, Emily turned and punched him in the shoulder, wishing it were his jaw. "Seriously, you're playing that stupid card after all we've been through?"

As he rubbed his shoulder, Mac glanced at her, his brows drawn close. From the fight in the SUV with their kidnappers, Emily noticed Mac had a black eye that grew darker by the minute.

Any semblance of a sexy five o'clock shadow now leaned closer to a guy who simply needed a shave. Obviously, a hit had turned his nose red, and that lump on his chin reminded her of a golf ball. Still, she never wanted to kiss someone so badly in all her life.

She recognized when the facts hit him.

"You…you don't have a boyfriend?"

"Oh, I have a dozen. But I'm not romantically involved with any of them. And I'm certainly not vacationing with one. So, give me a damn break." She looked out the side window. "Do you think I'm the kind of woman who would have sex with you while having plans with another man?"

"No, I know you wouldn't."

"Then cut the crap."

70

Thirty minutes later, he pulled off the freeway and into the parking lot of a motel. "Zoe handled the reservation. We'll stay in the same room, but it has two beds."

She closed her eyes and shook her head. "That sounds cozy."

He grimaced. "I'll be on my best behavior."

"You don't have a best behavior."

***

Goosebumps prickled Mac's arms as he stepped into the chilly motel room. The smell of floral air freshener and bathroom cleanser greeted him at the door, along with the sight of pea green walls and puke green carpeting…and *one* bed.

Trying to hold back his frustration, Mac tossed their few belongings Zoe had packaged before they left the office on the bed, scattering the contents across the floral bedspread. Knowing the inevitable, he turned to Em, "Maybe it's a mistake. There is this room and another one with two beds."

She was already so pissed he expected her to take out a gun and shoot him. He damn sure didn't want to fight over a bed, and if she starting crying again, he was going to commit suicide.

Picking up the phone from the nightstand, Mac dialed the front desk. Avoiding her gaze, he checked out the framed landscaped picture hanging next to the bathroom door, the open closet, the writing desk, and the TV.

Waiting through the uncomfortable silence, Mac chanced a look at Emily who'd barely stepped into the room. From the frown on her face, she wasn't moving any further.

The news wasn't good.

Dread mounting, Mac hung up the phone. "Desk clerk said there was a mix up. This is the only room." Knowing he'd never convince Emily to stay, he grabbed the envelope and scooped up the assorted toiletries. Finished, he turned to Emily. "Let's take the key back. You drive until we find another motel. I'm too tired."

"I can't," she said, inching into the room.

Confused by her statement, Mac stumbled backward. "You can't drive?"

"I have night blindness," she answered casually, like somehow he should have known that. "You sleep on the floor."

71

Mac tossed the toiletries back onto the bed. "Like hell." He folded his arms. "After flying from Russia, you want me to sleep on the floor when there is a bed big enough for both of us?"

She lifted her bruised chin. That gesture was starting to piss him off. "Yes."

Oh, she was itching for a fight. "Come on," Mac fumed, taking the keys out of his pocket. "I'll drive."

To his surprise, when he stalked passed her, Em touched his arm, pulling him to a quick halt. "And take a chance on us ending up as road kill? No thanks. We'll stay here and make the best of it."

Doom settled across his shoulders with the weight of a telephone pole. This couldn't be good.

For the umpteenth time since he'd connected with Em, Mac didn't know what to do. He felt like his face had been used for a punching bag because that's exactly what'd happened. He expected his head to explode any minute. Yet with all his aches, pains, and exhaustion, his concern for Em frightened him more than anything he'd ever encountered.

Deep in his gut, Mac knew this room, this motel, and them spending all this time together, wasn't good for either one of them. Taking a deep breath, he rolled his shoulders and said, "Let's get this straight," he said. "I'm taking a shower. Then I'm going to sleep on that bed." He pointed to the king-sized bed. "And that's the end of it."

The words were no sooner out of his mouth than Em's body drew tight as a bow. Her eyes glazed over with murderous intentions as she slowly turned to face him.

"Don't you dare give orders, demands, or even suggestions," she hissed. "You've been bossing me around since Moscow. You sleep in that bed with permission only." Emily touched her chest. "My permission!"

He jacked his fists against his waist. "So I have to ask to be invited?"

Defiantly, she lifted her nose and turned her back. "Yes."

Well, fuck me sideways.

72

CHAPTER EIGHT

The room reminded Emily of a small box. All it needed was a lid and packing tape, and she'd suffocate. Alone, with a dangerous man, Emily couldn't help wondering what to expect next.

Mac had managed to turn her life into such disarray she wanted to scream. And it was all because she'd helped him out of Moscow. Now, somehow she was stuck with him. At least until someone managed to figure this all out. That could take days, weeks, or months. Who knew?

Mac moved to stand in front of her, his cobalt eyes dark and deadly.

His intimidating gaze kicked up the tempo of her heart, and she had to remind herself to breathe. She refused to reveal evidence that she'd love to grab him by the shirt, drag him to bed, and make love until they were both drunk on lust.

She wouldn't dare; still, a girl could dream. Emily did not flinch when Mac reached over her head and shut the door.

Swallowing, Emily sighed then met his bold stare, just to prove she wasn't afraid. Somehow, the resounding thud of the door closing reminded her of a steel trap.

To hide her discomfort in a room that shrank by the minute, Emily cleared her throat and walked over to a small round table. Breaking eye contact with Mac, she put down her purse, briefcase, and laptop.

Looking at her airport purchased jeans and blouse, Emily thought about all her clothes left behind in the Russian hotel when those crazy guys tried to kill them.

Mac stood by the door, staring like a fox checking out his dinner. Ankles crossed, hands folded, he leaned casually against the wall. While he appeared to be in the comfort of his own home, she wanted to bolt. But where would she go?

Finally, he shoved away and said, "Relax, nothing's going to happen. I'm beat. All I want is a shower and a bed."

"A shower sounds nice," she said then cringed at the squeakiness of her own voice. She cleared her throat. "When you're finished, I'll take mine."

"I'm going to go get some ice. My head hurts. Do you want anything?"

"You all right?"

"I'll be fine. Just tired."

"Okay." She sighed with relief. "Do you want me to go get the ice? I don't mind."

"No, I'll only be a minute. You want me to bring you something?"

"A Diet Coke would be nice."

"That stuff causes brain cancer or some shit like that."

"I drink what I like."

He tossed her an *Of course, you do* look. After picking up the ice bucket, he stepped to the door. "Lock it behind me."

With him gone, Emily filled her lungs with air. The man was so big there was no space for her.

The motel was decent but had no amenities. No fitness room, no sauna, and no indoor pool. However, she did plan to make full use of the soap, shampoo, and towels. Just to be on the safe side, Emily bent down, lifted the corner of the bedspread and checked for critters. Satisfied, she connected her laptop, so she could catch up on her emails.

She wanted to contact Brenda and give her a better explanation for being late, but she didn't want her to worry. Then she needed to let Debbie, her dog sitter, know she wouldn't be home as expected. However, she wanted to wait until she knew for sure exactly when she'd be able to pick up Hershey.

Before sitting down, she clicked on the television, and the nightly news filled the screen.

Back in the room, Mac locked the door and placed the ice bucket on the table. He flopped down on the bed. "When you're through with your laptop, can I use it for a few minutes?"

"Sure, I only have a few emails."

"Don't tell anyone where we are."

74

Tossing him a scorching glare, she replied, "Really?"

He returned a stiff glance before the sports came on.

When she finished, she said, "Do you know nothing has been reported about that incident in London or that mess at DFW?"

"That's not unusual."

"What do you mean, not unusual? Someone tried to kill us."

He shrugged.

"Tell me that being threatened at gunpoint is not newsworthy."

Reclining casually, Mac looked up at her, his brows pulled together. "Did you see a newsman standing in the corner taking pictures?"

"No, but surely the police followed up. Filed a report?"

Mac shook his head.

"You live in a very dangerous world, Mac. You're lucky to be alive."

"I know."

"If I were you, I'd start a new career. Yours doesn't have a good retirement plan."

He laughed. A devouring smile traced across his lips. "I've never thought of retiring."

"No?" Blood pulsed through her, heating up her body temperature and making her squirm. Lord, she hated that Mac could control her heart rate with a simple look. In an instant, they were back on the plane and she felt him inside her.

Trying to distract herself, Emily popped the top on her drink and took a long swallow. Putting the can down, she stood. "I'm finished."

He took the chair she'd vacated and went to work on the keyboard. It surprised her that he actually typed faster than she did. How could he be quick with a gun *and* a speed typist? Beneath lowered lashes, she watched him as he worked on the laptop.

He must have felt her staring because his gaze collided with hers. "What?"

"Nothing," she replied. Uncomfortable with her feelings, she stepped away and fudged interest in the television.

Finished, he closed the laptop and put it back in the case. He removed a gun from the back of his waistband and put it on the table next to the bed.

"I'm taking a shower. Are you going to be out here when I'm finished?"

Stunned by his question, she asked, "Have I said anything about leaving?"

"No, but that doesn't mean the thought hasn't crossed your mind."

"It *has*, but where would I go? Have you forgotten? I'm blind?"

A crooked grin played with the corners of his mouth and her knees wobbled. "Maybe I'd better handcuff you to the bed anyway."

She shot to her feet, eyes narrowed. "You just try."

He laughed. "While the idea is tempting, I'm all out of hardware. I'll just have to trust you."

"Trust me?" she seethed. "I'm the one who trusted you enough to get on a plane with you. Get you across the ocean. And fight off a mob of guys at *two* airports."

Arms raised, he chuckled. "Okay, okay, so we trust each other. I'm going to go take a shower." While he kicked off his shoes, she took the toiletries out of the large envelope Zoe had handed her on the way out of Frank's office. Arms full, she put everything on the stand next to the bathroom.

Carefully, Mac pulled the tail of his shirt out of his pants. His face tightened when he shrugged it off and tossed it on the bed. His body was a mass of bruises. He went into the dressing room and stood in front of the sink.

His head came up and he looked at her in the mirror. "Do you have anything in your purse? Aspirin, Tylenol?"

Hoping drool wasn't leaking out of the corners of her mouth, she shook her head. "Sorry, just a small bottle of Midol, and that might mess with your testosterone and turn you into a menstruating woman. Wouldn't that be terrible?" She turned her back to him and picked up her can of Coke.

To her surprise, two strong arms wrapped around her waist and his mouth nuzzled her neck. Off balance, she fell backwards against a hot, bare chest, and Emily sucked in a nervous breath.

While she tried not to faint, he whispered into her ear, "You keep tossing out threats like that, Em, and you're going to force me to show you just how good I am, and I'm not talking about a damn quickie on a plane."

If she were a teapot, she'd be whistling loud enough to set off a fire alarm. His male scent accosted her, teased her, and taunted her feminine insides. Slowly, Emily stepped away from him with the pretense of a sudden urge to change the channel on the television.

"I'm not threatening you, Mac. I'm just letting you know, loud and clear, so there won't be any misinterpretations on exactly how I feel. No mixed signals, no subtle innuendos." She turned to face him. "And no sex."

Suddenly, Mac wiggled an *I got you* finger at her. "I didn't say anything about sex. You need to stop letting your imagination run so wild, Em." He came closer, and put his palm against her cheek. With deliberate slowness, he ran his thumb along her bottom lip, making her quiver. "But I can guarantee you I do my best work with a woman between me and the mattress."

Struggling to keep from swaying, Emily forced herself to stare at him without flinching. She'd been sweet-talked before, and it wasn't going to happen again.

Releasing her, he walked over to the bed. "I'll take the side closest to the door, if you don't mind." He stopped then turned to her. "With your permission, of course."

She shrugged her shoulders. "Whatever."

As he pulled his personal things from his pockets and put them on the table, he unbuttoned his pants. Emily hoped her knees wouldn't buckle as he slowly pushed his jeans down his narrow hips.

***

In his favor, Zoe had packed a set of clean clothes for him, but it would've been nice if she had found something for Em to wear. He made a mental note to stop somewhere, so they could pick her up a change of clothes.

The adrenalin had vanished, and Mac's battered body screamed with every move. A muffled groan tumbled from his lips as he stepped into the tub beneath the shower head. After a few deep breaths, he turned on the water and braced his hands against the tile.

Relief rolled down his back like a mudslide as the hot water pulsated against his sore, stiff shoulders. At this moment, nothing felt better or was needed more. God, exhaustion seeped from his pores, making it difficult for him to stand. After shampooing his hair, Mac thought about lying down and going to sleep in the tub with the water running.

Em.

That woman had such a hold on him Mac wasn't sure he could take anymore. In all his thirty-two years he'd never wanted a woman this badly. The whole situation was foreign. He didn't know what to do or how to handle her moods, her laughter, or her bravery.

Every time he opened his mouth, he sounded like a tongue-tied, sixteen-year old. And they were sharing a motel room together, in the same bed?

He didn't stand a chance in hell.

Reluctantly, he turned off the water and stepped from the tub. As he reached for the towel, it felt like a sledgehammer smacked him in the side. Shocked, Mac bit back a scream. Bending over, he held his breath and waited for the wave of nausea to pass.

This particular pain blew in with shadows of familiarity. Somehow he'd managed to crack a rib, and he didn't need a doctor or x-rays to confirm his diagnosis. Nope, been there, done that…way too many times.

Trying to refocus his gaze, Mac released the air from his lungs and gently dried off. He hopped around a few times, smacked the wall with his shoulder then finally managed to slip on clean underwear.

Leaving the steamy room, Mac ruffled his hair and kept his right arm pressed against his side. No need for Em to worry.

With only two towels in the room, Mac spread the towel out on the bar to dry, so he could use it again in the morning.

Turning around, his gaze fell to the bed, and he stilled. Em lay relaxed, her cheek pillowed on her bent arm. She appeared more settled now. Not strung out like in the car. Every word she'd said had sliced through his heart like a butcher's knife. But Mac didn't know how to fix that.

Hysterical women freaked him out more than a heat seeking missile. When Em went off on him, he'd wished she would've shot him instead. *That* he could deal with. He had no experience with women PMSing. His military training or intelligence knowledge didn't extend to a woman like Em.

Careful not to reignite her, Mac said, "You're next."

Wordlessly, she eased off the bed and stalked past him. A few seconds later the door slammed, shaking the cheap pictures on the wall.

As he stepped toward the bed, another sharp pain made him grab his side. Easing his way across the room with the aid of a chair, small desk, and an ottoman, Mac finally sat on the edge of the bed and released a pensive breath. Sweat peppered his forehead, and his stomach rolled.

Em stepped from the bathroom chased by the scent of mint toothpaste. Her face shiny and her hair free from the constraints of the rubber band. She glanced at him, her brow wrinkled. "Are you hurt?"

Not wanting to do anything that might upset her, Mac relaxed. "No, not really. I might have bruised a rib. But I'm okay."

Hands on her hips, she said, "Spoken like a true man." Like being a man was a bad thing, she turned and moved to the sink. "Get in bed and I'll fix an ice pack."

Stiff and sore, he crawled between the clean sheets. The air conditioner pumped out some serious cold air. Maybe he should raise the thermostat.

Before he could make a move, Emily pulled back the covers. With the ice bag wrapped in a small white towel, she put it on the table and handed him her Coke. He shook his head, but when she opened her fist and held out two round pills, his eyes locked with hers.

"Advil," she said. "Found them in the bottom of my purse. Best I can do."

Grunting, Mac pushed to his elbow. He popped the pills in his mouth and chased them with a swallow of the lukewarm, bitter soda. When he collapsed, she put the ice pack on his side then pulled the blanket to his chin.

"I'm going to take my shower," she said. "A word of warning. You stay on your side of the bed."

"Yes, ma'am." He waited for the sound of running water. When it came, Mac closed his eyes and listened to Jay Leno on the TV. Facing the door, he couldn't see the screen, but that was okay. All he wanted was a painless night's sleep.

He must have dozed because when he opened his eyes again he saw Em from the light reflecting off the screen of the TV. Quietly, she walked toward the door. Her wet auburn hair hung in shiny ringlets. She'd pulled on his T-shirt. She might be short, but Mac swore he'd never imagined legs that long or shapely before. And by God, he'd seen some legs.

Did she plan on leaving? He tensed, prepared to stop her. She pulled the curtain away from the window and looked out; then she checked the lock on the door. Just as she turned, Mac closed his eyes. His side felt much better.

The room grew silent when she turned off the television, and the hard mattress sagged slightly beneath her weight as she sat on the edge of the bed next to him. She lifted the covers to remove the ice pack, and cool air kissed his skin. Gently, she pulled the blanket over his shoulders.

Finally, Em stood and went around to the other side of the bed, but not before giving Mac a perfect glance of a pair of red bikini panties she must have bought at the airport in London shadowed beneath his black T-shirt.

It also caught him by surprise that he liked the idea of her sleeping in his clothes. Her body in his shirt seemed sexy as all get out.

Mac waited for her to get into bed. With the noise and light gone from the room, she slid in beside him and turned her back. She had to be hanging on the edge of the bed because she certainly wasn't anywhere near him. He wanted to chuckle, but he decided to sleep instead.

***

Long before daylight, Mac woke from a deep slumber. He stilled, gathering his bearing. Then he realized what had disturbed his sleep—a hot, little body pressed against his back like a second skin and a world-class hard-on.

Damn.

Mac knew he had to get some distance between him and Em, but at the moment, he was in a very awkward position. Em, the man-hater, was wrapped round him like paper on a present. To make matters worse, her smooth leg was wedged between his, her other stacked on his thigh.

She had him trapped and it felt *good*. Her warm body spooned his, with all the right body parts lining up perfectly. If he weren't on assignment he'd probably sleep like this for days.

But he couldn't.

Slowly, so as not to wake Em, he untangled himself. When he finally sat up and planted his feet on the carpeted floor, she mumbled something and rolled over.

After limping to the bathroom, Mac took a very painful piss. Now, what to do about the damn woody? No jacking off, he couldn't muster that. So he did the next best thing, he removed his underwear, picked up the bucket of ice, gulped half the cold water then poured the rest down his belly. His thirst quenched, his dick limp, Mac dried off, slipped on his shorts, and looked at the bed.

With help from the outside security lights, he saw her tousled hair fanned out on the pillowcase and his mouth watered, making the pain in his groin intensify. Em was prettier than he first imagined, and he rarely made mistakes like that. She had a certain natural beauty and wittiness he found refreshing and sexy as hell.

All his life, he'd been attracted to pretty woman. Models, stewardesses, tall blondes, chicks like that. He never went for brains, personality, or a sense of humor.

No, he was a hands-on guy. Not the type to spend a lot of time with one woman. Never settled for one when two was so much more fun.

Mac didn't engage in tight relationships and couldn't fathom ever asking a woman to marry him. The very words would probably choke him to death.

If marriage was anything like the hell his parents suffered through, he wanted no damn part of it. The accusations, the cussing, the drinking had made his childhood a living hell. The drugs came later. A strung out dealer shot his mother sixteen months after his father went to jail on a robbery charge.

When all was said and done, he'd ended up in the foster care system until he was old enough to join the Navy. His parents left him so bitter there was no room in his heart for love.

Marriage my ass. Give me a firing squad any day.

Besides, the life he led, the jobs he worked, and his personality in general, weren't ideal for a wife or family. He never knew where he'd be next, or if he'd be coming back.

Every time he went on a mission, the odds were he wouldn't return. So, why put a woman through that? Better he just did what he was paid to do and keep his relationships light. So far he'd had no complaints.

Mac walked across the room and stopped next to the bed. Mouth tight, he stared down at Em, who not only took most of the bed, but she had all the covers. Holding his side, he reached down, grabbed the corner of the blanket, and dumped her on the floor.

She jumped up like a drowning victim surfacing. Shoving her hair out of her face, she frantically looked around. "What! What's wrong?"

"Nothing," he said, wrapping himself in the blanket. He lay down and fluffed the pillow beneath his head.

"Hey," she said. "You took the covers."

He rolled on his back. "That's a switch because you had them and most of the bed all night. Now, it's my turn."

"I'm not a bed hog."

"The hell you aren't. Now let me get some sleep." He turned his back just as Em whacked his head with a pillow. He slowly tossed the covers aside, stood and faced her. Her hair all tangled, breasts pushing against his shirt, and those legs he'd dreamed about trapped in the sheets.

Mac fisted his hands. He was either going to take her down or make love to her like she'd never imagined possible. The choice was his. He was meaner, tougher, and horny as hell. Odds were Emily Richards, the great mediator, was about to learn what a real man could do.

CHAPTER NINE

Emily wanted to kill. "So, all I get is a sheet? That isn't fair. It's cold." For the first time in her life Emily wanted to jump up and down like a three-year old, but she refused to belittle herself in front of him.

"Tough."

Balling her fists, she shouted, "Fine!"

She stumbled around the dark room, stubbed her toe, bumped into a dresser then finally made it to where she'd left her shoes.

Angrily, she yanked on her jeans, walked over, and unlocked the door.

"Where are you going? Shut that door."

"I'm getting my own blanket. I'm sure the desk clerk has an extra one." She wasn't about to put up with him bossing her around.

"Come back here."

"I want a blanket." She stepped out of the room.

A strange male voice drew nearer, and Emily turned toward the sound. From the security lights attached to the eaves of the motel, a man wearing a black cowboy hat walked her way.

"Hey, little lady, you want to have some fun? Me and my buddies are having a party down there in 208. Wanna join us?"

This didn't look good, and Emily had no desire to put up with another jerk. "No thanks," she said as he drew closer. Without pause, she backed into the room and closed the door in the young man's face.

What else could go wrong?

"Lock it," Mac demanded.

As she turned the latch, a knock sounded from the opposite side.

"Come on out, sweetheart."

Emily leaned her forehead against the wall. What a night this had turned out to be. Before she could tell the guy to go away, Mac came up behind her. Wearing a dark scowl, he jerked his head, motioning her to move out of the way. When she did, he yanked open the door.

She couldn't help but notice with light streaming in from outside how Mac's black boxers hugged his toned rear.

Boldly, Mac grabbed the young man by the collar. "Get the fuck away from this door before you get more than you bargained for, cowboy."

With a grunt, Mac released the kid. He staggered backwards, his hands at his throat. "Hey, I didn't mean no harm. Ain't no cause to get all riled up."

"You mess with my wife, and I get plenty *riled*. And when I do, I go looking to hurt somebody." Taking a threatening step forward, Mac demanded, "Get back to your room."

Mac stepped into their room, slammed then bolted the door. He turned back to Emily, pointing a damning finger. "You're a lot of trouble."

"Me," she screeched. His insanity ran rampant. What had she done? "I was only going to get a blanket because you took the covers. So, now all this is this my fault? If you hadn't been so grouchy, I would still be sound asleep. I wasn't looking for trouble and don't you even hint I encouraged that idiot."

"I know you didn't give him the come on," Mac said wearily. "I'm just tired. I want some sleep."

Was that an apology? Probably as close as she'd get coming from him.

Guilt set in when she noticed the lines around his eyes. No doubt he was exhausted. His shoulders slumped and the dark shadow on the bottom of his face gave him a sinister look. A barrage of blame like Niagara Falls washed over her. She groaned. How much more of this could she take? Enough already.

"Look," Emily said. "I'm sorry about all this. I'm acting like a moron. I know you're tired."

"Yeah, I think that makes two of us. How about we just get some sleep?"

Together, they straightened the sheets on the bed and Mac crawled beneath the blanket with a heavy sigh. "Stay on your side of the bed," he grumbled.

"Yes, sir," she mimicked. "Gladly. Who wants to sleep cuddled up next to you?"

"Oh, I'm sorry I didn't pack my charming personality this trip."

"You don't own a charming anything. Go to sleep, Mac."

A strange, yet dangerous silence settled momentarily. Mac turned to her.

Quicker than she could draw her next breath, Mac had her pinned beneath him, straddling her.

He leaned over, placing his face directly in front of hers, his hot breath brushing against her cheeks. He yanked up her shirt. "Don't mess with me. I'm mean." Her gaze locked with his. "Now, let's get to sleep." His stare intensified. "Or do you want me to continue?"

Shocked, Emily opened her mouth, but no words came out. She blinked. Her breath trapped somewhere between her lungs and her nostrils.

Despite his injury, he smoothly swung off her then flopped on his side of the bed, leaving her exposed and stunned.

What in God's name just happened? He could have taken her in an instant, and she would have been helpless to stop him. He was quick and deadly, even wounded. In all her years, Emily had never seen a man move so fast.

With his back to her, Emily lowered her top, but remained rigid. No matter how much she tried, she couldn't ignore the loud pounding of her heart or her racing pulse. And she'd trusted the agent without question.

Foolish.

The darkness of the room closed in on her as she fought back tears. Frightened and shivering, Emily stared at the ceiling, as she clutched the blanket beneath her chin. Never had she felt so vulnerable. She realized for her own good, she had to get away before something happened.

Careful not to touch him, or breathe too heavily, Emily closed her eyes and prayed.

***

Mac was at the point he wanted to shoot himself. That was a dumb assed thing to do, he scolded himself.

What were you trying to prove? That you could overpower her? Was there any doubt? Shit, she doesn't weigh anything, and you just extinguished the only hint of guts you'd ever seen in a woman.

The look in her face damned him. The fear in her eyes taunted him, and his gut burned like he'd eaten a bowl of jalapenos. Realization hurt worse than his ribs. He'd cut his own damn throat before he ever again saw that look in Em's eyes. And he'd kill any other man who made the same mistake.

She moved slightly and Mac hoped she wasn't going to cry. If she cried, it would be all over. He was going to take the fucking Glock off the nightstand and blow his damn head off.

Of all the stupid things he could have done, this took the prize. If he wanted to punish her, it had worked. But he'd also done a good job on himself.

He wanted her, but he wanted her willing, eager.

Ever since he'd met her, he'd been a royal son of a bitch, and he didn't know why. What was it about Em that brought out the worst in him, even when he wanted to be nice? It was as if he deliberately shoved her away and did everything he could to show her what an ass he could be.

She didn't do anything other than provoke him a little. Hell, that just showed her spunk and tenacity. She shouldn't have to put up with his foul disposition and meanness.

Mac moved a little, trying to relieve his discomfort. All he thought about was Em's flaring hips and heavy breasts. He never wanted to taste anything in his whole life like he wanted to wrap his lips round her nipples and suck.

He was in for a long night, a very long night. The artificial light from the sign outside slithered through the gaps in the drapes.

What was she thinking over there? That he was a bastard? Damn, he wished he could get rid of her.

Well, after tonight he'd never see her again. He pulled up the covers. If he could get through the next few hours he'd be home free.

CHAPTER TEN

The sound of soft, whispery snores woke Emily from a sound sleep. Aware she wasn't home in her own bed, Emily blinked several times to get her bearings. Squinting into the dimness, she saw Mac McKinsey slumbering sweetly on *her* side of the bed. One of his legs stacked on hers, chest snuggled against her back, and his arms held her captive in a cage of flesh.

Dim light streamed through the window to confirm that the day was soon to begin. After the restless night she'd had, sunshine would be welcome relief. Rubbing her eyes, Emily swore this was the longest night of her life.

At first she wanted to wake her bed partner, and let him see that she was indeed on her side of the bed. But she didn't want the hassle. Much too early to argue.

However, she wasn't letting him off the hook.

Hell, no. After the little stunt he'd pulled earlier, she wanted to smother him with his own pillow.

She shifted away from him, but the moment she moved, his grip tightened and he clutched her closer. In a way, she couldn't blame him. The temperature in the room had to be close to zero. The air conditioner must be frozen. Regardless, she wasn't in the mood to cuddle.

After several minutes, Emily managed to untangle herself and sit up on the edge of the bed. The mattress squeaked loudly as she stood.

"Em," he muttered.

Well, at least he hadn't called her by another woman's name. Oh yeah, now she remembered why. *He forgets all his women the next morning.*

Lucky guy.

"I'm just going to the bathroom, but since you're awake, you might notice where you're lying. I'm not the only one who takes up the entire bed."

She didn't wait around to see if he followed her suggestion or not because she went into the bathroom and closed the door. Now, she wished she hadn't been so generous with her last two Advil. At the moment, she could use them to get rid of a raging headache.

Rubbing her temples, Emily would bite off her tongue before verbalizing that Mac had the most powerful and widest chest she'd ever been held against. That she loved the way he held on to her like a life raft. That, too, would never be said aloud.

She couldn't continue this constant friction between them. It was too unnerving and drained all her energy. She wanted him and his sexy eyes all over her, but Mac not only wasn't her type, he'd made it clear he didn't want to be anyone's permanent anything.

Flipping off the light switch, Emily opened the door and stepped out. Deliberately trying not to disturb Mac's sleep, she made her way to the bed by memory and shivered when she crawled beneath the blanket and fluffed her pillow.

Mac's arms instantly came around her waist, and he pulled her against his hard body. His scent raked over her like a thick mist of desire, wrapped around a body too long without affection. The rhythmic sound of his heart beating caused her to still.

Determined to safeguard her emotions, she wiggled away, but he held tight. His nose nuzzled her hair, his lips touched the rim of her ear, and Emily practically melted into the mattress. She tried to ignore the fact his touch scorched her body and made her want what she knew she couldn't have.

Him.

Slowly, Emily moved the arm from around her and put as much distance between them as she could by scooting to the far edge of the bed.

"Still mad?" he murmured, in a voice so sexy it should be used in every suggestive commercial in the world. "Come back over here. I'm cold."

God she wanted him.

"Mac, I don't want to cuddle with you." *Too dangerous.*

"Just look at it as a survival technique." That said, he snuggled against her. When she struggled, he said, "I wouldn't do too much wiggling around, if you know what I mean?"

"I don't want to survive with you. I want you on your side of the bed and me on mine."

He nestled closer. "I'm really sorry I penned you down. That wasn't a nice thing to do. I didn't mean to frighten you. I promise I'll never do that again."

His words sounded so sincere and caring she almost believed him.

"Now, you're claiming you have a nice side?"

"Shhh," he hushed in her ear. "Let's sleep."

Emily had no idea what to think of Mac. Was she safe or wasn't she? Would he harm her? She didn't want to think so because he worked for one of her best clients. However, she knew little about him. Ironically, here she was, sleeping with the guy and wanting him so badly her teeth hurt.

Emily closed her eyes and drifted off to sleep only to be roused by the loud ringing of the telephone on the table. Mac groped in the dark and finally picked up the receiver, then immediately hung up.

"Was that the wakeup call," she asked, burrowing deeper into the warmth of the blanket.

"Yeah, but we have a few minutes."

***

Mac rolled back over and resumed his previous position, which was them being as close as two people could get without going at it.

Damn, he was horny as hell. And Emily felt like heaven in his arms. They fit together like they'd been poured out of the same mold. Her hair smelled clean and intoxicating. The scent inflated his desire, making it hard to resist the urge to make love to her.

Horny or not, Mac knew better. Not only could it be stupid to get involved with the company lawyer, but he had a job to do. However, it wouldn't hurt to just lie here for a few minutes and keep her warm. Enjoy the feel of her feminine body, inhale her sleepy scent.

Slowly, Mac brushed his hands beneath his shirt she wore and cupped her warm breasts. Her breathing increased, but she didn't stop him. Reverently, he nibbled the back of her neck and kissed behind her ears. A soft moan tumbled from her mouth. A mouth he fully intended to kiss.

She turned so they faced each other; then he captured her mouth, and his lips nudged hers open. When she responded, he deepened the kiss and his tongue stroked the dark interior of her satin mouth. A whimper allowed him complete access.

Mac's whole body came to attention as his hard dick brushed against her soft stomach. She ran her fingers through his hair as her other hand on his back coaxed him closer.

Then he rolled them over, putting her on top. God, she looked beautiful, sitting on his lap with her body opened to him. All reasoning vanished from his mind. Uncontrollable need drove them both.

Mac rose to capture one perfect breast with his mouth while his thumb and index squeezed the other nipple. With a groan, Em threw her head back and closed her eyes.

For a moment, he released her only to pull off the shirt and her red bikini panties. She was naked and mouthwatering. Bucking up and ignoring the pain in his side, he pulled off his boxers.

Em gazed at his erection. Her smile gave him the ultimate compliment every man craved. Mac smiled at her Brazilian wax job.

His heart pounded against his ribcage, his head spun, and every muscle grew taut. He captured her mouth and kissed her long, hard, and demanding. He sucked on her bottom lip, nibbling softly with his teeth. Inhaling her familiar scent, he felt her warm, feminine body against his.

His hand went between her open legs where he rubbed her, parted her, and probed her with two fingers. She cried out in pleasure, as he withdrew only to slowly lick his fingers.

Delicious!

Mac wanted nothing more than to spend the whole day in bed, making love.

He flipped her over.

"Mac, I want you inside me."

"That's exactly where I want to be. Damn, you're sweet." He kissed her again as his hand fumbled for the wallet on the nightstand. He wasn't having any luck. Mac realized if he didn't get the condom soon, this was going to be the first time he had unprotected sex.

Em broke their kiss, took his wallet off the nightstand, and removed the foil package. Smiling, she waved it in the air. "Looking for this?" She arched her slender brow.

Once covered, he entered her slowly, sweat peppering his forehead. In then out, further in then back out, until finally Mac couldn't stand it anymore. Her body had such a hold on him he thought he'd explode.

Gritting his teeth, Mac pushed deep into her body and felt her squeeze tight as a clenched hand around him. She closed her eyes as he rocked back and forth, in and out, the pressure growing stronger and harder…fierce.

Em clutched his back, and he kissed her deep and hard and desperately. He raised his head. "Open your eyes, Em. I want to see you come."

She complied.

He took her hands in his, threading their fingers together. Out of need for a long-awaited release, he thrust hard, going deeper. He increased the pace and felt her body tremble with desire. Her honey brown eyes turned a soft golden color that pulled at his heart as his muscles tightened and he fought to hold back until she reached her satisfaction.

Then it happened. She arched her back as tiny pulses pulled at his dick, and Em cried out just as wave after wave of pleasure tumbled him right into paradise. Mac tried to hold on to that part of himself he never gave away, but he couldn't. The intensity almost blinded him. And it went on until they were both satiated and limp.

She lay beneath him, mellow and soft with a sexy smile on her face. Mac removed the condom, pulled her closer then kissed her. "You okay?"

"Oh, yes," she breathed out.

Wrapped in each other's arms, they both fell into deep slumber.

***

Later, Mac opened his eyes, yawned and stretched before he noticed he was alone. Worried about Em, he stood. The room spun. Closing his eyes, he shook his head to clear the cobwebs. "Em," he called.

Relief, like he'd never known, coursed through him when he heard the sound of running water and Em softly humming in the shower. Closing his eyes, Mac slumped against the headboard. Then all the memories of what had happened earlier slammed into his brain like an all-out offensive. Mac tried to take a deep breath only to find he couldn't. His emotions were too raw and exposed.

Remembering their lovemaking, he sat on the edge of the bed and scrubbed his face. His wristwatch lay on the nightstand. Once his eyes focused, he picked it up—nine thirty. They should have been at Stanley's by eight.

Since the day he'd enlisted in the Navy, gone through BUD/S training and became a SEAL, Mac had always done what he was directed to do. He rarely failed and never stepped out of line with something as serious as getting involved with a civilian.

A person he was trusted to protect. Even taking Angelina from the nunnery had been sanctioned by Frank and the Agency.

Frank was going to chew him up and spit him out then kick his ass to Canada.

The noise in the shower stopped. After a few seconds, Emily stepped into the dressing area outside the bathroom. Mac slipped on his pants and picked up his cell phone.

God, he wanted her again…and again.

After clearing his throat, Mac asked, "Ah, can I get in there?"

She turned and their gazes collided. She looked the happiest he'd seen since this mess started. "Yes, I'm finished."

She had a white towel wrapped around her hot little body and the other one twisted around her hair, which meant he'd be drying off on a small hand towel.

Em strolled toward him, a sultry smile that silently asked if he would be interested in a repeat of last night. Her warm brown eyes, delicate brows, and kissable lips all summed up one gorgeous woman. And that body was made for a man to love *forever*.

Uncomfortable as hell, Mac kissed her quickly on the forehead then practically ran into the bathroom and closed the door.

Man up, Slick, he tried to convince himself.

He stripped, turned on the shower then stepped into the tub. The warm water felt good against his cold flesh and his sore muscles. Maybe his ribs hadn't been broken after all.

After his shower, he dressed in the bathroom since he wasn't sure where Em was, and he was in no hurry to face her.

Yes, he felt like a royal jerk.

But he could never handle the next morning very well. That's why he never brought dates home. Never allowed anyone to spend the night and would rather be out the cost of a hotel room than experience the goodbyes. If he spent the night at a woman's place, he made damn sure to always be long gone before daylight.

And he made that clear in the beginning.

Yes, it was shallow and lot of other shit, but that was who he was, and the thought of changing never entered his mind.

Strange, but sex with Em had been mind-blowing and wonderful.

Special.

This meant he had to end it now. And make damn sure it never happened again. He was a smart man, and someone who couldn't screw with the emotions of a woman like Em. She deserved better.

Hating himself for what he had to do, Mac took his phone off the sink and dialed Frank.

"Mac?" Frank said. "Where are you?"

"We're still at the motel, but I can…"

Frank let out a sigh of relief. "Thank God."

"Really? Why?

"I'm glad Emily was able to get some extra shut-eye. She looked pretty roughed up yesterday."

"Ah, yeah, but…"

"Are you heading to the inventor's place?"

Mac cleared his throat. "Frank, I've been thinking." Rubbing the back of his neck, he fought for the right words. "Maybe you should send another agent to take care of Em. This way I can be out there looking for…"

"For what, Mac? We don't even know what the hell we're up against. Besides, Emily trusts you."

"Yeah, but it's getting…"

"Hold on, I have another call."

Silence.

As his eyes traced every inch of the small bathroom, Mac thought about how tough it was going to be to spend any more time with Em. He had never been in this situation. Still, he was determined to put Em in more competent hands and find out who wanted them dead.

Frank came back on the line. "Mac, you still have that lens camera, right?"

"Yeah, sure."

"Get that developed today and send me those pictures. Word's out that Emily might have managed to capture some serious intel. Tony found out someone followed her into the hotel in Moscow looking for information."

"Information about Em?"

"Yeah. Like who she worked for, why was she there. Stuff like that."

"Okay…but—"

"Get on it, Mac. We don't have a lot of time."

Well, that hadn't gone the way he'd hoped. Sticking the phone in his pocket, he stepped into the dressing area and expected to see Em's reflection in the mirror.

Instead, the room was empty.

"Em," he called, knowing she wasn't hiding under the bed. "Em?"

By instinct, Mac ran to the door and found the chain latch undone. He smacked the frame. Damn, where was she? Where could she go?

Disregarding everything, Mac yanked the door open and stepped out into the morning air. The black SUV sat parked where he'd left it.

Food!

Wasting no time, Mac ran down the walkway toward the vending machines. As he turned the corner, he plowed into the young cowboy from the night before. Surprised, the boy stopped and looked at Mac like his head was missing.

Mac grabbed the young boy by the shirt and pulled him close. "Where is she?"

The guy tried to draw back, but Mac held him too tight. "Who, man?"

"My wife?"

The redneck thumbed over his shoulder. "She's in there."

Shoving the boy aside, Mac darted into the small square room that held the ice machine, soda, and candy vending machines.

Mac rubbed his eyes and exhaled slowly. Emily Richards was the only woman who had the remarkable ability to scare the holy shit out of him.

Huffing hard, Mac saw her standing with a Diet Coke and a small orange juice in one hand, her other poised above the coin slot. She turned and looked at him, her fine brows drawn together. "What are you doing out here barefooted?"

"You lose track of your wife?"

"Mind your own business."

The boy inched backwards. "Fuck you too, mister."

Mac turned his attention to Em. "What do you mean leaving the room like that?"

"Like what?" she injected in a dry tone. "Opening the door and walking out?"

"You know what I mean. I thought you'd left."

She strolled from the vending room toward their room, him following close behind, unable to think of one word of small talk.

"Now, why would a woman leave a man as warm and cuddly as you, Mac?" Still walking, she handed the orange juice over her shoulder, and he took it. "No shirt, no shoes, no service."

He could only mumble like an idiot.

Outside their door, she slid the card key in place, and the door swung open. The coolness of the room wrapped around his bare shoulders. Before going out, Em had obviously adjusted the thermostat.

"Don't leave unless I know where you're going. You scared the hell out of me."

"I just went to get a drink for me and some juice for you. What'd you think? I'd stolen the car and run off." Her face brightened and her eyes rounded. "That's exactly what you thought

95

wasn't it, Super Spy." She slammed the Coke down on the table and faced him, her hands jammed against her waist. "You need to learn something about me. I don't run, I don't hide, and I never walk out on anyone."

"Fine," he muttered. "I was just concerned, that's all."

"Concerned that I'd leave you stranded. Is that all you care about?"

He wanted to argue, but what could he say. She was right. He'd thought she cut out on him, and he would be stuck here until Falcon brought another car. But what really scared him shitless was that while she was out there someone could have taken her. Maybe hurt her because she was with him. He couldn't live with that.

I've never left anyone. It galled him that some asshole had done a number on Em. Even before hearing the whole story, Mac hated every man who'd ever hurt Em and hoped they all suffered from chronic Erectile Dysfunction.

Was he any better?

Eyes averted, he untapped the cap on the orange juice and took a long swallow. It wasn't as cold as he liked, but it was wet and sweet.

"You ready?" he asked.

She knocked back a sip of Coke and shrugged. "Couldn't you get me passed on to another agent?"

His heart skipped a beat. "What?"

She nodded toward the bathroom. "The walls are thin as paper. I overheard you talking to Frank."

The pain and sadness in her beautiful brown eyes crushed his chest like a bug beneath his heel. He hadn't meant to hurt her. He wanted her happy and smiling. The only problem was he couldn't be the man to make that happen. He couldn't love her because he'd decided years ago to never go down that dark, scary ally.

"Your safety is what's important, Em. If anything happened to you—"

"Shut up, Mac. I'm sick of your lies and excuses. Morning after regrets setting in?"

"No."

"Liar." She put her hand on her hip. "Don't worry. You'll be free of me soon enough. I'm through playing Falcon's game. I'm going home, and you can all go to hell."

She wore her hair down, straight and shiny. To his surprise, it was longer than he'd thought. He tried to imagine waking up next to her every day for the rest of his life, but his mind went blank as trepidation and insecurity climbed up his spine.

After Em gathered her purse and laptop, Mac took her briefcase and opened the door. Assured it was safe, they left the room and walked toward the stairs.

He knew he had plenty of time to talk some sense into her head before they got to Stanley's.

As they passed room 208, the young cowboy stepped out in front of them. "Hey, Hot Shot. Me and you got a score to settle."

Surely this kid wasn't serious, was he?

"I'd like you to meet my big brother." The cowboy finished by kicking the door to his room open.

A man the size of a sumo wrestler moved in front of the kid, completely blocking the door.

Ah, shit. He wasn't kidding.

CHAPTER ELEVEN

Emily dropped her purse and laptop before wedging herself between Mac and the not-so-Jolly Green Giant. She nearly gagged on the stench of marijuana, stale beer, and an ashtray full of cigarette butts.

"Look, this is no way to start the day," she said, with a cheerfulness she didn't feel. "Let's all go along and mind our own business, okay?"

"Hell no, it ain't okay." The cowboy stepped from behind his protector. Face red and eyes spitting fire, he pointed at Mac. "That son of a bitch grabbed me up by the collar. Accused me of messing with his wife."

"You do that, mister?" the giant asked, in a voice deep as a cavern.

Mac shrugged then set Emily's briefcase on the concrete walkway. "Yeah, that's pretty much how it went down." With a wide stance and his balled fists hanging at his sides, he was ready for action.

"Don't listen to my husband," Emily interrupted quickly, waving her hands in the air. "He has Alzheimer's, and he never knows from one moment to the next what's going on." She tried to shove past the two men and move Mac and her to the safety of the SUV. She'd have better luck walking through a brick wall.

Mac snagged her back pocket and pulled her closer to him. "This could easily be a misunderstanding, but..."

"See," she said. "Just a misunderstanding. Let's go." Her feet moved, but she wasn't covering any ground.

Desperate to get away, Emily reached back and took Mac's hand. A grunt escaped her lips when she tried to pull him toward the stairs. He wouldn't budge. He might as well be super glued to the ugly carpet.

"Em," Mac said. "You go down and get in the car. I'll be right there." A menacing glint sparked in his blue eyes, telling Emily the inevitable. "Gentlemen, my room or yours?"

Emily gritted her teeth. *Grown people didn't act like this.* "Wait one damn minute. No one is going to fight. Do you hear?" She placed her palm on her heart. "I am a professional negotiator. I can talk anyone out of, or into, almost anything."

The three men continued to stare at each other. The giant cracked his knuckles, and Emily wanted to punch him herself.

"Why don't you come in here?" The big guy waved Mac inside.

Eyeing the young man carefully, Mac stepped into the room.

Emily moved in behind him. Inside, she noticed another man sat on the bed, drinking a beer, and smoking a cigarette.

Mac stepped over and tried to edge Emily out the door. "You go down to the car and wait," he said with a sly grin. "I won't be long."

"Oh, no. She stays," said the man, sitting on the bed. "When we finish beating the hell out of you, we'll take good care of your wife."

The younger cowboy reached out to touch Emily, but before Mac could react, Emily picked up the beige cradle phone and smacked the young man in the head. When he went to his knees, Emily drew back her foot and planted it solidly in his chest and shoved. Cowboy Bob dropped like a rotted fence post.

***

Damn, she was getting good at this, and that scared Mac in a proud kind of way.

The other two men looked on in shock.

"Now listen," Em said. "I tried to tell you we don't want trouble, but you wouldn't listen." Calmly, she reached behind her and Mac and opened the door, backing out.

Mac fought back a grin. She had the material of his shirt clutched in her fist. Obviously, where she was going, she planned to take his clothes with her.

The giant's bottom lip quivered, and Mac thought he was going to cry. Instead, he lowered his head then ran toward them. Mac pushed Emily to the opposite side of the door while he stood in the middle, waiting, his feet spread.

As the man came closer, Mac stepped aside, grabbed his arm and a belt loop on his jeans, and tossed the big guy over the wrought iron railing.

Silently, the giant sailed through the air like a missile. The loud thud of a body landing on metal made Mac cringe. Leaning over the rail, Mac saw the guy sprawled in the bed of an old pickup. He and Em turned in unison to face the last man.

He stood slowly then held up his hands in surrender.

That business taken care of, Mac and Emily grabbed her stuff and ran down the stairs, jumped in the car, and left.

"You knocked the hell out of that cowboy."

"Well, he shouldn't have touched me," Em said.

"Remind me never to piss you off."

"Humph, I've been pissed at you since Moscow."

"You never smacked me in the face with a phone."

"Not yet."

As he pulled onto the interstate, Em turned to him and cocked a brow. "Where are we going?"

He couldn't help but like and admire this tough little cookie. Most women in a situation like they'd just been through would have run screaming to the car or sat there with their eyes shut until it was all over. Not Em.

The troublesome thing about the whole matter was that Mac had a strange inclination that Em did what she did back there in the motel because she wanted to protect him. No woman had ever done that before. The thought sent a strange message to his heart, but he wasn't about to try and interpret.

***

Emily had her heart broken before, but for some strange and unimaginable reason Mac's coldness this morning sent her reeling into a dark void of regret, isolation, and shame. *Shame* being the most consuming.

Courageously, she'd fought her attraction to him since he showed up at her hotel room, now she had to face the fact that her heart had led her astray. Hadn't it always?

Wrong guy.

Wrong time.

Wrong place.

Mac headed the list of wrongs in her life when it came to men and love. Why else would she be single and alone at her age when all she'd ever wanted was a husband and a family? It simply wasn't meant to be. So, why did she want to get married so badly? Why was having a man to love in her life so important?

Maybe because she'd never had a steady boyfriend during those awkward teenage years. While other girls were picking out prom dresses and deciding who to go to the dance with, Emily had stayed home and studied. That's what she was good at. Besides, guys didn't date girls with glasses, braces, and twenty extra pounds.

Even after she was older, had Lasik, lost her braces and the weight, every guy who caught her eye was a heartache waiting to happen. One right after the other. In all her years, she'd only had one serious relationship. And look how that had turned out.

As uncomfortable as Emily felt at the moment, she had to get her life back into her own hands. That started now.

"What's Stanley's address?" Mac demanded.

"Why?"

"That's where we're heading."

"Now?" she said around a lump in her throat. So much for her tough strategy.

"Yes, right now. I want to see those pictures."

"Ah, I can't…I mean, I don't know… Maybe."

"Now, Em," he growled. "I'm through messing around."

"He lives at 4231 Heritage."

Mac put it in the GPS. "What city?"

"Bedford."

As Mac pulled onto 820 East, Emily made the quick phone call to Stanley then dialed her neighbor. "Hi, Debbie."

"Emily. Are you back?"

"Almost, did you pick Hershey up for me?"

"Yes, and he was ready to be busted out of the doggie hotel."

"Good, I'll be over shortly to pick him up."

"Okay, but don't hurry, the kids have enjoyed him."

"Thanks so much, Debbie."

Emily finished the call and placed her phone in the console of the vehicle.

"Who's Hershey?"

"My dog."

"That's a candy bar or a frickin' cake."

"I like chocolate."

"Yeah, but you don't label your dog with a handle like that. It's a male dog too, isn't it?"

Refusing to be drawn into an argument, she nodded. She now realized that's what Mac hid behind. Words, anger, insults. Anything to stay away from the real issues in his life.

"He must be a real terror. What is he, some little miniature thing you stuff in your purse?"

"Hershey is a very brave dog, and I love him."

***

"What's wrong with Butch, or Killer, or Rover?" Caustic words rolled off his tongue, taunting her for a comeback, because he could handle an argument. But being ignored or attacked by a hysterical woman, like she'd been yesterday, threw him off his game. Today, she was a different woman.

A scorned woman.

"Those are dog names. A dog deserves a decent name."

Mac slapped the steering wheel and blew out an aggravated breath. He frowned. "Do you holler out," Mac raised his voice to a high pitch, "come here, Hershey! Mama wants you to come home now." He chuckled. "If you had a cat, you'd probably name it Lasagna. This way you'd have a whole damn meal. Your neighbors must think you're crazy."

Emily shrugged her shoulders. "Maybe."

"Maybe?"

"I personally don't think what I name my dog or what my neighbor's think of me is any of your business," she said tartly. "You're probably jealous. I imagine a man like you doesn't even own a dog."

Well, that pissed him off. "What do you mean, a man like me?" Mac scowled. "What's wrong with a man like me, and why wouldn't I have a dog?"

She turned to him with a solemn gaze and replied in a soft, mellow voice. "You don't collect things, remember? Plus, you don't allow yourself to become attached."

His mouth tightened. "I don't have a dog because in my line of work I travel a lot." Mac glanced out the side window. "A dog would be left alone all the time."

"What if you worked a nine-to-five job, would you have a dog then?"

"Sure, I would."

"You're lying, again," Em said. "I can tell."

"I'm not lying. I'd like a dog. A big one. Like a Rottweiler or a Doberman. I like big, mean dogs. Tough ones that eat those named Hershey for a snack."

"You're even competitive with pets? Who has the biggest?" Em shook her head. "That's pathetic, Mac."

CHAPTER TWELVE

Every commuter within a fifteen-mile radius inched toward Dallas, and Mac and Emily sat stuck in the middle of a snarled string of cars.

Emily had maintained her calm and silence, while much to her delight Mac squirmed.

"Are you hungry?" he asked. "We could grab breakfast and allow the traffic to die down a little."

"I'm not hungry," she said, staring out the window. "How am I going to explain you to Stanley?"

Mac clutched the wheel with both hands then cleared his throat. "Tell him I'm your new boyfriend. We met on the plane and hit it off right away."

Emily took two deep breaths before answering. "I'd cut my throat and bleed to death before I'd ever say that."

Mac drew back defensively. "I knew you were a little pissed at me, but…"

"But nothing, I won't lie for you. You're on your own. My agreement ends when I get you in the door. After that, I'm home free."

"Listen, about you going home—" Mac slammed on the brakes as a car cut in front of him. "Idiot."

"Don't talk to me, Mac," Emily gritted out. "I'm going home, and if I have to call Frank and tell him why, I will."

"Dammit. Em, I'm not good at this stuff." He dragged his fingers through his hair and frowned.

"Tough." She crossed her arms. "Why don't I just say you're a spy, and we're being chased by a bunch of crazy people who want us dead?"

"They wouldn't believe that."

"What makes you think they'd go for you and me meeting on a plane and you following me home?"

"I live here."

Anger started at the soles of her feet and traveled through her veins with the same speed as a double shot of expensive tequila. "You what?" she screamed.

"Right off Highway 183 in Bedford. Stanley could be my neighbor." He made the statement so casually Emily wanted to use his head for a battering ram.

"At a formal hearing last year, you said you lived in Virginia. That's one more lie I can chalk up, isn't it?"

"I wasn't sure I could trust you."

"I'm a lawyer, for heaven sakes. *Your* lawyer! What did you think? I'd stalk you or something?"

He glanced out the driver's window. Emily reached over and slugged his arm as hard as she could.

"Ouch." He rubbed the wounded area, glaring at her. "What was that for?"

"For being a big fat liar. The biggest one I know, and as an attorney, I know plenty." Way more than her fair share, and true to form, most were men, just like him. And she'd spent the night with him in a motel! Damn, what she wouldn't give for a do-over.

"It was only a precaution. Nothing personal."

"Nothing is personal to you, Mac." She snatched her purse and put her hand on the door handle. "Stop the car. I want out."

Mac grabbed her arm, and a shot of electricity hummed through her body. "Are you crazy?" He edged closer to the car in front of him. "The car is stopped, but in case you haven't noticed, there are two lanes of traffic between you and the shoulder. Settle down."

She yanked free. "Don't you dare tell me what to do. I've had all of you I can stand."

"Why you are so angry?"

"You lied." But that was merely the first thing that came to mind. What really bothered her was the idea of being lured into thinking he cared. That they'd made *love* and not just had sex. The idea that she'd responded to his touch in a way she never imagined possible, made it difficult to face him. Just sharing a ride made her yearn for his touch, his kisses…his love.

She felt small, used, and insignificant. Her skin no longer fit her body. She wasn't the same person as before. Mac had managed to seduce not only her body, but her mind and more dangerously, her heart.

And now they were going to Stanley's house. God, could her life get any worse? She nibbled on her bottom lip and prayed to be somewhere else.

Mac turned and looked at her. "Do you realize that almost everyone who works in my line of business with a top security clearance lies?" He took a breath. "Em, it's part of the job. Half the time, wives married to agents have no idea what their husbands do, where they go, or when they'll be back." He turned away. "The job is designed that way to protect innocent people, as well as those who put their lives in danger every day. If you were my wife, you'd be in the dark like other wives."

"You don't get it do you, Mac?"

He released a tired breath then replied in a warm voice. "Yes, I do get it, Em." He laid his hand on hers.

At his touch, she nearly lost all self-respect. She wanted him to care for her the way she cared for him. But she knew now that could never be.

"I understand. And I'm sorry I can't be what you want me to be."

She blinked back tears that threatened to flood the car.

He squeezed her hand. "Last night was the greatest moment of my life, but that's all I can give." His deep blue eyes held a glimmer of sadness. "Believe me, I don't own a heart worth having. Too much sadness. Too much hurt. No room for love." He exhaled. "Right now, you're my responsibility and I will protect you with my life. You're caught up in something that you knew nothing about. I'm just trying to make it all right."

She pulled away as a ping of regret washed over her heart and ducked her head, hoping he wouldn't notice how deeply he'd hurt her.

She scooted over and leaned her head against the window. "You don't need me for Stanley to develop those pictures. I'll tell him you're coming; that's all he needs. He could care less if I'm there."

Mac looked at her bewildered. "What's he going to say when I walk in with your contact lens?"

"Nothing."

"My ass. He's going to want to know how I came by it. Where you are. And why you didn't return home when you were supposed to. How am I going to answer all that, huh?"

"Lie. That's what you're good at."

Mac angrily slapped the steering wheel with the palm of his hand. "Women."

He looked at her and narrowed his eyes. "You're coming with me if I have to drag you."

"Then plan on doing just that."

CHAPTER THIRTEEN

Thanks to a fender-bender that kept traffic at a crawl, Mac and Emily didn't arrive at Stanley's until ten forty-five.

Stepping out of the vehicle, Emily hugged herself, struggling to protect what little pride she had left. What hadn't been shattered, tattered, or battered by past mistakes now hung in obnoxious shreds that swirled and reminded her what a fool she'd been.

Much to her consternation, Mac came around the vehicle and took her arm. Reluctantly, she'd agreed to act like a couple just to speed the process, so she could be rid of him.

When this was over, she planned to barricade herself at home with a bottle of wine, her dog, and a Keith Urban CD. What she wouldn't give to be leaving for Belize today instead of tomorrow afternoon.

As they walked toward the house, their gazes clashed, and Emily forced a miserable smile. Mac looked partly apologetic and vaguely annoyed. No doubt, he couldn't wait to get rid of her and get back to his fanciful life of love 'em and leave 'em rituals.

It took every drop of willpower she possessed to keep from sitting down on the sidewalk and bawling her eyes out. Biting on her lower lip, Emily shook her head. She might be a loser when it came to men, but she wouldn't give Mac the satisfaction of seeing one single teardrop fall from her eyes again.

Not today, not tomorrow, not ever!

With no way out, she squared her shoulders, straightened her spine, and prepared to be struck by another of life's lightning bolts.

She hadn't seen Stanley in months, and she never imagined their next meeting would be like this. What would he think? More important, why did she care?

When they reached the door, Mac lifted one shoulder. "What? You going to knock or walk in?" He shoved his hands into his back pockets and looked around slowly. "Let's get this over with."

Emily pressed the doorbell and waited. The sound of Dumb and Dumber barking and yapping inside made her cringe. Those two miniature dachshunds were the stupidest dogs she'd ever met and rightfully named. Of course, it wasn't their fault. One had only to consider the dogs' owner.

The tapping sound of dog toenails on tile floor drifted outside.

Mac raised an eyebrow. "Any chance we'll be eaten alive once we get inside?"

"No, but you might want to commit suicide before they finish licking you."

"Emily!" Stanley used his foot as a barrier to keep the dogs from breaking free. "I'm so glad to see you." His boyish grin scrunched up his face and made him look ten years younger than his thirty-eight years. "How was Russia?"

Before she could answer, Stanley's eyes went from her to Mac, and his enthusiasm melted like a chocolate bar on a summer day. "Who's this?"

Emily gently shoved Mac into the interior, causing Stanley to have to reach down and grab the dogs by their collars. He looked awkward and uncomfortable staring up at them.

Emily's sister Victoria came around the corner. "Oh! Do my babies have company?" The minute she spotted Mac her mouth instantly curled into a "come get me, I'm all yours" smile. That well-practiced look could turn lemons into pancake syrup and send a diabetic into shock.

An absolutely glowing Victoria pressed a hand, the one with a rock the size of Montana on it, to her perfectly styled hair and tugged at her expensive summer cardigan sweater. "Emily," she said smoothly, without glancing in her direction. "Who's your friend?"

Sadly, Emily couldn't take her eyes off the engagement ring. It was the most beautiful thing she'd ever imagined. She blinked back tears as her heart shattered into a million pieces.

"Oh, you haven't seen my ring, have you?" Victoria held up her hand and admired the jewel. "It's so expensive I can hardly believe Stanley insisted on getting it. You know, he designed it himself." Victoria giggled. "Isn't that sweet?"

"Lovely."

Victoria looked over Emily's shoulder and smiled so hard her dimples sunk in two inches. "So, who's the guy?"

Emily turned to see Mac smiling as ridiculously as her sister. She inwardly groaned. This was the story of her life. She'd never brought a guy around that her sister didn't take a liking to.

"John McKinsey. You can call him Mac."

"My," Victoria said slowly, offering her hand. *The one with the ring, of course.* "I'm very pleased to meet you."

Mac waved the contact lenses container in front of Stanley.

Adjusting his glasses, Stanley's eyes widened as he took his newest invention from Mac's fingers. "Let's see what we have here."

Solemnly, Emily followed Stanley to his office off the foyer. Glancing back, she grinned at Mac dancing around while the dogs clawed at his pant legs.

The little dachshunds had him trapped between them, the wall, and Victoria. He didn't know it, but he wasn't going anywhere.

"Nice doggies. Good doggies. Now go away," Mac said, as he tried to follow.

"Have you heard back from Sony yet?" Emily asked Stanley.

"No, and the government hasn't notified me either. It's just a matter of time. You know how it goes. I'll sell the patents."

"I'm sure you're right."

Stanley was a handsome guy in a Clark Kent kind of way. Most people referred to him as a geek, with his thick glasses, carefully combed hair, and casual dress code. But it never offended Stanley because he *was* a geek. What most people didn't know was that he held the honor of being the best in the State of Texas. He'd made a fortune with computer programs and games he'd developed and marketed over the years.

Emily looked back to find Mac and Victoria standing close to each other at the end of the hall. No doubt, Victoria would do what she did best—wrap unsuspecting men around her little finger. One would think by now she'd have run out of fingers because God knew she'd never run out of men.

From outside, Emily heard the dogs barking and scratching at the back door. Evidently, Victoria had banned them to the yard, so she could concentrate on her latest victim.

A glance at her sister's sparkling engagement ring sent another wave of sadness coursing through Emily's body.

An arrow of betrayal right to the heart!

Shaking her head, Emily silently vowed to ignore them and reminded herself that Mac didn't mean crap to her either. All she wanted was to be left alone.

Stanley took the chair behind his massive cluster of computers, disc drives, CD burners, and a staggering amount of papers with high tech designs scribbled on them. She sat next to him and watched the screen as he inserted the disc into a tiny piece of equipment that reminded Emily of a dental floss container.

She looked up when Mac came in the room, only to notice Victoria hot on his trail. When he moved to stand next to Emily, her sister's breasts rubbed against Mac's arm. He tensed then shifted his questioning eyes to Emily.

You're on your own, buddy.

"What is that, Stanley?" Victoria asked. "Are those pictures you took in Russia, Emily?"

"Yes, they are."

Victoria laughed and clapped her hands, trying a little too hard to convince anyone in the room that she really cared.

"Oh, I'm dying to see them." Victoria turned to Mac and asked, "So, how did you and my sister meet?"

Mac backed up and cleared his throat. "On the plane."

"How romantic!" Victoria licked her lips. "So are you two…" Her sister leaned closer and smiled. "So, are you dating or what?"

Emily gritted her teeth and growled before muttering, "I can't stand the man; he's all yours."

Then Emily turned back to the screen as Stanley tried to pull up the images. She wasn't concerned about Stanley taking her remark the wrong way because when he sat in front of a computer screen, he was completely oblivious to everything around him.

Victoria huffed loudly then said, "That's a cruel thing to say. You're still jealous, aren't you?"

Emily shot her sister a cocky smile over her shoulder. "I'm not jealous, Victoria. There isn't a single thing you have I want." She turned back as the pictures came into view. "You're a genius."

Stanley glowed. "It works…it really works." His finger danced across the keyboard, sharpening the photo-images. Scenes of the Kremlin, Red Square, and several local businesses filled the frames. The pictures were sharper than any she'd seen before.

"Those are great," Emily said, truly impressed. "I have to be honest the lens was so small I didn't think it would work. And with it being in my eye and all, it just seemed impossible."

"I had my doubts too, but as you can see, these are great shots. And the clarity is far better than anything else that size."

Mac leaned across her to get a better look at the screen. There were twelve different frames on the screen, each one taken at a different location. "Is that all the pictures?"

Emily looked up at him and grinned, quiet satisfied with her part in this project. "There are over a hundred pictures on that little chip."

Mac straightened, rubbed the back of his neck, and blinked his tired eyes. "Do you think we could flip through them real quick, so I can take a look?"

"Sure," Stanley said. "Each click of the mouse will bring up twenty different photos." He demonstrated and several pictures ran across the screen.

"I'm afraid most of them are boring because I ran out of things of interest. So I just started clicking."

"You did a great job, Emily," Stanley said as he continued clicking the mouse. His brows came together. "What happened to your eye?" he asked her. "Did you have an accident?"

She gently touched the area. "No, I walked into a wall."

"Stop!" Mac shouted then smiled uneasily. "I mean, can you go back to the last two frames?"

"Sure."

"There." Mac pointed to several pictures Emily had taken the last night she was in Moscow. Wanting to complete the frames she'd randomly shot everything and everyone in sight.

"Those on the second line, can you blow them up?"

"No problem."

The screen pulled up a picture of three men talking. One smoked a cigarette, while the other two looked directly at the camera lens—or rather the young woman wearing it.

Emily sucked in a deep breath and said, "That's the man who tried to kill us."

CHAPTER FOURTEEN

Ramón Marino stood, walked to the liquor cabinet where a bottle of scotch sat, and poured a drink. He took a long drag from his expensive Cuban cigar and blew the rich smoke into a thin cloud overhead. Without permission to enter, Bruno waited in the doorway. When his boss decided to talk, Bruno would listen, but he would never be the first to speak.

The waistband of Bruno's casual tan slacks and the bright tropical shirt he wore absorbed droplets of sweat running a race down his back.

Being summoned to Marino's study was never good. Bad things happened here. Bruno knew this because he had both witnessed and partaken in carrying out the man's orders.

In the left corner of the large room, deep in the shadows, a young naked girl laid covered in blood. She couldn't be older than sixteen. It appeared Marino had used her callously and when finished, beaten her to death.

Bruno suspected less pleasure came from the sex than the killing.

Staring back at a man he loathed, Bruno resigned himself to whatever fate his boss decided. Those who failed paid the ultimate price. One didn't hang around long making the mistakes he'd made.

No, when Ramón Marino wanted a man dead, he wanted the job done quickly, quietly, and flawlessly.

"Bruno," Marino called from across the room. He turned, his dark features handsome, yet more dangerous than anything a normal person could imagine. His thick hair was dark as midnight, and he wore it long, slicked back, tied with a simple leather strap. Those who looked into his hard, cold eyes saw the devil and a soul too corrupt for God's mercy. "What is this I hear?"

"I don't know, *jefe*. What have you heard?"

Marino took the icy glass of scotch, along with the cigar between his fingers, and sat in his favorite bamboo chair. It reminded Bruno of a throne where a monster sat while tossing out dire punishment to the poor and innocent people of Columbia.

Putting the drink on the table, Marino took a slow drag of his cigar then picked an imaginary piece of lint from his perfectly pressed white suit. "I hear McKinsey still breathes."

Bruno did not react. They'd played this game before. Like a perilous chess match, accept the wrong move, you die, the wrong reaction, your wife and children die, the wrong words and your whole family is annihilated. A man's lifespan tended to be short around Marino's cartel, and Bruno had been with him longer than others.

Bruno bowed. "*Sí.*"

"How can that be, Bruno? How can it be when I told you to kill the bastard in St. Petersburg?" He took a sip of scotch. "Did I not?"

Bruno watched as the pool of blood surrounding the dead girl grew larger, seeped into the grout of the tile then careened in a straight line to the back of Marino's chair—like a living spirit seeking revenge. Silently, Bruno sent up a prayer for the innocent child murdered with no feeling or regret.

"*Sí*, I had three men waiting when he left the snitch's apartment. They were trained assassins. The best money could buy."

"Now, they are dead assassins."

"*Sí*, Señor Ramón. McKinsey killed two of them; then one got away."

"How does a man who travels with no identity, no papers, and no contacts manage such a feat?"

"Agent Jake Taylor was nearby on a diplomatic mission. I'm sure he had a hand in all this."

Marino puffed on his cigar then blew out the smoke in a thin line. Taking a sip of scotch, he placed the glass back on the coaster and studied the ceiling. "We all know Taylor has remarkable skills, but he's not..." Marino waved his hand. "How you say, *magical?* He is but a man. And a man can be killed." He took another sip of his drink. "Besides, I know for a fact that Archuletta is in Columbia looking for me.

"I had not heard that. But it's true all Falcon agents seem to have nine lives."

"I want one of those lives." Marino stood and stomped across the room, shouting. "Can you not simply kill the son-of-a-bitch? I want him dead! Yet, he leaves St. Petersburg, gets to Moscow to meet up with that woman who took the pictures. Together, they escape the country on a private plane, get away safely from Heathrow, and now he's back in the US."

"I sent men to the hotel room. I sent men to the private airport. I had men waiting in London," Bruno said.

"I've heard nothing from the men in Dallas. And since there is no word they captured or killed McKinsey, I have to assume he is alive, and your plot at the airport there failed as well."

Marino's dark face reddened with anger as he threw the glass of liquor across the room. It crashed on the white floor, next to the dead girl. A snarl of hatred masked his face. Black eyes burned evil.

Bruno swallowed hard. The open-handed slap came as a surprise…and a relief. At least Marino hadn't pulled out a knife and stabbed him to death.

Bruno touched his cheek. "I'm sorry."

Suddenly, a brutal backhand knocked Bruno against the expensive leather chair where he caught himself. The kick in his left thigh hurt, but did no damage. For that, he silently gave thanks.

Marino swiped his mouth and brushed back strands of hair that had broken free of the leather strap. Staggering with anger, he moved to get another drink. Filled with visible rage, he gulped the liquor, leaving only cubes of ice rattling in a new glass. After another inhale on the cigar, Marino dropped back in his chair. One leg hung over the arm.

Bruno stood and wiped blood from the corner of his mouth on a white handkerchief. He watched as Marino raised his arms and cupped folded hands behind his head. His gaze remained deadly, unforgiving.

"Bruno, I took you off the streets when you were just a boy. I care for your family. I give you all that you have. And you repay my kindness by failing at the one thing I asked you to do."

Bruno wanted to argue Señor Ramón had done little to make his life easier. At twelve, Bruno was a street thug. At fifteen, a mule in

Marino's drug trade. On his seventeenth birthday, he'd been given control over the prostitution and gambling rackets. By eighteen…he was a killer. Yes, his family lived well, but Bruno had given up his freedom for that luxury.

Since joining up with Ramón Marino, Bruno knew he could never leave. Not alive, anyway. And if he died, his family would suffer unbearable pain. Traitors were always made an example. The boss ruled with fear and brute strength. There was nothing Ramón Marino wouldn't do.

Nothing!

"I will see it done, *jefe*." Bruno wiped perspiration from his face. "I swear McKinsey will die."

To hide his disgust, Bruno turned to leave, the determination to please his boss strong, as was his desire to live. Just as Bruno reached the door, Marino said, "Kill that fucking bitch, too. I don't know how she fits into all this, but I know she took pictures that no one can ever see. Do you understand?"

Bruno looked over his shoulder. "It will be done."

"And get that goddamned film from whatever camera she was using. If the wrong people see that, my strategy will be ruined, and everything I've planned could fail."

Grudgingly, Bruno nodded. "This is the first I heard of the camera. Did you see it?"

"No, but on her phone, she said she had all the proof she needed. How did she get that without a camera?"

Bruno shrugged.

"Don't fail me again Bruno, or your pretty young sister will meet the same fate that *puta* did." He nodded toward the bloody body discarded in the corner. Marino grinned. "Oh, I bet she's a virgin. And you know how much I love virgins, don't you, Bruno?" Marino's cruel laughter echoed, like a taunt from El Diablo.

Bruno gritted his teeth and swallowed the bile in his throat. He refused to allow his mind to go there. He'd kill McKinsey and the woman before his family suffered.

CHAPTER FIFTEEN

Gently, Mac pulled Em closer, knowing her seeing Stanislaw in the photo would mentally transform her back to the hotel. Without resistance, she leaned against him for support.

Adrenalin swam through Mac's veins like an illegal drug. Squinting, he leaned closer to verify the other man. Lev Stanislaw had been a henchmen for Nicholas Belskavia, until Mac had shot him in the Moscow hotel.

Everyone in the underworld knew Nicholas Belskavia would sell anything left over from the Cold War. Some referred to the Russian as *The Wholesaler* because he sold everything—bio chemicals to make dirty bombs, nuclear bombs or any other serious weapons he had access to—and could sell to the highest bidder.

Ramón Marino.

So why was Marino there? What was the connection? And why would they be foolish enough to meet in the open?

Separately, these men were dangerous, if they hooked up, it could be disastrous for the entire free world.

Mac's phone rang. Releasing Em, he went to the other side of the room, so no one could hear the conversation.

"Yeah, Frank?"

"What's your twenty?"

"Stanley's house. We're looking at the pictures."

"Well?" Frank asked. "What the hell is it?"

"A picture of Ramón Marino, Lev Stanislaw, and Nicholas Belskavia. I took Stanislaw out in the hotel. My guess is The Wholesaler sent him after Em."

"It's coming together, Mac. The guy in Oak Cliff said someone from Russia has been talking about a dirty bomb. Ten minutes ago, I received an alert from the NSA saying they spotted Bruno Reyes."

"Marino's top guy. Where?"

"He's heading our way."

Mac disconnected and tried to figure what the three men could possibly have to meet about, besides something illegal or destructive. Did Marino have access to that kind of firepower? If so, they'd be used to destroy Falcon and inflict as much damage to America as possible.

After his sister had been killed, Marino had done everything possible to hold Mac accountable. When the US government denied Marino's claim, he turned against the American justice system as well.

"Em, do you remember taking that picture? The place or time of day?"

"Yes, I was leaving the next day. I went outside my hotel to finish up, and I walked around for about an hour shooting pictures. This one wasn't far from a coffeehouse. And see right here? That's the north corner of Red Square."

So, they were hiding in plain sight. Together, right out in the open. Very clever move. This way they couldn't be accused of conducting a secret meeting.

"Who tried to kill you?" Victoria demanded, hands planted on her shapely hips. "What have you two gotten yourselves involved in, Emily?"

"Nothing," Mac answered. Hugging Em, he whispered, "It's okay. Just breathe through it."

She nodded and gripped the edge of Stanley's desk.

Slowly, Mac massaged the tension from her body. "Can you scroll through the rest of the pictures?"

"Of course." Stanley went back to doing his magic.

"There, that picture!"

Stanley froze the frame. Then again, but this time Marino and The Wholesaler were exchanging briefcases. Mac suspected one briefcase held a fortune in small, unmarked bills and the other, bad news for America.

"Did they see you taking these pictures?" Mac asked.

"I don't know. I had my gloves on, and the clicker kept getting stuck." Then Em tapped her bottom lip and stared out the window. "But when I went to my hotel that night, I had the feeling I was being followed." She shook her head. "I don't know why. Once in my room, I just blew it off. Later, I met a few Russian lawyers for a drink."

"Stanislaw is staring right at the camera. Could they have suspected you were taking their picture?"

She shrugged. "Perhaps."

Obviously annoyed to be excluded from the conversation, Victoria asked, "Why in the world would you even think you were being followed? Were you doing anything wrong?"

"Of course not."

Victoria waved her diamond-studded hand in the air. "See how silly you are? I'm surprised the Russian police didn't lock you up for acting so suspicious." She then turned to Mac and placed her hand on his arm. "She's the biggest coward I know. And a company sends someone like her to Russia? Can you believe it?" Victoria slid her hand into Mac's. "Let's go into the kitchen and have some coffee, shall we?"

Mac pulled out of her grasp. "No, thanks." It hadn't taken him long to figure out he didn't like the woman. Her remarks about Em being a coward proved Victoria to be as dumb as her dogs. Mac had met a lot of women, and he'd take Em anytime. On the other hand, if stranded on a desert island with Victoria, Mac would probably end up drowning her at some point.

"I think Em handles herself pretty well," Mac said.

Victoria's smile crumbled. "*Em?*" She reared back and looked down her nose at him. "Really?"

Mac smiled. "You bet."

"You sure we're talking about the same woman." She pointed to her sister. "She's afraid of her own shadow."

Mac reached over and put his arm around Em. Before a protest could escape, he leaned down and captured those pouted lips. Immediately, they were back in the hotel, in each other's arms, hot, sweaty. Need wrapped around him like a warm blanket on a winter's night, as they climbed heights he'd only imagined.

After raising his head, Mac looked at Victoria and smiled. "Yeah, we're talking about the same woman."

Victoria huffed out of the room, and Mac practically applauded. What a pain in the ass. How in the world did poor Stanley put up with her?

120

Mac looked back to the computer screen. "Stanley, can you print off all the pictures of those guys?"

"Sure." A few clicks later and the sound of the printer filled the quiet of the room.

As Stanley selected the pictures to be printed, Mac saw another familiar face. "Stop!"

Blinking, he leaned closer. "Where did you take this one?" He touched the screen.

Brows furrowed, Em studied the monitor. "I don't remember. Probably the same as the others. That's the only night I took pictures of people. The rest were buildings and stuff like that."

"This is about two miles from the Kremlin," Mac said. "I've been there before."

"I guess so. Like I said, I was just using up the memory."

"I need that one too, Stanley."

***

After what seemed like hours of arguing, Emily convinced Mac they were going their separate ways, even if it involved the police, CIA, and the FBI.

They stood outside Stanley's home, neither apparently knowing what to say. Too much had happened to ever go back to what they had been.

Finally, Mac broke the silence. "Take me home. Then drive the car to your house. I'll have several Falcon agents keeping a close eye on you. When you get home, call Falcon and have them pick up the Taurus." Hands in his jean pockets, Mac looked around. "Make a list of all your expenses, and I'll turn it into Frank. He'll be glad to reimburse you."

Realizing how she hated good-byes, Emily lowered her eyes and got into the car without speaking. They'd never see each other again. She'd make sure of that. They truly were strangers, not meant to share a life. She knew no more about Mac this morning than when he'd accosted her in the Moscow hotel room.

Well, everything happened for a reason. Besides, having a man hanging around would only complicate everything. As Mac drove them toward the freeway, he said, "That Stanley is a pretty smart character."

"Yes, he is."

"When are they getting married?"

"Next month."

"Hmm, they make an odd couple."

"What do you mean?"

"Well, he's kind of nerdy, and she comes on pretty strong. If you know what I mean?"

"I know," Emily replied. "I'm amazed she let you out of the house without getting your address and phone number."

"Doesn't Stanley mind her openly flirting with other men?"

"Probably not."

"He sure was looking at you."

She shot him a questioning glance. "What is that supposed to mean?"

"I don't know. I got the feeling he wanted to reach out and latch on to you."

"He doesn't, believe me."

"He sure…"

Emily turned to him. "Stanley doesn't want anything to do with me. He's madly in love with Victoria. I know."

"How?'

"What do you mean, how?"

Mac shrugged. "How do you know he's madly in love with Victoria?"

"Because he broke up with me to marry my sister."

CHAPTER SIXTEEN

Mac slammed on the brakes, causing the car to skid to a halt in the middle of the side road. Dumbfounded, he turned to Em. "You dated Stanley?"

Apparently unfazed by his question, Em lifted her pretty chin. "Yes."

Unbelievable! Grumbling, he faced forward, and gripped the steering wheel. "Did you sleep with him?"

Oh shit, that's a pathetic thing to ask a woman.

The answer presented itself when Em turned pink from neck to forehead. "That's none of your business." Nostrils flaring, she tightened her mouth and stared out the windshield.

Even from the opposite seat, Mac heard her teeth grinding. So, he'd hit a nerve.

Since Moscow, Em had deliberately given him a hard time, and here she'd dated a geek like Stanley. Mind you, not some hunky guy you'd expect to be on the cover of GQ, or some calendar pinup fireman or police officer, or even a good looking attorney.

Hell, no!

Not one of those. Instead, she'd fallen for a nerdy little professor with a paunchy gut, telescopic lens glasses, wearing clothes that didn't fit from Goodwill.

Oh boy, that pissed him off.

Mac pointed behind them. "You're telling me that Mr. Genius is the reason you've signed off on men? He's the one who broke your heart so badly you didn't want anything to do with the male race again?"

Her sober expression and pinched lips confirmed the truth. All respect for Stanley evaporated. No way would Mac believe any man with half a brain would take Em's flighty, egotistical, come-fuck-me sister over her. Side by side, Em was twice the woman Victoria ever dreamed of being and nine times prettier. That brilliant asshole just morphed into a god-damned idiot.

From his standpoint, Stanley and Victoria deserved each other. The big question was how could Victoria do that to her sibling? Surely some universal female law existed that once your sister had dibs on a guy, he was off limits to the rest of the family? What possessed Victoria to make a play for a man whose only claim to fame was intelligence?

And Mac knew a sorry SOB when he saw one, and that described Stanley perfectly. That guy had really cared for Em at one time, and now he'd lost her forever. How could a man be that stupid?

Em.

Her ex-fiancé and her own sister had condemned her to watch on the sidelines as they went through life in wedded bliss. How sad, how awkward, and how damn cruel. No matter what Em said, Mac saw regret in Stanley's eyes. That man had shit in his own nest and ended up making a mistake of a lifetime. One he'd never forget.

Had Em fancied herself in love with him?

Mac's gut tightened, and a sigh of regret silently slipped through him. He wanted to slam the smartass's head against a concrete wall. "Stanley is a dimwit, okay? And an idiot."

"He graduated from MIT. He's very intelligent."

"Well, brains aren't everything."

"I like men who are smart."

Mac continued driving. Well, if she thought Stanley so freakin' smart, she needed to rethink the whole idea of men.

He drove to the next intersection then slammed on the brakes again. Em braced her hands against the dashboard. She looked at him.

"Holy shit, is that ring on her finger yours?"

Em reared back, her eyes wide. "What?"

"Did that son of a bitch give her your engagement ring? Because if he did, I'm going back there to show him *my* new *invention.*"

Shaking her head, she rolled her gaze upwards before drawing her brows together. "Stanley would never do that."

"Then, where is your ring?"

"I don't know." She thought for a moment. "I assume he returned it to the jeweler."

"So, he traded one ring in for another? One sister for the other."

"I don't know why this matters to you."

"Because you think I'm a jerk? Well, in my opinion, we just left the throne of the King of Jerks. Any man that would ask a woman to marry him and then turn around and dump her for her sister is an asshole."

Gritting his teeth, Mac wanted to go back and hurt, really hurt, Stanley. Instead, he put the car in gear and headed toward his place. In less than ten minutes, they had pulled into his apartment complex. He took the pictures with him.

Em came around to the driver's side then slid behind the wheel and adjusted the seat.

"Look, since you refuse to let me protect you, Frank has sent agents to watch you around the clock." He pointed to the second floor. "I live in 207. If you need anything, let me know. The security code for the gate is 7741."

Emily put the car in gear but kept her foot on the brake. "I'll be fine." She wouldn't meet his gaze.

Mac knew their time together had run out.

"It's been exciting, but I'm glad to be back to my nice, boring, but normal life."

Mac leaned down, but before he could reach her lips, she rolled up the window halfway. He stepped back, his gaze falling to the ground as he wondered if he too had made the same damn mistake as Stanley.

He reached in and stroked a strand of her hair. "Listen, Em," he started. "There is a special guy out there just waiting for a woman like you to rock his world. Forget Stanley. You're too good for him."

He withdrew his hand and Em pressed the accelerator, pulled out of the parking lot, and turned left. Mac realized he didn't know where she lived. But he did have her cell phone number and hell, as a spy, he could find almost anyone. If he ever wanted to find Emily Richards, he wouldn't have to work too hard.

His problem would be leaving her alone.

Once in his apartment, showered and wearing a clean set of his own clothes, Mac picked up the phone.

Frank answered on the second ring. "Mac, I don't like this shit with Emily. What in the hell happened?"

"You know what a bastard I am."

"Mac," Frank breathed out. "Emily's life is in danger because you acted unprofessionally. I should pull you in for that."

Mac didn't reply. Frank couldn't worsen his pain.

"I'll call her tomorrow and try to piece things back together. In the meantime, what else did you learn at Stanley's? I can't believe all this is over a couple of damn snapshots."

"It's not. You know who else Em took a picture of?"

"Who?"

"After looking at all the frames, I saw one of our old buddies. Do you remember Youssef el Jabir?"

"The Bomb Maker?"

"Uh huh."

"Jesus, were they all together?"

"No, but the photos proved his location. How can he do that and be on every watch list in the world? Interpol wants him, Germany wants him, and Israel has a bounty on his head. Everyone wants him. Dead or alive."

"Youssef el Jabir is responsible for killing thousands of innocent people," Frank said. "And he was in Moscow at the same time as Marino and Belskavia. Marino has the money, Belskavia the material, and el Jabir is the best bomb maker in the world…"

"That's what I'm thinking," Mac said.

"God, this is big. Can you scan me those pictures?"

"Sure."

"I'm calling the President and the National Security Council. This could be another 9-11."

"I'm going to be working my contacts. Where is Archuletta?"

"At the airport in Columbia."

"We need him in Moscow."

"I can make that happen, but I'm not sure that's safe," Frank said.

"When have we ever played it safe?"

Frank grunted then said, "I'm worried about Emily."

"So am I. But I know you have her wrapped up like a Christmas present."

"Yeah, I do. No thanks to you."

∗∗

Emily turned onto her street, and a strong sense of homecoming washed over her. The brick house she'd bought seven years ago rendered a sense of security and warmth that she seriously needed today. Even at a distance, the gold Texas star hung above her garage sent a surge of heritage and pride through her body. Looking at her neighborhood, Emily smiled at the prospect of being home.

Releasing a heavy sigh, she allowed the past few days to run through her mind. She was lucky to be alive. She couldn't count how many laws they'd broken, or how close they had come to death.

She pulled into her driveway and got out of Falcon's SUV. It felt as if she'd been gone months instead of days. Glad the ordeal between her and Mac no longer existed, Emily wanted to take a shower, change clothes, curl up on the couch, and take a long nap. But first, she had to stop at her neighbor's and get her dog, Hershey.

With it being Friday, in the middle of the day, and everyone at work, the side streets and the neighborhood quietly welcomed her home. Emily filled her lungs then let out a sigh of contentment.

But she couldn't ignore three cars with Falcon agents outside. They were across from her front door, down the street, and around the corner.

Sadly, she hated Big Brother watching, but it would be impossible to convince Frank she didn't need to be guarded.

She got out of the car, slammed the door, and jogged across the street to her friend's house. Debbie welcomed her back into her own private world.

"Come on in," her friend said, as she pulled Emily into her arms for a hug. They both walked toward the back of the house.

"How was Moscow?" Debbie asked, smiling. "I see the Russians didn't frisk you off to Siberia." Her friend looked closer. "Or did they? What happened to you face?"

If you only knew. "Nothing but a minor misunderstanding."

Debbie paused. "But you got the contract, didn't you?"

"Yes, I did, and made a lot of money in the process."

"Cool."

They high-fived and entered a small, cluttered kitchen. A pot of chili simmered on the stove and a pitcher of iced tea sat on the counter. With three boys, Debbie rarely had a quiet, sane moment.

"Where is Hershey?"

"He's out, digging holes in the yard."

Emily knew that rascal would be up to no good. "I'm sorry I was late."

Debbie laughed, deepening the creases around her eyes. "Don't mention it. The kids had so much fun with him I was afraid if you came when they were home, they wouldn't let you have him."

"Well, I certainly thank you for watching him, so he wouldn't have to spend an extra weekend in the doggie hotel."

Debbie waved her hand. "After what Whiskers did to your couch while we were in Disneyland last year, don't mention it. Besides, he wasn't any trouble at all." She walked over and opened the backdoor. "Here, Hershey. Here, boy."

The large brown Labrador came bouncing into the house, sliding on his rump when he lost his footing on the slick tiled floor then struggled to make his way to Emily. He barked jovially when she bent down and slapped her knee. "Come here, boy," she called out. "Come on."

Hershey managed to get his feet under him, bounced toward her, and slammed into her thighs, practically knocking her down.

"Hi, baby," Emily crooned. He licked her cheeks then whimpered and squirmed with excitement. She buried her face in his silky fur, glad to be where she was loved and appreciated.

Leaning back, she ruffled his ears, grateful for his warm welcome. "Come on, boy. You ready to go home?"

Debbie met them at the door with Hershey's dog dish. "Sorry he finished off the bag last night."

"That's okay. I have to run to the supermarket anyway. Thanks again, Debbie. When I get rested up, I'll come back and tell you all about my trip."

"Hey, I'm glad you're home."

With Hershey leading the way across the street, Emily took her keys out of her purse and opened the front door. The wonderful comforts of home and familiarity greeted her like a parent with open arms to a lost child.

Today, she needed this normalcy more than any other time in her life. While Hershey trotted all over the house, Emily put her briefcase in her home office, along with her laptop. Further in the house, she dropped her purse on the counter and went straight to her bedroom.

She turned on the shower and stripped. These clothes had to go. Something familiar would feel wonderful. She wadded up the jeans, knitted top, and flip-flops and threw them in the trash can. Absolutely no memories allowed.

In the shower, she shampooed her hair and scrubbed her body clean. After rinsing, she left the shower to dry off.

Hershey waited for her outside the bathroom door.

"I know you're hungry," she crooned. "Give me five minutes, and we'll go to the store and buy dog food. Are you hungry, boy?"

Hershey barked and wiggled his body.

"Real hungry?"

He barked twice, prancing and dancing all over the place.

"Okay, in a minute."

Emily blew dry her hair then applied a small amount of make-up. She slid into a pair of black jeans, a white frilly blouse, and a pair of sandals with a small heel. Being in her own clothes felt wonderful.

Once in the garage, she called Hershey to get in the car for a trip to the store. The shower, clean clothes and her friendly dog made Emily almost forget about Mac.

As she pulled out of the driveway, she looked at the black SUV and made a mental note to call and have the car, along with all memories of Mac, picked up.

***

Mac paced the carpet again. He urgently had to get those phone calls, but he wanted Em to be safe. What if something happened to her? What if Marino got his hands on her? Unable to stand her being away from him, he fought the urge to pick up the phone, but couldn't muster the nerve. What would he say?

His hand hovered over the phone for a moment before he walked away. Running his fingers through his hair, Mac reminded himself Em had her own life to live, and Frank had her secure.

Closing his eyes, he tried not to think about last night when their hot bodies lay entwined, and he'd entered heaven. Her lips were so ripe and eager. Her body pulled at him like a magnet to metal.

God, he needed her.

The phone rang and Mac jumped.

"Hello?" He'd hoped it would be Em's voice on the other end, but it was an informant he'd contacted earlier. He hung up, confident his hunch had been right on target.

He decided to check in with Frank to see if Brody had found out anything.

CHAPTER SEVENTEEN

After leaving the grocery store, Emily tossed the bag of dog food in the trunk and wondered why she didn't have a smaller dog.

One that ate less.

Inside the vehicle, Hershey barked and wagged his tail with excitement. Even though he could be a pain at times, she adored the fact that he loved her so completely.

Maybe it was the goofy way he shook his head and tail in sync, or maybe those big bright, orange/brown eyes, but...she'd taken him in and loved him ever since that visit to the animal shelter. Life would be unimaginable without him.

Walking around the car, she opened the door and shoved. "Move over, Hershey, let me get in." Her being away had made him more hyper than usual.

"Settle down, boy. Sit. Sit. Let's get home." She rubbed her hands on the sides of his face then pressed her nose to his. "You hungry?" He wiggled like a worm. "Yes, my handsome boy is. Okay, we'll go home." Hershey licked her cheek several times before allowing Emily to pull out of the parking space.

The sun settled into the west as she turned onto Bedford-Euless Road and headed for her quiet neighborhood. As she pulled up to a stoplight on Harwood Drive, a loud explosion shook her car. Instinctively, she looked at the sky, wondering if a plane had crashed.

Strange.

All clear overhead, Emily slowly turned onto her street and drove toward her house.

What happened?

Rubble lay everywhere. Clothes were strewn in the trees and a large plume of smoke billowed into the sky.

She stopped and stared at where her house had once been.

Fire, smoke, smoldering charred wood occupied the corner lot. Her neighbors ran out of their homes, and Emily bit back the urge to scream.

In shock, she realized she'd just lost everything. Even Falcon's SUV resembled a mess of melted steel.

She looked around at her stunned neighbors then searched for the cars the Falcon agents had occupied earlier. They were gone. But further down the street a black sedan sat with its engine idling. She couldn't identify the driver because of the tinted windows.

Slowly, she backed into her neighbor's drive and drove away, constantly checking her rearview mirror. Nothing moved, so hopefully, no one followed.

Somehow, she managed to get on the freeway and drive to Mac's apartment complex. She pulled her Honda up to the gate, but couldn't remember the combination. Looking up, she saw Mac running toward her. He pressed the combination and waved her inside the complex.

Frantically, she pulled forward and into the same parking space as earlier when she and Mac had parted. She killed the engine. Hands shaking, she reached for the door handle. As she staggered out of the car, warm summer air slapped her in the face.

Mac ran to her, and before she knew it, a pair of strong, male arms wrapped around her and held her in an unbreakable grip. She buried her face against his shoulder, breathing in his familiar scent.

His hand came up and cupped the back of her head. "I'm sorry, Em. I'm so damn sorry you're messed up in this."

Tears streaming down her face, she leaned away from him and looked into his eyes. She didn't care if he saw her crying. It didn't matter anymore. "Everything is gone. Even the SUV."

After kissing her forehead, he put his arm around her shoulders, and they walked toward the stairs. His eyes searched the surrounding area. "Come on, let's get out of the open."

As they reached the steps, she stopped, remembering Hershey. "Wait, my dog is in the car."

Mac looked over his shoulder at the blue sedan. "Does he bite?"

"No."

Mac released her and approached the car. When he opened the door, Hershey ran to her, almost tackling her to the ground.

"Settle down," she said. "You have to be a good boy."

Pointing her finger at him, she continued, "Can you do that for Mommy?"

Hershey actually nodded his head, but Emily had seen that before, and this was no time for his nonsense. "I mean a really, really good boy."

Hershey rolled over on his back and whimpered his disapproval at having to be really, really good.

"No, I mean it this time. You have to be nice or you get locked in the bathroom."

Hershey jumped up and barked furiously.

Emily looked at Mac. "He hates the bathroom." She turned her attention back to the dog. "I want your promise now."

As usual, he whined and growled. Then, when she didn't relinquish, he sat on his haunches and nodded.

"Can we discuss all this inside?"

They entered the small apartment, and Hershey walked ahead of them into the living room.

"Oh, I left the bag of dog food in the car trunk."

"I'll get it." Mac took her keys and motioned for her and the dog to stay inside.

When he returned, Emily and Hershey were standing in the middle of the living room, staring at the cleanest and most organized apartment in the world. Neither of them knew what to do.

Mac passed them on his way into the kitchen and opened the dog food bag, sitting it on the floor. As soon as Hershey heard the paper ripping, he charged and started eating like he hadn't been fed in a week.

Mac looked at Emily then Hershey, who now had his face buried in the bag. "When's the last time you fed him?"

Emily wrapped her arms around her body. "Debbie, my neighbor, fed him last night. Hershey is just a natural born pig. Don't you have something you can put the food in? He'll eat until he's sick."

"Won't he stop when he's full?"

"Not a chance." She looked over her shoulder at him. "You ever cleaned up dog puke?"

He moved past her into the kitchen, frantically looking for a bowl. "No, and I don't intend to."

When the search didn't immediately reveal anything, Mac reached down and took the bag away from Hershey, who wasn't through eating. Poor dog, he managed to sink his teeth into the bottom of the bag. As Mac pulled one way, Hershey tugged the other.

"Let go, mutt," Mac snarled.

Hershey growled and continued.

"Stop it both of you or…"

The bag ripped, and brown nuggets spilled all over Mac's spotless, white floor.

"I'm sorry, Mac. I tried to warn you."

Hershey acted like he was in doggy heaven. He sucked up kibbles faster than a vacuum cleaner.

The phone rang.

Mac looked down at the mess and shook his head.

"Answer the phone. I'll clean this up," Emily said, pulling at Hershey. "You've had enough."

The dog stopped and licked his chops. The phone rang again.

"Didn't I tell you that you had to be really, really nice?" She pointed at the living room. "Now go over there in the corner until I clean this up."

He barked and the phone rang again.

"No arguments. Go."

Mac reached the phone just as the dog dropped his head, ran his tongue over his nose, and trotted toward the corner.

Hershey turned and looked up at Mac with big amber eyes and growled softly.

"Hey, don't blame me, you're the pig," Mac responded.

***

Mac put the phone to his ear and listened carefully as the informant told Mac everything he needed to know about Marino's activities. Just to be sure, after hanging up, Mac made two more calls that confirmed what his snitch had said.

Several of his contacts said they'd heard rumors about a bomb, but they didn't know anything solid.

He hung up and looked at Em, tears running down her face as she swept up the dry dog food. He looked over at Hershey and saw he now sat with his nose pressed against the corner.

Emily had found a dustpan and a plastic bag to dump the dog food into. He walked up and relieved her of those and put his arms around her, pulling her up against him. "Tell me what happened."

"Well, I went to the store to get Hershey some dog food because he'd eaten the bag I left at Debbie's. On the way back, as I neared the house, I heard this loud explosion. When I got closer, I saw my house engulfed in flames. Then I stopped and…" Emily took a deep breath. "Mac, everything is gone. There's nothing left."

Mac couldn't believe it. Emily could have been in that house. She could be dead right this minute. And all because of him. This mess belonged to him. Yes, she took the pictures, but if Marino wasn't so hot and bothered about killing him, maybe none of this would be happening. Now, her life was in a complete shambles.

He pressed her closer, loving her scent, enjoying the feel of her body against his. Being this close to her drove him crazy.

For someone to find out where Em lived wouldn't be hard, but to know if she were home or not meant that someone had been watching. *Or had they?*

Emily pulled away and walked over to sit on the arm of his couch. "Mac, how did you know I was outside the gate?"

"What?"

"You knew I was coming?"

"The agents in front of your house called me."

"But they're gone."

"They never left you unprotected. A set of agents followed you to the store. Then the agents in front of your house received a bogus call to return to base. But the caller didn't know to use the code word before saying anything. They drove away only to transfer to another car and drive back to see your house explode.

"They couldn't get to you before the blast because right now, they're following the black car that was parked down the street from your house."

"How did they know I was coming to you?"

135

"They followed long enough to figure out where you were headed then informed me you were on the way. I knew as scared as you were you probably wouldn't remember the code."

"God, you guys are clever. But I could have been killed."

"Yes, but you weren't." Mac picked up her purse. "Em, where is your cell phone?"

She covered her mouth. "Oh no, I left it in the rental car. Now, I don't even have a phone!"

"Thank God."

"What?"

Mac picked up the phone and called Frank, who answered on the first ring. "Frank, I think I know how they've been able to track us."

"How is Emily?"

"Em and her dog are fine. However, Hershey is in time-out."

"Huh?"

Mac shook his head. "Never mind. Listen, Emily's house was blown up because her cell phone was in the rental parked in her driveway. They've been using her GPS system to keep tabs on her. They blew up the house thinking she was inside."

"I'll be a son-of-a-bitch."

"Yeah, me too. I should have figured that out in the beginning. I just assumed since our phones are non-traceable, so was hers."

"I have to admit I hadn't thought of that either, Mac. But it makes sense. Now they think Emily is dead. That leaves only you."

"Jake and A.J. are tracking the black car seen in Em's neighborhood when the bomb went off. They're keeping me informed. Is Brody heading this way?"

"Yes, but I think I might come and stay with Emily until we see where that vehicle leads us."

"No, you're better off there. No one knows Em is alive. Should they happen to spot you, they'd know their plot failed."

"You're right."

"I have a call into Archuletta. I think I'm on to something."

"Keep me informed. If you need help, let me know."

"I will, Frank."

"Above all else, keep Emily safe. And you better be on your best behavior, Mac."

"Sure." Yada, yada, yada. Like he *wouldn't* keep her safe. Dame that's his job, for Christ Sakes. He'd died before Em was harmed.

CHAPTER EIGHTEEN

Hershey climbed onto the couch next to Emily and Mac and put his head in her lap as if he sensed something wrong. "I'm so glad to have you. You're such a good boy."

Rubbing her dog's soft fur, Emily's body shook uncontrollably. The explosion raced through her mind, scene after scene in rapid procession. She squeezed her eyes shut to block out the memory of seeing everything she owned destroyed.

Emily hid her face with her hands, as if that would stop the images, and inwardly fought against the mess her life had become. She didn't know who was responsible for blowing up her house, but hatred for the act of injustice and brutality made her heart ache.

What if they find her? A sob escaped from her lips, and Mac pulled her against his chest. "I'm…I'm so scared."

"I know," Mac said, stroking her hair. "But you're safe, Em. We'll get through this. We'll find the people responsible and punish them. I promise."

Emily clutched the front of his shirt, wanting to crawl inside him where she would feel safe from harm. And yet, she had the urge to run as fast as she could away from the damage in her life. With no strength left, she went limp and sobbed until the tears were gone. All feeling left her body, and she surrendered to complete devastation.

The life she'd once known had not always been a happy life, but it was her life. The one she'd built alone after her parents had died and she'd been left to care for her younger sister. Through tears and heartache, she'd never asked anyone for anything. She'd paid for her and Victoria's education by working two jobs. She'd gone to law school to make a difference, to serve as an honorable example of how one should live.

Never in her whole life had she ever harmed another human being. Clean morals and a sincere belief in integrity were the foundations of her whole existence. And while there were things she would've loved to change…a husband, children, an extended family, she was still grateful for each milestone she'd passed along the way.

Desperate for something to do besides cry, Emily asked, "Should I call my insurance company about the house?"

"No, Falcon Securities is taking care of everything." Mac brushed her hair back. "If you call the insurance company, someone might find out you're alive. Frank is getting you another phone. Same number, but no GPS. Brody will bring it over soon."

"So, is this entirely my fault? The pictures, my phone?"

"It's nobody's fault, but Ramón Marino's. He's the one to blame. He wants me dead. You just got caught up in his shit. That's all."

"Why does he want you dead?"

Mac let out a deep breath. "I managed to bust up his organization pretty good the last time I went after him. He lost a lot of money. The CIA wanted me to bring him back to the States to stand trial for killing two DEA agents. I tried, but Marino crawled into a hole and wouldn't come out. Frank gave me the go ahead to kidnap his sister as a bargaining tool."

"What happened?"

"We'd made a deal. Marino for his sister. Once we had Angelina, Marino agreed to surrender if we let her go. During the exchange, in the middle of a dirty road on the outskirts of Columbia, with Marino fifty yards away, someone took a shot. Angelina was killed."

"How horrible." Emily placed her hand on Mac's shoulder to offer comfort.

"I was on this side of the border. The shot came from the other side. The murder weapon belonged to a Mexican policeman, and we proved it. But Marino refused to believe anything, except I murdered his innocent sister. For that reason, he's vowed to kill me."

Mac's cell phone rang and Tony's ID came up. He answered then walked into the kitchen. Emily continued petting the dog, now sound asleep and snoring softly.

"Tony, can you get to Moscow?"

"I'm on my way. Why?"

"I think I'm on to something. Do you remember that CI we pulled out of Bogotá?"

"ATF, right? I remember."

"Do you recall what he said about Marino dabbling in a new market other than drugs?"

"Yes."

"Before you leave, can you have a conversation with Nicholas Belskavia?"

"He's a strange duck. We aren't exactly on speaking terms. But I sort of owe the bastard a favor. He gave me an exit when I needed one. Never knew why. What's on your mind, Mac?"

After finishing the conversation, Mac returned to the living room, only to see Hershey's head pop up. That damn dog lay stretched across Em's lap on Mac's expensive leather couch. With all that had happened lately, it must've gotten to Em because she was sound asleep.

Mac called to the dog, but Hershey put his head down and stayed put.

Determined to let Em rest, Mac dropped into the chair across from the couch and patted his knee. "Come here, boy. I'm not going to hurt her."

Slowly, the dog came off the couch and sat beside Mac to get his head scratched. Watching Em sleep, Mac felt horrible. They had been on one rough joyride, and Em definitely deserved that vacation in Belize. Instead, unless Falcon came up with some serious information fast, Em's life would change drastically.

Sad eyed, Hershey put his chin on Mac's knee and whimpered.

"What is it?" The dog padded to the door. "You need to go outside?"

Hershey pawed the door. Realizing he didn't have a leash, Mac went into his bedroom closet and buckled two belts together. All he needed was to lose Em's dog.

After securing the belt to the dog's collar, Mac opened the door. Obediently, Hershey walked beside Mac as they went down the stairs to the designated doggy area of his apartment complex.

At dusk, few people were in the park, but Mac was reluctant to let the dog off the leash. He squatted down and took Hershey's head in his hands. "Can you be a good boy off your leash?

Hershey barked.

"No, I need a nod."

Hershey obeyed, and when Mac released him, he ran to the nearest patch of grass and hiked his leg. Then he went sniffing everything, including the butts of every other dog in the vicinity. Being the biggest mutt in the park, Mac didn't worry about him getting hurt, and with Hershey's disposition, there'd be little chance he'd bother anyone. Even with all that, Mac wasn't going to let him get too far away.

After several minutes, Mac called, and Hershey came and sat while Mac clipped the belt on. Then they went upstairs to check on Em.

Mac expected Brody any minute. With the make-shift leash tossed aside, a knock sounded at the door.

Surprisingly, Hershey didn't bark, but crawled toward the door and growled low in his throat.

Mac bent down and patted Hershey's head. "He's one of the good guys." Confident his fellow agent wasn't going to be eaten alive, Mac opened up and Brody stepped inside.

The agent looked at the dog then Em lying on the couch. "What's going on?"

Hershey sniffed the bag in Brody's hand and started licking his chops. Mac quickly snatched the food from Brody and held it up in the air. "This is Em's dinner."

Hershey's eyes followed the brown bag.

Brody laughed. "When I used the drive thru, I didn't know it was for *Em.*" He raised a brow and the dimples in each cheek deepened.

"Frank tell you her house got blown?"

"Yeah, what kind of yahoo blows up a woman's home?"

"I finally figured out they were tracking us by Em's GPS. You bring the new phone?"

Brody reached in his pocket. "No contacts or anything like that, but same number."

"Good, at least she can make and receive calls."

"So, what's the deal?"

"Unaware anything was wrong, Em accidentally left her cell phone in the Falcon SUV and drove her own car to the store. They read the signal from the phone, figured she and I were there, and they detonated the bomb."

"Damn, if that isn't enough to get every Falcon agent pissed, I don't know what is."

"Frank is plenty *pissed.* He wants these bastards caught," Mac said.

"When I left the office, he told me to do whatever needed to be done to wrap this up."

"I know Em wants it over, so she can get on with her life."

Brody rubbed the back of his neck and slapped his Stetson against his thigh. "Jake is hot on the trail of the black car that pulled into Emily's neighborhood and parked down the street just minutes before the blast. So, we need to get going."

"Okay, let me get things situated. Meet me downstairs."

"Hey, Mac, that's a good-looking dog. He yours?"

"No, that's Hershey. He belongs to Em."

"Who names a big boy like that, Hershey?"

"Em." Mac petted the dog's head. "He's pretty well behaved, except when it comes to food."

A low growled sounded.

Pointing his finger, Mac said, "You know I'm not lying."

That got a bark, which woke Em.

She rubbed her eyes and sat up. "What's going on?"

"It's okay." Mac turned to Brody. "Wait for me at your truck."

Em stood on wobbly legs.

"Brody brought you some dinner. I put it on the counter. Hershey had a nature call, and I took him downstairs."

"Thank you, Mac."

"I want you to sleep here tonight. Brody and I have to go check out a lead."

***

"I hate to intrude," she said, looking numbly about Mac's apartment. It surprised her. Situated in an elegant, gated community, she could only imagine how expensive it must be.

This apartment is so unlike Mac.

Meticulous and über clean. Never one to bet, but in this case, Emily would lay money down you couldn't find a speck of dust in this place with a magnifying glass or a white glove. And here, Hershey was shedding everywhere.

Earlier, she'd cringed when her dog and Mac had a tug-of-war with the bag of dog food, and the kitchen floor lost. Although she'd quickly cleaned it up, she didn't miss the shocked look on Mac's face before he'd turned away.

So much for the conversation they had about him owning a dog. An apartment this spotless didn't allow for any kind of animal. Still, it surprised her that Mac lived in such a fastidious environment.

When she'd been alone with him, he didn't seem to care if he had a toothbrush, nor did he mind using hers. The clothes he'd showed up wearing at her hotel in Moscow weren't fit for a homeless man. In her mind, if necessary, he'd drink sewer water.

Then to walk into this?

The guy was a conundrum. Just went to show, you never knew a man no matter how much time you spent with him.

He cupped her face. "Listen, pretty lady. You're not intruding. I want you here when I come back. Besides, it's Frank's orders." He bent and kissed her.

What started out as a simple good-bye kiss turned into something miraculous to never be forgotten. His head lowered until his breath brushed against her face and then her mouth.

Emily hadn't been with a lot of men, but the woman in her reached out to his masculine side, and she felt the hard firmness of his warm body against hers. His lips, hungry and on the prowl, captured her mouth, and without hesitation, his tongue slipped in to taste and sample, leaving her panting and wanting more. He nibbled her lower lip before breaking the kiss.

"Mac…"

"Eat, watch TV, take a hot bath, and relax. Nobody knows you're here. If Hershey has to go out, the dog park is to the left of the building. You'll see a sign."

"I'm afraid I'll make a mess of the place."

She stared at the floor, but he tilted her face toward him. "I don't care how dirty this place gets. It's nothing more than a place for me to crash."

Emily spread her arms out in a circle. "It's so neat and sanitized." She rolled her shoulders and ducked her head. "I feel out of place."

Mac laughed. "You want to know why this place looks so clean?"

She nodded.

"My cleaning lady lives three doors down, and she's from Japan. When I moved here, her older brother was harassing her because she refused to settle for an arranged marriage. I handled that for her. Ever since, she's kept my apartment like a shrine. She bought everything you see. I could walk away from all this, and it wouldn't matter one bit."

"I think it's lovely."

"Then enjoy the hell out of it." Mac put his arm around her and walked into the kitchen. "Listen carefully. See that small screen with four squares mounted on the wall?"

She nodded.

"If anyone besides me, Brody, or Frank knocks, call 911 and lock you and Hershey in the bathroom. The door is solid steel."

Her nerves tightened her skin, but she managed another nod.

"That's the best security system money can buy. On this screen, you see Brody downstairs by his pickup, the view of outside the front door, the entrance gate, and the stairs leading to this room. Check the screen constantly. That's all that stands between staying alive and someone taking you."

"But they don't know I'm here."

"Should by some miracle they find out, and Em, the easiest way is for you to tell someone." He held up his hands. "I realize your family needs to know you're safe. However, do your friends a favor by keeping your location secret. People can't repeat what they don't know."

Emily lowered her head. "I need to tell you that I called my sister." She swallowed nervously, knowing Mac would be pissed. "But if she found out about my house, she'd be worried sick. I couldn't do that to her."

Mac paled. "I hope that doesn't come back to bite us."

He pulled her against his chest, his lips capturing hers, and Emily drank in every ounce of feeling he offered. The kiss deepened when he moaned.

Trying to get closer, she slung her arms around his neck. She didn't know what she felt, only that right now it would be foolish to try and analyze the sensation.

After breaking the kiss, he moved across the room and squatted down. Hershey trotted over. "Take care of her, okay?"

Emily smiled as Hershey licked Mac's face from chin to hairline.

"I'll take that as a yes."

CHAPTER NINETEEN

Ramón Marino puffed on a cigar before answering the phone. "Yes," he replied calmly.

"It is done." Bruno's voice rushed with excitement. "They were both in the house when we blew it up. They could not have survived."

"You got proof, Bruno?" He didn't believe in taking chances. For that reason, he didn't know if his head man told the truth or not. Bruno had been wrong before, and McKinsey proved to be one hard bastard to kill. For the last two years, countless attempts had been made against the agent's life, and he always came out on the other side alive.

"We'll know when the police carry out what is left of their bodies. I have a man near the scene, posing as a concerned neighbor. I expect to hear soon."

He wanted to believe Mac McKinsey had been killed. Also, he needed the girl out of the way. Maybe he'd finally let it all go. He only wished McKinsey had died by his own hands.

For years, he'd dreamt of the day he would squeeze the life out of the Falcon agent. He wanted justice for his sister. It was McKinsey's fault she was shot down like a dog on that dusty road on the Mexican border.

His beloved sister was dead because that Falcon agent had kidnapped her. McKinsey had destroyed the only good thing in Ramón's life.

Pain pierced his body like poison arrows, and he silently screamed to the gods for revenge. Everything had changed that day. Every dream he had, destroyed.

She would have been eighteen in two weeks.

Now every American would suffer for what one man did. For one man's cruelty.

Hatred burned Ramón's gut like cheap tequila and seethed below the surface, begging for an escape. Why hadn't McKinsey died that day?

"Keep in touch, Bruno. I want to know beyond all doubt they are both dead."

"I will, *jefe*. I promise."

Ramón hung up the phone and walked to the bed. A young village girl lay stretched out, anchored to the frame. A rope tied her hands and ankles. Naked, she laid with legs open wide, inviting him to fuck her. However much they protested, he knew they were all whores at heart and wanted him. Oh, they cried out, they screamed, they begged, but he knew their black hearts. For that, they must be punished.

None of them were as good as Angelina.

Nude, Ramón picked the knife off the table next to the bed. Smiling, he stretched out beside her, his dick hard as granite. He rubbed the flat blade of the knife against his erection. The need to be inside the whore grew with each breath.

But, he had to pace himself. Too often lately he'd been overzealous, and the girls died before he had finished *playing* with them.

That would not happen now. The girl, gagged and bound, tried to kick and squirm. He slapped her. "Don't you realize how lucky you are to be here with me, *puta*?"

Tears stained her face. He gently kissed her cheek as he cut a straight line from her naval to the small patch of dark hair between her thighs. Not too deep, just enough to smell the blood mixed with her essence, all wrapped neatly in fear.

He licked the side of her face and tasted salt, dirt, and perspiration. Slowly, he leaned over and sucked the nipple of her small, firm breast, before biting hard.

She bucked, and Ramón rolled over, balanced on his knees. He looked down at his prize and kissed her stomach. Then gently, with the sharp knife, he carved a heart surrounding her opening, putting her femininity on display before the game started.

As blood poured from her wounds, he smiled. He planned to thoroughly enjoy this pretty little morsel.

With a loud grunt, he plunged deep into her tight pussy. His knife in one hand, her long black hair twisted in the other. Slowly, he rocked back and forth. With each stroke came a slice on her face, her arm, her shoulder…until the sheets were soaked with blood, and he came close to exploding.

With the knife against her throat, he cried out, "My sweet, Angelina." Then he shoved the weapon deep into her jugular as he climaxed. Only the sound of his heavy breathing filled the room.

Ramón looked into the young face and smiled. His first of the day.

CHAPTER TWENTY

The delicious aroma from the paper bag on the counter had Emily's stomach growling. Mouthwatering, she pulled out the food and realized she hadn't eaten all day. Sitting at the white kitchen counter on a barstool, Emily devoured the hamburger and fries in a matter of minutes. With the last sip of Diet Coke, she looked across the room and saw Hershey sitting with his nose pressed against the window, waiting for Mac to return.

Even her dog liked the man.

She licked her fingers, then crumpled up the paper and put it in the trashcan. Casually, she strolled into the bedroom. She stopped short of stepping over the threshold and blinked.

The bedroom walls were a faint, soft green, accented by bamboo floors, a tan bedspread, and a large vase water feature in the corner. No clutter, nothing on the dresser, nightstand, or chest of drawers. Only nature prints clung to the wall.

The lure of quiet, peaceful water, and serene surroundings relaxed Emily immediately. Tension rolled off her shoulders like rain during an April shower. Stress tentacles clutching her spine released, and she stretched the kinks out of her neck. Stepping into the Zen world of Mac's bedroom, peace and calm embraced her.

She couldn't find a thing out of order, and the sparseness unruffled her instantly.

Emily met heaven and loved it immediately.

What a contrast from Mac's personality. He was big, bad, mean, rude...a spy, for crying out loud. This room belonged to a monk. Not the man she'd been on the run with for thirty hours.

Peeking around the corner, his bathroom gave her another shock. White Spartan walls encased by earth-toned tile, a multi-spray shower, large Jacuzzi, and oyster colored double marble sinks. Emily marveled at the shiny brass faucets, a large mirrored wall, and a walk-in closet big as her bedroom had been.

Maybe it would be wise for her to go to Brenda's and stay. Mac had instructed her to remain here, but how could she? This belonged to him, his apartment, his personal space, even if it didn't parallel his personality. Even if Frank ordered it, Emily still felt the uninvited guest.

Touching her lips, Emily recalled the kiss they had shared. She wanted to capture that moment as she slowly ran her tongue over her mouth. She could spend a lifetime in that man's arms, and not feel like she'd missed a thing.

Shaking her head, Emily reminded herself to stop dreaming of something that didn't exist. Looking at the tub, she practically sighed. Those powerful jets would do wonders for a tired body. Reaching down, she turned on the water and undressed.

***

They took Brody's pickup and headed east toward Colleyville. If Jake's information was accurate, they were only blocks away from where the mysterious car had turned in.

Two blocks from the other Falcon agents they planned to connect with, Mac and Brody drove past the house with security gates. Hidden in the back of a cul-de-sac, Mac and Brody exited the pickup and met up with the two agents Frank had put in charge of watching Em.

"What did you find out?" Mac asked.

Jake Taylor, a former Ranger operative replied, "The place is a rental. Leased about a month ago under the name Mike Kent. Any info we found about the guy proved to be bogus."

"Pretty smart move when you got the call that Em's watchdog force had been pulled off."

"You know Frank. He leaves nothing to chance. When the caller didn't say the password right away, we knew something wasn't kosher."

"Yeah, that's how he rolls," Brody said with a chuckle. "Still, pretty smart to have two agents hidden nearby, so you could follow and not be tagged."

"It comes with the job."

Mac faced Jake. "So tell us about what's inside? I noticed a fence."

"Yeah, but almost no security," replied ex-Ranger A.J. Roddio. A.J. and Brody were best buds. They'd both been in the service together before becoming Falcon agents. "I don't think those guys holed up there are expecting company."

Mac and Brody looked at each other and smiled.

"Well, they're in for a good ole shit-kicking surprise," Brody said.

"From what we saw, the west side of the building is completely unguarded. No cameras, no dogs, and no security gate. Just a brick wall."

Brody chuckled. "Piece of cake."

Mac punched him in the shoulder. "Last time you said that I got my butt kicked, big time."

Brody laughed. "You're right. You did get an ass whooping…by a guy the size of a ten year old."

"That's when I realized, size really doesn't matter."

Mac turned to Jake and A.J. "You guys find a safe place across the street from our target. If anything goes south, come in with all the fire power you have."

"I counted eight outside. Not sure about inside. Four vehicles and a man on the roof. Probably a sniper," A.J. offered.

"Let's go," Mac said.

Brody and Mac drove toward the house. Mac wondered what he would find behind the walls. Whoever occupied that compound better be ready for hell because the devil was on his way.

To stay hidden, they parked five hundred yards away, behind a school then sprinted to the house the back way through a field of mesquite trees and small shrubs. They crossed an empty side road then backed up against the wall.

Immediately, the sniper came into view on top of the building, looking bored out of his mind and evidently not taking the assignment seriously. And unlike Mac and Brody, he didn't wear night vision goggles.

Mac had his Glock, a knife, and a couple of smoke grenades. Brody's weapons of choice were a double-barreled shotgun, a Smith and Wesson .45, and two knives.

After a few minutes, Brody reached behind him and took out a rope with a grappling hook tied on the end. One small swing and the hook latched onto the other side of the wall. Brody climbed up first then Mac.

While Mac was stockier and more powerful than Brody, Brody made up for it by being tall, lean, and faster than a roadrunner. As an ex-Ranger, Brody could take out a target in seconds, and nobody would even know he'd been there.

Brody was a wild-hair, loosey-goosey. Rarely did anything conventional, and anybody dumb enough to draw on him learned real fast they'd made a fatal mistake. Tonight, he'd replaced his Stetson with a black sock hat.

Mac climbed the rope, and they both laid flat on the top of the warm brick, waiting. After a few seconds, Mac swung over and adjusted the hook. Silently, they slid down and looked for an easy access to the interior of the house. The longer they stayed undetected, the better.

Backs against the house, Mac slowly edged around a corner, and spotted three guys smoking a joint next to an SUV. They were loud little dumb asses, but armed.

Brody squatted down and crawled to the opposite side of the vehicle. When in position, he tossed a pebble toward Mac, who waited with a cocked fist.

When the first guy came to check out the sound, Mac took the stoner out with a left jab and a right hook. When his friend called and received no reply, he raised his gun and moved in Mac's direction. He missed tripping over Brody by inches.

Brody rose and smacked the guy in the back of the head with the butt of his shotgun. Mac gave the third guy a jump kick and a roundhouse to the head. He went down with a thud.

"That's three." They moved the bodies to the far back against the house and went hunting.

All eight guys were either tied up or out cold in ten minutes flat. Now to learn who occupied the house. Mac gave Brody the signal to take out the sniper.

Brody stepped into center of the yard and threw his knife with killing accuracy. The sniper's body rolled off the roof and into the large holly bush at the edge of the house.

Mac looked in the window and held up six fingers.

Brody nodded, went in first, and Mac followed with a smoke bomb and a hail of gunfire. Six men lay dead when they started up the stairs.

Hugging the wall, weapons ready, Mac saw an armed man step from a room and walk toward the banister.

Brody threw another knife and caught him in the throat. He stumbled to the railing then flipped over, sprawled on the floor below.

They were halfway up the wide staircase when two guys burst from the opposite side of the house with AK 47's. Mac and Brody took them out before they fired a shot.

Sprinting up the rest of the stairs, Mac darted to the opposite side of the double door. On Brody's nod, Mac threw in his last smoke grenade, and they dropped to their knees and waited.

A big man ran out, coughing and firing blindly. Mac grabbed his ankles and yanked his feet from under him. The man went down hard, and the weapon slid across the floor.

Brody tied the big man's hands behind his back, while Mac checked the rest of the upstairs. He found no one. When Mac returned, Brody rolled over their hostage.

Mac stamped his foot down hard on their captive's chest. "Well, hello, Bruno. Welcome to hell."

Mac heard a familiar click behind him.

CHAPTER TWENTY-ONE

Moscow

Tony Archuletta took a chair at the small diner and ordered a cup of coffee. Blowing into his fists and huddling deeper into his coat, he waited for the drink to arrive. When the waitress placed the cup on the table, he grasped the hot brew with both hands.

Seeing his frosted breath, Tony murmured, "Damn, this place feels like a meat locker."

The tiny corner coffee shop reminded Tony of an over-crowded diner from the old TV show *Happy Days*. At the counter where patrons sat elbow to elbow, their fat asses hung over the sides of their little round stools. On the other side of the room, red plastic booths lined a grimy window the size of a wall. The view was nice, but Tony surmised the gaps around the panes probably added to the freezing temperature inside.

He'd carefully selected a small table in the middle aisle, but now, every time the waitress walked by, her hip bumped his arm, but it gave him a great vantage point.

Watching the steam rise from his coffee cup, Tony noticed the pattern on the plastic tablecloth no longer resembled anything, due to age and frequent cleaning. In the middle of the table sat a wire tray with sugar packets, salt and pepper shakers, and napkins.

Restless, Tony shifted his tall frame and watched the door. Unfortunately, he sat in a vinyl-covered chair as ugly as it was uncomfortable. The waitress, with a grease-stained apron stretched across her broad belly and fingernails crusted with dirt, asked if he wanted to order breakfast.

Not in this lifetime.

Tony shook his head and stared into the black coffee. It looked strong enough to sharpen a knife. He picked up the small tin of cream and poured.

On second thought, the stench of boiled cabbage, unwashed bodies, and burnt coffee had Tony shoving his cup and the creamer to the center of the table. He refused to punish his stomach with that crap.

When the door opened, Tony watched Nicholas Belskavia enter the diner, walking between the tables and booths to join him. Inwardly, Tony smiled. He and Nicholas had never had a real run-in. Shrewdly, they'd always managed to tip-toe around each other in a diplomatic way. Both avoided a confrontation that stood a good chance of only one of them surviving.

While Tony could tolerate Belskavia, he'd hated the Russian Mac had shot in Emily's hotel room. Lev Stanislaw had been one messed up psycho. Scary and into torture, brutally corrupt, he took too much pleasure in killing. Rumor had it he'd murdered both his parents and his brother. All over a bottle of beer and a cheap hooker.

Nicholas sat down with a grunt.

Tony smiled.

The older Russian reminded Tony of a retired boxer going bald. His nose covered the center of his face, his slack jaw and dirty teeth, along with a drooping eyelid made him the ugliest man Tony knew.

Poor Nicholas, he had been KGB all his life, and when Russia changed to the Federal Security Service, Nicholas couldn't adapt, didn't fit in, and had finally decided to go rogue. According to certain sources, he'd made a good career move.

Snapping his fingers in the air, Nicholas asked for coffee in Russian before removing his jacket. Slinging it over the back of the chair, he pulled a pack of cigarettes from his shirt pocket. Just as the waitress put the coffee down, Nicholas lit up. Pulling a strong drag from the cigarette, he blew out the smoke then took a sip.

Since Nicholas had set the time and place, Tony figured the offending filth and foul odors didn't faze the Russian.

After a few more loud slurps, Nicholas flipped the ashes of his cigarette into the ashtray and asked, "What you want, Archuletta?"

After straightening the front of his Valentino jacket, Tony leaned back and propped his ankle on his knee. "I have some information I think you might find useful."

"I don't know what you are talking about. You and I don't have anything to discuss."

They both knew better then to bring up the incident from two years ago. Tony had desperately needed an alibi to cover taking out a target, and of all people, Nicholas had walked in and said that they'd been playing poker together with several of his Russian friends. Later, Tony learned Nicholas had wanted the target eliminated more than the US.

"You're right, we don't and never will, but information is a good thing to have."

"Okay, so what you got?" Nicholas sounded like a gangster from New Jersey.

Tony folded his arms on the table. "Word on the street says Ramón Marino and you conducted a little business a few days ago."

"I don't know anything about that." Nicholas took another deep drag.

"Where is Lev?"

Nicholas's face turned red, and he puffed out his chest. "When I get my hands on the shithead that killed him, I will tear off his legs."

"Ouch, that sounds so gruesome, Nicholas. Why not a bullet between the eyes? Much neater." He knew that remark would wiggle the Russian's memory about the target Tony took out.

Nicholas batted that thought away. "*Nyet!* I want him to suffer."

"Good luck with catching the guy. But why did Lev go after the girl?"

"I don't know what you are talking about."

"Word has it you might have overheard her saying something about pictures she'd taken."

Nicholas scooted his chair back. "Our business is finished. I have done nothing wrong."

"Really? Since when is selling illegal weapons not against international law?"

After a careful look around, Nicholas leaned closer. "I don't know what you are talking about."

Reaching inside his jacket pocket, Tony pulled out the pictures from Mac then spread them on the table. "Look familiar?"

Nicholas reared back from the photos as if to distance himself from the obvious. "I was just out for a walk that night. I did nothing wrong."

"And this?" He showed him the picture of Marino passing him the briefcase.

Nicholas shrugged.

"You know this guy?" Tony laid down a picture of Bruno.

"Never seen him in my life."

"You're a liar. But let's not worry about him right now, okay?"

"What do you want, Archuletta? Do not play with me or they will find your body floating in the Moskva River, face down."

Tony clutched his arms. "Brr." He faked a shiver. "It's so cold."

"Cut the shit."

"I have to assume there was money in that briefcase Marino gave you. Probably a lot of money."

Nicholas remained stoic.

"My question, Nicholas, is have you tried to spend any of that money?"

"Only you are assuming Marino gave me money. Money for what?"

"I think you sold him something he could unleash on the United States. So, if you did, these pictures are pretty incriminating."

"They prove nothing. Nothing, I say."

"Until something happens. Then these pictures will lead right back to you. Now, Nicholas, the way I see it, you sold Marino bio weapons, so he could detonate a bomb on American soil. If that happens, you won't need to worry about proof. Frank Hamilton will send every Falcon agent he has at his disposal to hunt your ass down. And when we catch you, ripping your legs off is the least we'll do."

Tony pushed back his chair and stood. As he walked toward the door, Nicholas grabbed his arm.

"What has money got to do with this? You asked if I'd spent any. What did you mean?"

Tony paused and looked down at Nicholas. "I should let you find out on your own, you dumb shit."

"Find out what?"

157

"If Marino paid you in American dollars, they're probably counterfeit." He waited a moment for that to soak in. The widening of Nicholas's eyes revealed his horror.

"Counterfeit? He is a fucking drug dealer."

"A drug dealer who recently learned how lucrative making phony money can be."

"You are shitting me. He not got that kind of balls to play me like that."

"Check it out, and when you do, I have the perfect way for you to get even."

Nicholas stood and jerked on his coat. "I'll get that fucker."

Tony handed him a card. "I'm gone in eight hours. Once I leave Moscow, I can't help you."

***

Mac stilled as the barrel of a weapon pressed against the back of his head. He looked at Brody who had the guy in his crosshairs. In one swift move, Mac spun, knocked the weapon out of the thug's hand then finished with a right hook to the jaw. The guy hit the floor, and he wasn't getting up anytime soon.

Jake and A.J. busted through the downstairs door. Mac let them know everything was okay. They rounded up the gang of thugs and headed for Falcon's office in Dallas.

Mac checked on Em. The phone rang twice before she answered.

"Is everything okay?" he asked.

"Yes, I just stepped out of the tub."

Mac's imagination went from a life and death struggle to images of Em's naked body in record time. He enjoyed the thought of her sleeping in his bed, her touch making an imprint on everything in his apartment. He swallowed. "Why don't you get some sleep? I'm going to be a while."

"Mac, did you get the bad guys?" Her voice sounded soft, inviting, and real after what he and Brody had been through.

For the first time in his career, Mac wanted to go home. Let someone else deal with the bad guys. He only wanted to curl up and make love to Em. "Yeah, they're on their way downtown. As soon as I finish, I'll be home."

"Are you still mad at me for telling my sister?"

"No, I don't have a family, but I can understand your need to protect them."

"I've been with you all this time. I didn't know you didn't have a family," Em said, slamming a fist into his soft spot. "Your parents are dead? How horrible."

"It all happened when I was a kid, so I've gotten used to the fact that it's only me."

Silence followed by a deep sigh. "Mac, everyone needs a family. Weren't you even adopted?"

"Naw, I got dumped into the foster care system. When I turned fourteen, I took off. Lived on the streets for a while until I joined the Navy."

"That's so sad."

"That's reality." He paused unable to continue. He'd already told her more than any other woman. "I gotta go. Sleep tight."

CHAPTER TWENTY-TWO

Mac brought Bruno back to Falcon's interrogation room. Frank followed. After shoving their prisoner into a chair, Mac handcuffed him to the table, and they stepped into the hall out of Bruno's earshot.

"Easy as hell to get him," Mac said with a hint of uncertainty. "I kept thinking we're walking into a trap or something." He shrugged. "Nothing happened. We threw him in the back of his own car and drove him here."

Brows furrowed, Frank shook his head. "That's not like Bruno."

"I'll say. Did you hear from Tony?"

"He baited the trap."

Mac grunted. "Bet the Russian bites."

Frank shook his head. "Tony could talk a nun out of her habit in one minute flat."

"Let's go inside and talk to the man who blew up Em's house."

Frank opened the door then followed behind Mac. They leaned against the wall.

"Bruno, imagine our surprise when we found you right under our noses." Frank pulled out a chair on the opposite side and sat. "You probably aren't in a talking mood, are you?"

Beads of sweat bulleted Bruno's brow. His hands gripped the edge of the table, so tightly his knuckles showed white, as his black eyes darted around like a cue ball searching for a pocket. "Not really," he muttered.

"That's too bad because before the night is over, we'll get what we want." Mac casually examined his fingernails. "Your decision is how we go about it."

Marino's henchman looked up. "It's simple. I came here to carry out Marino's orders. You guys know that. I do what I'm told."

"He tell you to kill Emily Richards?" Frank asked.

Sadly, Bruno nodded. "*Sí,* he did."

"Because he wanted to destroy the pictures?"

"*Sí.*"

Mac tossed the photos on the table. "These?"

Bruno's head moved slowly as he looked at the snapshots. "I guess. I wasn't there when these were taken. I only know Marino didn't want anyone to see him with The Wholesaler."

"What do you know about that?"

Shrugging, Bruno looked away. "Not much." Turning back, he nodded to Mac. "You know he keeps everything to himself. He don't confide in nobody."

Pushing away from the wall, Mac said, "Yeah, but you've lasted longer than anyone. You do that by being one step ahead of your boss?" He leaned down and placed his palms on the steel table. "Marino might not tell you what he's doing, but you know a lot more than you let on."

Bruno shifted and cleared his throat. "I know he is a monster."

"We want to know what he bought from The Wholesaler?"

Bruno shrugged then looked at Mac. "Drugs and weapons. They are the way Marino makes money. But his real crime is against God."

"What are you talking about?"

Bruno bowed his head and held his silence.

"Why didn't he take you to meet with The Wholesaler?"

"My job was to take *you* out, McKinsey," Bruno snarled. "Marino did not tell me he was going to meet the Russian until afterward."

"So, you flew to and from Moscow with Marino?"

"*Sí,* but Angel Diaz went with him to make the exchange. I was sent to kill you."

"Who is this Diaz?"

Resigned, Bruno glanced away. "Probably my replacement."

"What about Miss Richards? Why would you kill an innocent woman?"

"Marino is convinced she is a spy. Sent by Falcon to rescue you."

"Your boss is wrong. She knows nothing. She's just a lawyer."

"Marino did not know that. But if she is innocent, why did she take pictures of the transaction?"

"She was just testing a prototype for a friend who invented a small camera."

"Does she not know how dangerous that is? To take pictures of Marino making a deal?"

Mac shook his head. "You don't get it. She's just a…lawyer."

"But she has the proof."

"Really? She just had a bunch of pictures until you goons turned it into a fucking war."

"But you met up with her."

"No, I didn't. All I needed was a ride out of Russia."

Bruno looked down.

Did it bother him that his boss had sent him to kill a woman who'd done nothing to intentionally harm Marino's operation? Mac doubted that. Bruno was as callous as his boss. They'd wallowed in the same blood and destruction for years.

"If you think Diaz is your replacement, then you have nothing to lose by giving Marino up. There probably isn't much left for you after you botched killing me and Miss Richards." Mac looked at his watch then at Bruno. "And the clock is ticking."

"I know what you want, but I have a family. They are all that matters to me."

Pushing away from the wall, Frank said, "We can protect your family, Bruno. I give my word." He leaned closer. "We can get them out of the country and settled in a place where they'll never be found. And we can do it in less than twenty-four hours."

Bruno slumped back in his chair, his eyes downcast on the table. He was a big man, younger than he looked, older in many ways than someone twice his age. He'd never married. Mac figured he'd avoided the altar because Marino knew how to use a man's weaknesses against him. He knew how to make a man sweat and control him to the point he'd do anything Marino ordered.

162

"Bruno," Mac said. "You were there the day Angelina was shot. Who pulled the trigger? You and I know it wasn't me or any other Falcon agent."

"I was there that day." The hard lines in Bruno's face softened.

"Why was she shot when we went to make the exchange?" Mac banged his fist against the metal table. "It could have all been so simple."

Bruno shook his head slowly and bowed. "No, it had to be."

"What do you mean?"

"Marino was convinced you seduced his sister, and she was no longer a virgin. He gave the signal for her to be killed. He no longer wanted her."

"But she was his sister." Mac ran his fingers through his hair. "Damn, she was so young. How could he?"

"You don't understand do you, McKinsey?"

"What's to understand? She was his flesh and blood." It angered Mac that Marino would kill his only sibling when Mac had no one.

"He loved her in an unnatural way," Bruno said. "She was his bride."

Frank let out a deep breath. "It's enough to make a strong man sick."

"Bride?"

"*Sí*, when she was thirteen, he paid a priest to marry them. He'd planned to bring her home in the summer, and they would live together as husband and wife."

Mac narrowed his eyes in disbelief. "His sister?"

"Aw, shit," Frank said.

"Angelina did not love him that way. She wanted to stay in the nunnery. Even the priest forbade her to go home. They found the padre dead. Hung on the wall like the Holy Christ."

Mac closed his eyes and squeezed the bridge of his nose. He couldn't comprehend any of this. "So, he thought I'd touched Angelina, or his bride. And for that he's been hunting me for years?"

"*Sí.*"

Mac glared at Bruno. "No one touched that girl. I stayed with her twenty-four-seven. I kept her safe." He shook his head. "He killed her in cold blood."

"That is why he keeps killing the young girls of his country. He rapes, tortures, and mutilates." Bruno's mouth turned down. "Then he murders them and tosses their young bodies into the garbage like rotted food."

"Bruno, you have to help us stop this."

The Columbian looked up, and Mac knew he was looking into the eyes of a man with little time left. "I think we are too late."

"You're smart, Bruno. No man lasts as long as you have without a few tricks up his sleeve."

Bruno leaned his head back and closed his eyes. "I have a little money set aside, a place to go, and a few passports. But I also have a family. Anything I do to help you, my family will pay for."

"I meant what I said about protecting them, Bruno," Frank reminded.

Bruno looked like he considered the offer before he glanced at Mac. "When Marino finds out I didn't kill you, my life is over, anyway."

"But we can save your family," Mac offered.

Bruno looked at Mac. "It is not my family you should be concerned about. I left a man at the girl's house to wait for the bodies to be removed after the bomb exploded. This way we'd know the job was done."

Mac's breath caught in his throat. "So, when two body bags aren't carried from the house, the gig is up for you?"

Brody burst into the room, snatched up the TV remote, and clicked on the television. "You won't F-ing believe this!"

Em's sister, Victoria, stood in the middle of the screen, explaining that Em wasn't in the house when it exploded. She was at a friend's place in Bedford.

Mac dropped to his knees.

CHAPTER TWENTY-THREE

The car Mac drove turned the corner on two wheels as he pulled to the gated entrance of his apartment complex. After punching in the code, he sped to his apartment and raced up the stairs, leaving the car running.

He and Brody came to a halt when they noticed the door was open and heard Hershey barking inside. Mac rushed in and called Em's name. The only sound was Hershey. Mac went to the bathroom and let the dog out. Hershey leapt on him and continued to bark.

The dog was unharmed, but Em was gone. Her purse lay abandoned on the coffee table and her new cell phone on the kitchen counter. He picked it up and dialed the last call Em had made.

"Hello," a female voice answered.

Mac took a stab. "Hi, is this Brenda?"

"Yes, it is. Who's this?"

"I'm Mac, Em's friend. Her phone shows your number as the last one she called. What did she say?"

"Well, she mentioned you. Said she was safe, but she didn't tell me where she was. She called to let me know she was fine, that's all."

"She's not safe now, Brenda. I'm at my apartment, and Em is gone, and Hershey was locked in the bathroom."

"What! Emily said she had no intentions of leaving until you returned. Is her car there?"

"Yes, parked where she left it."

"What are you going to do? Do you think the men who blew up her house found out where she was hiding?"

Mac didn't know what to say or think. Em in Marino's hands scared him so much he could hardly breathe.

"Oh God, no!" Brenda shouted. "It was her dumb-assed sister, wasn't it? That bitch with the fake boobs and big mouth?"

"I'm sorry, Brenda, but you might be right."

There was a wrenching sob on the other end as Mac blinked back tears himself.

"Okay, Mac, you go get Emily. Give me your address, and I'll pick up Hershey and bring him here so he'll be safe. But I'm telling you right now, I'm going to Victoria's and Stanley's and I'm kicking some serious ass. I'm about to rock their sick, twisted world."

Mac liked Brenda. She was the kind of friend Em needed. One willing to stand up and fight when other "fair weather friends" hid behind silence. After telling Brenda how to get to his place with the code to the gate and a promise to leave his apartment unlocked, Mac and Brody went hunting.

Mac dialed Jake. When Jake answered, Mac said, "Go to the office and find out from Bruno where Em might be. We don't have a single clue to go on. None of my neighbors saw a thing."

"Got it," Jake replied.

"Don't be nice. Em could die any minute."

"You can count on me."

"I know, Jake. That's why you're the one I called."

***

Jake made it to the office in record time. He went downstairs and kicked in the door to the interrogation room. When he saw Bruno, he pulled out his weapon and laid three loaded clips on the table.

Long, unbroken lines of sweat streamed down Bruno's face. His shackled hands shook and fear bulged his black eyes. He stuttered and stammered, unable to form a complete word. His crumpled face revealed his certainty that negotiations were over.

Jake fired a bullet and took off the lobe of Bruno's left ear. The next shot clipped his right shoulder.

Bruno screamed in pain as tears fell from his eyes and the stench of his fear filled the room. Jake cocked the gun again and fired. Bruno lowered his head as the bullet creased his temple. Stomping his feet, he tried to yank free of the cuffs that held him bound to the metal table.

"Please stop!" Bruno cried. He hunched his shoulders and squeezed his eyes shut.

Emily Richards was the only thing Jake thought about at the moment. Bruno had made a lot of bad choices in his life, and now the devil was here to collect his due. Jake didn't care how much he hurt a man who'd tried to kill an innocent woman. All he wanted was results.

"Where did Marino take the girl, Bruno?"

"I swear I don't know."

Jake shot his right ear off. "School is closed, Bruno, and I don't play nice. If I don't find out where Emily Richards is right now, I'm going to kill you piece by piece. It'll take an army of crime scene investigators to clean up this fucking mess when I'm finished. Now start talking."

"I swear——"

Jake shot him in the left shoulder. "Try again."

Bruno screamed at the top of his lungs. He cried, he pleaded, he begged. None of it mattered to Jake. All he wanted was Emily's location.

"I don't know what to do."

Jake cocked his weapon and shot Bruno in the left kneecap.

"Wait! Wait!" Bruno screamed.

Jake released the trigger. "I'm listening."

"I can reach him by phone. Maybe I can call him and he'll tell me where she's at."

Jake walked around the table where Bruno sat in a chair pooled in blood. He reached inside his pocket and took out a phone. He put it on speaker then slid it toward Bruno.

"Make the call, Bruno, and hope you learn where she's at because if you don't, I'm going to take four hours to kill you."

Jake's phone was programmed to put out a tracer, record the conversation, and determine the person being called.

Bruno dropped the phone several times before he managed to dial the number. "Yeah, Marino, where are you?"

"Where are you, Bruno? With the fucking Falcon bitches?"

"No, no, I got away. When the shooting started, I ran out the back into the field. I made my way to a local store where I stole a car. I'm on my way to meet you."

"Why do you want to find me, Bruno? You have done nothing I have asked you to do. I don't need you anymore. I have Diaz. He is a man who gets results. Not you, Bruno."

"But, *jefe*, I've—"

Silence. Bruno dropped the phone on the table and lowered his head. "He hung up."

Jake left the room and took the stairs two at a time. He walked into Frank's office just as he picked up the phone.

Jake went to the console set up by the NSA and read off the message. "Marino is at 1206 Mockingbird Lane in Southlake."

"Did you hear that, Mac?"

Frank put the phone down. "You're backup. Get going."

Jake turned to leave.

"How bad did you leave Bruno?"

"Alive."

CHAPTER TWENTY-FOUR

Emily struggled to breathe. Every stitch of clothing clung to her sweat-soaked body. Her feet burned like fire ants had feasted on them. The smothering dark hood forced her to control her breathing or hyperventilate. Panic riddled her mind as terror spiraled down her spine.

Surrounded by darkness, not knowing where they were taking her, Emily tried to chew at the tape across her mouth with no success. She stubbornly blinked back tears and thought of Mac. He was out there hunting for her, and he wasn't one to quit.

Earlier in the apartment, she'd hung up from Brenda when Hershey started barking. Thinking he needed to go outside, she foolishly opened the door without checking the security screens. Three men with guns pushed inside. They threatened to kill Hershey if she didn't keep him quiet. A short, stocky man followed her to the bathroom where she had to fight with Hershey to get him to stay.

Then they grabbed each arm and pulled her from the apartment. She lost her sandals in the struggle. As soon as they cleared the door, Emily screamed like a crazy person. She kicked, squirmed, and tried to bite the man on her right. She managed a solid kick to the ankle of one guy, and the other got a jab in the ribs. Then before she knew their intent, they smacked a piece of duct tape against her mouth.

Following Mac's instructions, she dug in with her bare heels and squatted down. They yanked her up, but she struggled backwards, stalling for time. Hoping someone would hear her plea for help or see the abduction.

Angrily, she'd twisted, kicked, pulled against their tight grip and continued to dig her feet into the hard cement. She didn't get much for her efforts, but she got the satisfaction of refusing to give up easily.

Finally, the two men grabbed her legs and threw her into the backseat of a car. With one on each side, they shoved her onto the floorboard. Moments later, they squealed out of the apartment compound then made a left.

Leaving her only sanctuary behind, the guy next to the window covered her head with a black canvas bag. He propped his feet on her shoulder and hip. The hump on the floorboard in the back of the car dug into her side.

From that moment on, Emily was helpless. She didn't know where they were taking her, how long they drove, or their intent. But something told her this would not end well.

The car came to a stop. The men yanked her out with more force than necessary. The soles of her feet were so raw she stumbled forward when released. They removed the hood and shoved her through the open door of a large, two-story brick house.

With her eyes still adjusting, Emily fell several times before she came to the living room where a tall, handsome man greeted them. The coldness in his eyes twisted a knot in her stomach. Without being told, she knew this was Marino. The man determined to kill Mac. Obviously, she would play the part of a pawn.

Emily knew with all her heart that Mac would come. The confident smirk on Marino's face told her he also had no doubts.

When they ripped the tape off, she licked her lips and asked, "What do you want with me?"

"You will see," he replied smoothly. "You are McKinsey's lover, are you not?"

His blatant remark gave her pause. *Were they lovers?* To this point, she'd never considered their relationship or lack thereof. She cared a great deal for Mac, but at the same time, she knew he wasn't the settling down type. Besides, with her luck in the romance department, she wasn't about to hold on to any hope.

"No, we are *not* lovers. I represent Falcon Securities as their attorney. I barely know Mac. I was in Russia and he came to my hotel room needing a lift to the States. That's all there is to it."

A bitter, ugly laugh bubbled from his throat. Pointing a mean finger at her, he said, "You play me for a fool?" He stepped forward and tilted her chin. "Or are you the fool, Miss Richards?"

"I don't know what you mean, and I have no idea why you want to harm me. I don't even know you."

"But you know McKinsey. The one I am after. The one I will kill."

It took every muscle in Emily's body to keep from reacting to Marino's statement, but she managed, barely. "Then I suggest you go after him and let me go. Are you blind? I'm not McKinsey."

In a breath, Marino slapped her so hard she fell to her knees. Blackness swelled and blinded her. With the metallic taste of blood in her mouth, Emily shook her head. Refusing to remain on the floor, she shoved herself up. Rage brightened his face.

With his feet spread wide, he squared his shoulders. Madness glistened in his eyes. He pointed at her. "You are not him, but he cares about you. And now I am going to kill someone he loves like he did to me." Marino thumped his chest. "I promise he will watch as I slice you into small pieces while your heart still beats."

Emily stood on wobbly legs and shook her head to get her hair out of her face. Blood trickled from the corner of her mouth and no doubt Marino's hand imprint on her face would be added to her other bruises, but still Emily couldn't resist. "I hope he kills you for the animal you are." Then she spit in his face.

A horrible growl erupted from his mouth, and he lunged for her with both hands. Before he could reach her, a small man shot between them and warned, "*Jefe*, we need her alive. Dead, she's worthless."

The two kidnappers forced her into a large bedroom. Without a word, they cut the hand restraints and slung her on the bed before banging the door shut. She rubbed her wrists and lay quietly, waiting. The bolt slamming home from the other side echoed in the sparsely furnished room.

CHAPTER TWENTY-FIVE

Moscow

A loud thumping on his hotel door brought Tony to his feet. He picked up his smartphone to see who waited on the other side. Tony never left anything to chance. A tiny camera across the hall showed the back of Nicholas Belskavia. He was alone. Clicking off his phone, Tony opened the door and waved the Russian in.

"Glad to see you came to your senses. So, Marino gave you *fugazi?*"

"I do not know what that means, but the money is no good." He threw his hat on the chair and sat on the edge of the bed. "I'm going to kill that fucker. He thinks he is safe in America. Wait and see how long is my arm."

Tony strolled further into the room. He opened the mini bar and poured his guest and himself a glass of vodka. "Be smart, Nicholas. Get legal. In today's world with all the technology, it's hard to get away with much."

"I think maybe after I kill Ramón Marino, I will retire to the countryside. My wife hates Moscow. My son is in the army and my daughter is married to an engineer and they live in Kiev."

Tony leaned against the wall and crossed his ankles. "I've known you for years, Nicholas, but I never took you for a family man."

Nicholas tilted his glass and chuckled. "I have been married to the same stupid woman for a million years."

"Giving up crime is a move in the right direction. You're too old for all this."

He blew out a frustrated breath. "*Dah*, I'm too old for all this killing." He looked at Tony. "So, what is your plan?"

Tony shrugged his left shoulder. "Kill Marino."

Nicholas took a drink of his vodka. "I like it."

"How much money did you lose?"

Nicholas stood and paced the room. "Not as much as you might think."

Tony raised his eyebrows. "Really?"

"You see," Nicholas said. "Those weapons I sold him? The nuclear ones that he could make into bombs?"

"Yes."

"Well, they're not exactly *nuclear*. If you know what I mean?"

"You old son-of-a-bitch." Tony laughed. "What a pair the two of you make. Now, I don't know who to kill."

"I do. That fucker screwed me good. That was my retirement fund." Nicholas stared out the window. "It will be a matter of honor. I go teach Ramón Marino never to double cross a Russian before he thinks."

"I need a favor, Nicholas."

Nicholas stood and walked to the large window overlooking Red Square. "I owe you nothing, Archuletta."

"I turned you on to the counterfeit money."

Nicholas shrugged. "I would have eventually found out on my own."

"Right, but it would have taken you time, and I saved you a lot of embarrassment. You try using that money, and people will think you're an idiot."

Nicholas rubbed his bristled chin. "You are right there. And I could have been arrested. Not good for a man my age." He finished his vodka and helped himself to another glass before turning to Tony. "You tell me what you want and maybe we can settle on a price."

"No money is going to exchange hands. Remember, I still have the pictures. I could hang your asses. You and Marino both."

Nicholas raised his hand. "Okey-dokey," he said. "And you Americans say Russians are rude." He waved Tony aside. "What is it you want?" He paused and raised his finger as if remembering something. "But when it's all over, Ramón Marino must be dead...and the pictures become mine."

"That leaves one little issue we have to solve."

"What's that?"

"The man who killed your right hand man, Lev."

173

"*Nyet, nyet, nyet!*" Nicholas shouted. "That man must die. He killed my friend."

Tony took the glass from Nicholas's hand and pointed at the door. "Then get out. We have no business to do. I can find others who will help."

Nicholas walked toward him, his eyes narrow. "Did you kill Lev?"

Tony shook his head.

"It was a Falcon agent, was it not?"

"Yes, it was. Lev broke into his hotel to kill the woman who innocently took the pictures, and the Falcon agent protected the woman. She didn't do anything wrong, but go sight-seeing."

"I heard her on the phone say, 'I have all the pictures I need'."

"She has a friend who invented a camera. She was testing it for him. Nothing more."

Nicholas took his drink out of Tony's hand and slumped into the overstuffed chair. "I loved Lev. He was a good friend. And loyal, too."

"Nicholas, we know for the right amount of money he would have killed you. That's not a friend; that's just a killer."

Nicholas shrugged. "Probably, you are right." He let out a loud sigh. "We are in an ugly business, Archuletta. The whole world goes on about normal living, they drive their cars, they cook dinner, raise their kids. Us, we kill people. It is sad."

Tony nodded. "Necessary evil. But maybe you can escape to live in peace with your wife."

"Okey-dokey, how do we go about getting what we both want? I will tell you; I have men in your big state Texas. They stand by should I need them."

"You know Marino's in Texas?" Tony had just spoken to Frank, so he knew where the Columbian was, but how did Nicholas find out?

"I have people everywhere. You never heard of the Russian Mafia?"

"Yes, I have, but I didn't know you were connected."

"I'm not, but my brother is. He owe me favor."

"Okay, this is what we do."

174

CHAPTER TWENTY-SIX

Bedford, TX

Brenda Sullivan walked up the three steps to Stanley and Victoria's ranch style home. She rang the doorbell. Dumb and Dumber barked like a Rottweiler who'd just sucked on a helium tank. Brenda wanted to squeeze their little heads until their brains popped out.

After a second ring, Victoria answered the door with a flourish. Maybe she expected more TV cameras. Stanley stood behind her. That's good, Brenda thought.

"Hello, Brenda," Victoria said with a smile. "Did you hear what happened to Emily's house?"

Brenda stepped into the foyer, doubled up both her fists, and planted her right one directly in the middle of Victoria's perfectly made up face. She dropped like a ten pound weight. Stanley, the idiot, didn't seem to know it was his job to catch her.

Standing over Victoria, with the dogs yelping like air heads, Brenda waited for her eyes to open. In a matter of seconds, Victoria sat up and raised her hand to her bloodied nose. To fix the nose, thousands, to replace the bloody sweater, hundreds, but the look of shock on Victoria's face…priceless!

As Emily's sister looked up at her, bawling like a two year old, Brenda said, "Listen, you stupid brat. You went on TV and told the whole world that your sister was still alive. Then went on to say where she was hiding."

"Brenda," Stanley said. "Victoria didn't mean any harm to come to Emily."

"I don't believe that, stinky Stanley. She knew what would happen. She got her ugly, plastic surgery face on the air."

"I didn't mean to slip and give them the address."

Brenda leaned down. "Liar."

"I'm not."

"The hell you aren't. All your life you've wanted anything and everything Emily ever had." Brenda looked at Stanley. "Even this weirdo."

"Brenda!" Stanley stuttered, his brown eyes wide with shock.

"Mac called me and said that Emily has been kidnapped. I'm calling my brother to see if he can help. But I don't think this is a police matter."

Victoria picked herself up off the floor and buried her bloody nose in the front of Stanley's shirt. "I'm completely innocent. And you come in here attacking me."

"Be glad I didn't bring my gun."

Stanley patted Victoria on the back. "You need to leave, Brenda," Stanley said, "before I call the police."

"Oh, I'm going, and I'll be the one calling the police. My brother. And if I see *her* face on TV again, I'm going to black both her eyes." Brenda turned and stomped back to her car. Anger shook her whole body. How could Victoria be so damn stupid?

She couldn't.

Tears blurred her vision as Brenda imagined her best friend being harmed. Emily never hurt anyone. She'd always been a good person. Now someone had kidnapped her.

Batting away the tears, Brenda drove to the Fort Worth Police Station on Belknap. There she parked her car and fed the meter. After whisking away all the tears and straightening her clothes, she stepped into the precinct where her brother worked.

A female officer sat at a desk near the door. "Can I help you?" she asked.

"I'd like to see Detective Sullivan with CID."

"May I ask your name?"

She took a deep breath. "Tell him it's his sister, Brenda."

Within seconds, she watched as her brother came walking toward her. He was a tall, handsome guy if you were into bald heads and hairy mustaches. "What brings you here, sis?" He smiled, reached down and gave her a big hug.

"I guess you heard about Emily?"

"I heard her house blew up." His hand on her back, he propelled her in the direction of his office. "She okay?"

Brenda took a chair after her brother closed the door. "I don't know. She's been abducted from a friend's apartment, and I think this is some kind of spy thing."

"Spy thing?" he said, sitting in the chair behind his desk.

"Well, see, she met this guy. He's actually one of her clients. Anyway something happened and the bad guys blew up Emily's house."

"Did you call the police?"

"No, Mac is looking for her."

"Mac, the client?"

"Yeah, she said his name was John McKinsey. He works for Falcon Securities."

"Oh, those guys." Her brother leaned back in his chair. "Not much to say about that company. I know they do a lot of undercover stuff."

"Yeah, I guess so."

"If one of those agents is on the case, I don't think you have a lot to worry about. I hear they're the best of the best."

Brenda couldn't hold back the tears any longer. Her brother stepped around and pulled her against his chest, hugging her.

"I'm so worried, Kenny. What if something happens to Emily?"

"Let's just pray it doesn't." He released her and grabbed his jacket off the hook next to the door. "Let's get out of here and grab some coffee."

"Sounds good." Brenda paused at the door and looked up at her brother. "Oh, by the way, I socked Victoria in the nose."

Kenny patted her on the shoulder, and grinned. "Good girl."

As they moved toward the exit, two policemen walked in, escorting a man wearing tattered clothes and reeking of liquor. "This guy says his name is Rayland McKinsey, and his son is a cop in Dallas."

Stunned, Brenda stopped short and grabbed her brother's sleeve.

***

Mac's cell phone rang just as he and Brody pulled out of his apartment complex parking lot. Hershey hadn't wanted him to leave, but Brenda would be there soon. He wouldn't be alone for long.

"This is Mac."

"It's Tony. You on your way to Marino?"

"Yeah, I'm headed there now. Frank just sent me the address."

"Okay, well, I have Nicholas Belskavia backing us up. He has thugs in the area."

"Look, Tony, I don't want some stupid Russian screwing this up. Marino has Em. There's no telling what he'll do."

"We'll get Emily out of there. You know that, and I know that. This is what we do; it's our job. But beware, buddy. You're driving right into a trap. Get your head on straight and don't go barging in there and get killed in a hail of bullets. This isn't something you can shoot your way out of."

Mac wanted Em back so badly he could hardly see straight, nor could he keep his car in the right lane. He had the pedal almost to the floor. If a cop didn't stop him, he could arrive in Southlake before Marino knew he was coming. "I don't plan to shoot my way out, Tony. You know me better than that. Once I get there, I'll come up with a plan. I always do."

"I know, but first of all, slow down before you manage to kill Brody. I know you're driving like a maniac."

Mac lifted his foot off the accelerator. "How do you know that?"

"I know *you*."

"How did you get Belskavia's help?" Mac asked as he pulled up to a stop sign. "I thought you two were arch enemies. Like Batman and the Joker."

"No, we just kid around. But it just so happens that dumbass Marino paid The Wholesaler in counterfeit money."

"We suspected that."

"Marino just crossed the wrong man."

"We're almost there. Wish me luck."

"Keep your head, Mac. Know it's a trap and be smart enough to do what you have to do."

"One last thing, the Russians," Mac asked. "Does Marino know?

"That's your edge. He's completely clueless."

Mac clicked off his phone and turned to Brody. "Tony sent us some help. Russians. It seems Marino bought his nuclear weapon with Monopoly money."

"How stupid can that man be?" Brody replied. "But I don't like messing with Russians. They're so damn blood thirsty."

"Today, at least, they're on our side."

"That's a switch." Brody checked the GPS. "We're one block away. Turn left at the next street and the address Frank gave us is the second house on the right."

"Let's do a drive-by," Mac said, fighting the urge to slam on the brakes, run up to the house, and start shooting. But he knew Marino hoped he'd do just that.

As they slowly passed the house, Mac saw nothing unusual. There were three cars in the driveway. Two black SUVs with dark windows, and a white Cadillac, right out of the showroom.

The blinds were drawn, the landscape perfect, and a round, flowered ornament with the word *welcome* hung on the door. From the outside, nothing appeared amiss. There wasn't a hint to what was taking place inside, and Mac wasn't going to let his mind go there. He had to remain focused and alert. One screw up and Em could die.

Mac stopped the car after they turned the corner. "Nothing unusual," Brody said. "You want me to hop a few fences and do some recon?"

Mac pulled from the curb and turned at the next block. Driving slowly, he found the house behind where Marino hid. It had a For Sale sign out front and looked empty. Mac turned and grinned at Brody.

Brody reared back. "That still doesn't mean this isn't a trap. It simply means we may get a look-see into the yard. But my guess is we're going to see a bunch of armed men."

Mac put the car in park and stepped out with Brody right behind him. They eased to the side of the house and approached the gate to the back yard. Mac saw a swimming pool, several shrubs, and two shade trees.

Carefully, he pulled down on the lever of the entrance and opened it a few inches. Through the slats in the privacy fence, Mac saw Marino's guys armed with assault rifles. They lined the back of the house like Storm Troopers in Star Wars, except they wore black. Brody had been right; the weakest area was well covered.

Quietly, Mac and Brody backed out of the yard and got to the pickup without being seen.

"Well, that didn't work," Brody said. "What next?"

"I'm thinking." Mac pulled away from the curb.

"I know you hate that Emily is in there, and you don't know what's happening to her, but be strong, Mac. I know she is."

"Marino is a killer." Mac's chest constricted. "She could be dead for all I know."

"I don't think he'd kill her. He's more likely to use her to pull you in."

"Maybe we should let that happen. I'll wire up, you get Jake and A.J. I can let you know what's happening inside, so you'd know when to attack."

"The first thing he'll do is check you. And we don't know when the crazy Russians are coming."

"I don't like the idea of Russians saving our ass."

"Stop!" Brody shouted.

Mac braked in the middle of the street.

Brody smiled. "I have an idea."

***

Emily eased off the bed. She nearly screamed when her bare feet touched the rug. Looking down, she saw they were bleeding from being scraped over concrete. Her wrists burned from the zip ties and her hip was sore from being held down on the floorboard of the car by a heavy foot.

A hundred bees stung her face from Marino's slap. Her mouth throbbed and her lip felt like an inflated balloon.

As she managed to move around the room, Emily looked for something to help with an escape. The room smelled stuffy and closed up. Apparently, no one had been here in a while. Dust covered the furniture, and there were no pictures or decorations.

She inched the curtains back from the French doors leading to the backyard only to see men walking around with weapons. No escape route there.

Turning, she looked for other avenues. She had to get out before Mac learned she'd been kidnapped and came looking for her.

That's what Marino wanted. Emily knew Mac would be walking into a trap that would get him killed.

Determined not to remain a captive, Emily went to the bathroom and pulled out the drawers, hoping to find something sharp.

No such luck.

However, on the floor, beside the Jacuzzi tub laid a small, cylinder shaped candle. She quickly plucked the candle up and placed it on the vanity and went looking for matches. Start a fire. Make the smoke alarm go off. Then hide behind the door. When everyone rushed inside, she'd sneak out.

In her mind, it all sounded like a good idea, but she knew in her heart that it only worked in the movies. Emily continued to search for another way out. There were no windows in the bedroom. Only the French doors. The bathroom had a large opaque window, but it faced to the backyard. At the end of the bathroom was a closet.

Emily stepped inside, looked up, and smiled.

CHAPTER TWENTY-SEVEN

"Okay, Lone Ranger," Mac said. "What hair-brained scheme have you come up with now?"

"Well, Kemosabi, watch and learn."

Mac's emotions resembled a tornado, knowing Em's life was in Marino's hands.

"Follow me," Brody said, climbing out of the vehicle. He opened the metal toolbox in the bed of his truck. From inside, he pulled out a zip line and hooks.

"I'm not following."

Brody stopped and turned to him. "Listen, we can't blow up the place because Emily is inside. We can't go in guns blazing either since we don't even know what room she's in."

"Okay."

"There's no way to get in without being seen unless…" Brody looked up. "We go housetop to housetop. And since these damn mansions are so far apart we can't jump from roof to roof like Mary Poppins. I thought we'd rig a line and zip across."

Now was not the time to imagine how badly they could screw this up. There were far too many possibilities. With Em's life in danger, the plan had to work because it was the only thing they'd come up with.

Knocking on the door was foolish because he'd never make it to the driveway before Marino's guy laid him out.

Brody was right. A zip line was the only way since his unspoken idea of digging a tunnel would take too long.

Sweat rolled off Mac in buckets. He couldn't remember the last time his nerves had been this strung out.

"We'll use the house on the left," Brody said, his gloved hands working frantically. "I don't think anyone is home. But the closer we get to five, the less likely that becomes."

"I know. It's just so damn hard to concentrate when I'm not even sure Em is in there. They could have taken her somewhere else."

"Frank said when Bruno called Marino, this house came up. It's the only lead we have."

Mac started the truck and steered toward the address Frank said Jake's phone had traced. Since the info came from the boss, Mac was confident it was legitimate. Frank hadn't been wrong before. Jake and Brody also had his back, and they'd been on hundreds of missions before.

But now Em was involved.

What would he do if anything happened to her? Marino's crazy mind could always come up with something diabolical, or one of his associates playing suck-up to the boss could run with Em.

It also didn't help that guilt gnawed at Mac's conscience like a hungry dog on a bone. Inside, his gut twisted.

Brody reached over and touched his arm. "I know you're blaming yourself for all this, but don't."

Mac looked out the side window and blinked hard. "Yeah, I know. But if I hadn't gone to her hotel room…"

"She'd be dead, Mac. Bruno said that Belskavia, The Wholesaler, had sent that wild assed Russian to kill her for taking those pictures."

"I keep wondering how this got so damn out of control."

"Mac, we go after the meanest sons-of-bitches in the world. When has it ever been easy?" Brody took a piece of gum from his shirt pocket and folded it in his mouth. "Would you really expect any less from Marino?"

"No, not really."

"Then I say, let's man-up and kill that motherfucker once and for all."

They exchanged glances.

"We *are* good at this shit, aren't we?"

"Damn straight."

Wiping the sweat from his forehead and commanding his hand to still, Mac turned the corner. Thoughts of what they'd been through in the last few days made Mac's heart hitch a beat and his jaws lock.

Quietly and unselfishly, Em filled a void he never knew existed. He'd gone through his whole life deliberately avoiding any type of commitment.

In his own way, he'd kept on the move. Never home for any length of time. Wasn't he always the first to volunteer for a tough assignment? Daring, risky, a tad too bold, perhaps. All the signs were there, but Mac had never taken the time to analyze his lifestyle.

In his mind, it all came down to his job. The next assignment. Being the best at what he did.

Now that Em had walked into his life, none of that mattered. Not even his job. He only wanted her safe and in his arms.

Mac parked the truck and took a deep breath. After hiking the wire onto his shoulder, he and Brody headed down that imaginary dark alley where only the brave or foolish dared to venture.

***

Emily turned the light on in the closet and reached up to pull down the attic stairs. Slowly, trying to prevent noise that would alert her captors, she held her breath and hoped no one heard. As soon as the ladder touched the carpeted floor, Emily rushed up the stairs. She wasn't going to give herself time to talk her way out of this. Not the darkness, or the insects, or anything else that might be in there besides her.

Instead, she'd find an exit.

Turning around, she went back down to the closet. She then locked the bathroom door, switched off the light and ran back up the attic stairs. Once there, she squatted and pulled the folding ladder up to close the opening. Coughing from all the dust, Emily struggled with a couple of two by fours she found between the rafters. She wedged one in the brackets to prevent the door from being pulled down.

After the exertion, she sat on the attic floor panting, her palms resting on her thighs, head down as she struggled to catch her breath. All the while, she wished Mac was there. He'd know how to get them out. But he wasn't here, and she had to move forward.

Standing on bare feet, she prowled around, looking for light. Far off in a corner of the eave, a sliver of light guided her to a square, wooden vent. As badly as she needed out, she had to be careful and silent. Crawling over air ducts and making sure her feet stayed on the

184

wooden beams, she managed to make it to the other side of the house.

She prayed no one below could hear her.

With her face pressed against the slats, Emily could only see bricks on another house. She grabbed the middle board and pulled with all her strength until it gave a little. Encouraged with the small success, she braced her foot against the wall and yanked with both hands.

One side gave way and she fell backwards with a palm full of splinters. Convinced she'd made enough progress to continue, she disregarded the pain and wrenched off the other end of the board. With it free, she looked out at the side of the house next door. Then her gazed plunged to the ground. A good ten-foot drop, but she would take any chance she could to get away.

Once the other boards were removed, she had about a fourteen by fourteen inch square window. She saw the front of the house on her left and the back to her right. Not a single person in sight.

Maybe she'd get lucky.

Turning around, she rolled onto her stomach and scooted her legs out of the vent. Just when she tried not to think how hard the ground would be, Marino's men pounded on the attic door.

Knowing her chances were slim to zero, Emily wiggled until her body was free of the attic. Frantically, she hung on the ledge.

Suddenly, the sounds of tires squealing, and guns firing filled the quiet neighborhood. Emily screamed. Men shouting *in Russian* had Marino's men in the back rushing to the front of the house.

Emily felt she'd been suspended for hours. The rough wood dug into her already painful palms. One glance down and the thought of letting go jacked up her heartbeat and had her rethinking her actions.

Her slippery hands made her tighten her grip.

Shouts came from below. Emily closed her eyes and prayed she wouldn't break a leg when she hit the ground.

She released her grip.

For a moment, she sailed through the air...too fast. Eyes squeezed shut and holding her breath, Emily gritted her teeth and forced her body to go limp.

An involuntary squeal split her lips.

In seconds, she landed on something…*soft*.

Her eyes flew open when two strong arms curled around her, and Mac pulled her to his chest. "Oh my God, you're alive."

"Mac, where have you been?"

"Trying to save you. Brody and I were about to rig a zip line when all the Russian's came barreling down the street. Then I saw you hanging out the vent up there and decided to get here before you broke your neck." He took her by the arms and held her away from him. "Are you okay? Did that bastard touch you?" He turned her chin. "What happened to your face? And your mouth is bleeding."

"I'm fine. They locked me in a bedroom." She buried her face in his chest and drank in his scent, enjoying the safety of his muscular body.

A gunshot chewed up the dirt next to where they stood. Mac looked up and drew his weapon in one smooth motion. He fired and the man fell out of the attic and landed at their feet with a loud thump. Neighbors must have called the police because sirens coming their way sounded in the distance.

Mac grabbed Emily by the arm, and they sprinted through the gate leading to the backyard of the house next door. Hand in hand, they raced toward the opposite side of the house. Mac pressed his ear and said, "Brody, I caught her. When the Russians get away, tell Jake to let it rip."

As they dashed along the side of the pool, Emily clutched Mac's hand, afraid to let him go. They turned the corner and crawled through the fence where several slats had been kicked out.

The front of the house, where she'd been held captive, blew up, giving them the opportunity to make it to the waiting vehicle.

Mac released her hand and guided her to Brody. "Take her to Falcon." He grinned at her. "Find some shoes while you're at it." He stepped back. "I'm going after Marino and I'll meet you there."

"No!" Emily grabbed his shirt and pleaded. "Mac, let it go." She released him and stepped back with her arms spread eagle. "Look at me. I'm safe. No harm came to me. I want you to walk away from this, Mac. For both of us."

Determination hardened his jaw and gave his beautiful blue eyes a sinister look. "I can't, Em. This ends today." He lowered his gaze. "One way or another."

Without another word, Mac turned and stalked toward the house and Marino. Brody guided her out of the yard and into the pickup. Emily took one last look back. Mac had a gun in each hand, edging around the corner. She blinked back the tears as they drove away.

CHAPTER TWENTY-EIGHT

His men shouted the bitch had escaped, and Ramón Marino ran toward the bedroom door. A blast came from the front of the house, knocked him down, and filled the house with smoke. He crawled across the carpet toward the French doors. With his men protecting him, he made it out the side gate where an SUV waited for him.

Angel kicked open the rear door, and Marino dived into the vehicle. Once secure, the SUV took off and sped down the street. Shots rang out in the quiet neighborhood. Afraid to lift his head, Marino remained on his stomach. The stench of stale cigarette smoke assaulted his nostrils and curled his lip.

When the sound of gunfire lessened, Marino flipped onto his back. He thought of all the times he'd been so close to killing McKinsey and never once had been given the pleasure of watching the son-of-a-bitch suffer. He was like a fucking snake. Somehow McKinsey crawled his way out of every dark corner in the world.

Angry, Moreno grabbed the man next to him by the shirt. "What the hell happened, Angel? Who's the snitch that told McKinsey where we had the girl?" He shook the man violently. "Who?"

Defeat left a cruel bitter taste in his mouth. Sweat popped out of every pore in his body. He wanted answers and could no longer stomach the bitterness of knowing the man he hated still lived.

Covered with dirt and grime from the explosion, Angel stuttered, "I don't know. Maybe Bruno?"

"Bruno did not know where we were."

The driver spoke up, "*Jefe*, you know Falcon. They probably had a tap on the phone Bruno used when he called you." The man behind the wheel looked back. "Don't you remember Bruno calling you?"

"Of course, I do," Marino spit out. But he never expected the boy he'd taken off the filthy streets of Bogotá, without a single morsel of bread, to turn on him like a dog.

Hot anger blurred his vision. His body trembled with rage. To think that Bruno, of all people, would betray him. Dark images of how he would torture the traitor played out in Marino's mind. His family would suffer the most. Before putting a bullet in his brain, Bruno would watch as everyone he cared about died a slow, torturous death.

"Where in the hell did the Russians come from?" he asked. "Who called in the Russian mob?"

"I don't know," Angel insisted.

Determined not to let this end with McKinsey still alive, he ordered the driver to pull over in a nearby strip mall.

He jumped out of the van and went to the side of the SUV. Then he yanked the driver out of the seat and onto the concrete. When the man looked up, Marino shot him. He was through messing with fucking idiots. Idiots like that bastard Bruno. His time on earth was coming to a close.

When Angel stepped around the side of the vehicle, Marino motioned him to get into the passenger side of the van. With the gun pressed against that guy's nose, he said, "No more betrayals and no more mistakes. Today, McKinsey dies or I will blow up the whole fucking place."

He enjoyed the fear in Angel's eyes because fear and fear alone was what controlled men.

Kicking the dead body out of the way, he slid behind the wheel and headed toward Dallas. Speeding west to the 183 freeway, Marino thought about the circumstances that had placed him in this situation.

Nothing was right when a man dragged family into business, and that's exactly what McKinsey had done. What kind of crazy man would break into a convent and kidnap a young woman?

Tears welled in his eyes as his thoughts turned to Angelina. She was so pure and so much a part of him. For her, he would have done anything. Anything she asked. But McKinsey snatched that opportunity away from him like Russians grabbed money. That bastard had robbed him of his only true love.

189

Killing McKinsey was too good for him. No, this would not be so quickly done. McKinsey would suffer as much as Ramón had. The time had come for the agent to get his heart ripped from his chest. To watch the one he loved die, knowing there was nothing he could do to stop it.

Ramón knew what some of his hired guns thought of him. A man in love with his younger sister was not natural. Not ordained by God. But how can anything be more natural than to love your own blood?

And on that fateful day, when he'd signaled her death, no one knew what pain it had caused him or the torment he'd suffered ever since. The many nights he lay awake and whispered her name in the darkness.

Tears dripped from his chin as he whispered, "Angelina, tonight I avenge your death, or I join you."

CHAPTER TWENTY-NINE

Mac jumped from Jake's SUV, and they both walked into the office of Falcon Securities. Em ran into his arms, and he buried his face in her hair, inhaling the lingering scent of her floral shampoo and spearmint clean body. A smile tugged at the corners of his mouth as he remembered she'd made good use of his Jacuzzi.

She leaned back and he looked into her gorgeous honey brown eyes. His heart sped up and raw need burned inside his chest.

"Is it over?" she asked. "Is he gone?"

"I don't know. We still have people going through the rubble. But one of our surveillance guys said he saw a black SUV drive away. He couldn't see anything because of the tinted windows."

The smile slid off her face. "So, he might be out there?"

Frank came over and put his hand on Em's shoulder. "You're okay, and that's what matters most."

"But he'll just come for us again." Em's brows wrinkled and she looked at Frank, then back at him. "He wants us both dead."

"What he wants and what he gets are two different things," Brody said.

"And," Jake added, hip against the desk, "he could be dead."

She looked at him. "Do you think he's dead?"

Mac stepped away from her and ran his fingers through his hair. At a safe distance, he turned. Foot braced on the wall, he leaned back and folded his arms. "My guess is he's alive and on his way here."

"I agree," Frank said. "That's why I want you to take Emily as far away from here as you can. Go to the lake house. I want you to disappear until we confirm Marino is dead."

Mac didn't like that idea. Marino belonged to him. That bastard was his kill, and right now being cheated out of that pleasure didn't sit well. "Maybe Jake can take Em." Mac pushed away from the wall. "I want to be here when, and if, Marino shows up."

"Mac," Frank began. "Be reasonable. Let me, Jake, and Brody handle this. You worry about Emily."

"I *am* worried about her; that's why I'm staying."

"Mac," Emily said. "Either leave here with me now, or..."

He turned to her. "Don't say something you'll regret."

Her mouth hardened and anger narrowed her eyes. "Don't worry. I won't." She stepped to Jake. "Can you get me to a hotel? I'm leaving now." She turned to Mac. The visible hurt and rage turned her features stoic and sad at the same time. "Stay here with your crazy vendetta and get yourself killed."

She stalked out with Jake behind her, although his fellow agent paused between the doorjambs and gave him a questioning glance.

Mac shook his head. This was something he had to do, and he wasn't going to change his mind. Hopefully, Jake would talk her into going to the lake house where she'd be safe.

But at what cost?

His heart felt like it had been trampled by the Budweiser Clydesdales, and his breath was trapped prisoner somewhere between his lungs and his throat. Nerves tightened with the realization his only chance for happiness had just disappeared. Mac sighed and let all the pain Marino had caused roll over him, surround him, and seep into his psyche.

Frank squared his shoulders. "Son, you have to get past this Marino thing. Emily is a wonderful woman. I think you made the mistake of your life."

"I just saved her."

"That's a matter of opinion," Brody said, cleaning his nails with a pocketknife. Head bowed, he continued, "Sometimes a bullet hurts less than a broken heart."

As Mac took his gun out and checked his rounds, shots vibrated through the building. Mac hit the door first with Brody right behind him. Frank grabbed his gun and followed in pursuit.

When they got to the elevator, unlit lights announced the power had been cut. Mac slammed back the door to the stairwell and darted down the stairs. The thunder of feet followed behind him.

They crashed open the garage door and drew their weapons. As they ran to the vehicle Jake would use, they saw him sitting on the cement.

His Glock had been tossed a good ten feet from his position. He'd taken a slug in the leg, but was okay. Brody ran over and pulled Jake out of the line of fire behind a concrete pylon.

A man jumped out of the SUV and ran down the parking garage to safety. In the dim light, Mac's focus clashed with Marino's hard glare. He had his forearm around Em's throat and a 9mm at her temple. Mac's heart paused for a second before slamming hard against his ribcage. Air left his lungs and the color red filled his peripheral vision.

At this very moment, a DVD of his worst nightmare played out before him. Em was in the hands of a man who wanted him dead more than he wanted to breathe.

Mac stood perfectly still, pushed Em from his mind, and focused on one thing.

Killing Marino.

"You think you are some badass motherfucker, don't you, McKinsey?" Marino pulled Emily closer to him and pressed the gun's muzzle harder. Em squeezed her eyes tightly and hunched her shoulders. "Well, you ain't so fucking bad." Spittle flew from Marino's tight lips. His harsh features deepened in the dim light. "I got your bitch, man. What you gonna do about that?"

With his gun at the ready, Frank said, "Let the girl go, Marino. You know if anything happens to her, you won't leave here alive."

"Shut up!" Marino shouted. "All of you clear out of here. This is between me and that son-of-a-bitch."

"Then let her go, and you two can shoot it out," Frank said.

Marino's evil laugh echoed through the covered parking garage. "Oh, no. He dies and so does she." Marino leered at Mac. "But she dies first. Just like my Angelina."

"Bruno said you ordered her murdered," Mac shouted. "You killed your own sister."

"No! It was because you spoiled her. You ruined her as my bride, my wife, the mother of my children."

Mac shook his head. "I never touched her. Yes, I was with her every minute she was in my custody, but an armed female agent was her bodyguard. I was never alone with her." He pointed his finger. "Angelina didn't have to die."

"No!" Marino shouted. His face raw-beef red. "You lie." He staggered slightly. "I'm going to blow her brains all over the place."

***

Her body numb with fear, Emily slowly opened her eyes and looked at Mac. The gun barrel against her temple hurt. How much pain would she feel when the bullet sliced through her brain? How long would it take her to die?

Quickly, she prayed.

Brody held Jake while keeping his gun trained on Marino. Frank stood next to Mac, his gun staring at Marino. On the other hand, Mac's weapon hung next to his thigh.

The last four days fast forwarded through Emily's mind, and she realized how very little she knew the man across from her. Yes, they'd made love and had gotten close, but she didn't know the man inside his skin. While they'd been through so much, Mac had always kept a part of himself separate. A place she couldn't touch because she hadn't been invited.

Now it taunted her like a bully on a playground.

The knowledge that he didn't love her in return and never would crumbled her heart. He'd go on fighting the bad guys and keeping danger at bay. But the real man would never be revealed.

Warm tears of sadness, not fear, glided down her cheeks as she listened to her heart break.

"Why don't you just leave this between me and you? Let the woman go."

"Oh, you'd love that, wouldn't you?" Marino tightened his arm around her neck. "Not going to happen."

"You know Angelina didn't love you."

"You shut up."

"She loved Bruno."

"No, that is a fucking lie."

Mac shook his head. "No, it isn't. She told me one night. But I think you've known all along."

"Enough!" Marino shouted. "This ends now."

194

Emily watched as the air in the parking garage stilled. The outer noises silenced, and everything fell away. She, Mac, and Marino were all that existed.

Time slowed to a crawl.

Knowing that at this moment Mac was alive, yet stared death in its ugly face, she could only pray.

He blinked.

Was this the end?

He braced his legs and sucked in air through his parted lips then slowly released it. Without moving any part of his body, Mac pulled his gun and fired.

The deafening noise sounded like Big Ben had just struck with her in the bell tower. It seemed to echo and reverberate in her heart, seizing her breath in its wake.

Nothing moved.

Marino's hold on her lessened. Then he slumped to the ground. His black eyes stared into emptiness. A trickle of blood oozed from the perfect circle between his eyes.

Emily's body went limp. If it hadn't been for Frank and Mac, she would have face planted on the concrete. Her body trembled, her thoughts swirled, and it all became too much.

Darkness closed in like a fog rolling off a turbulent sea. Mist engulfed her completely, sealing her off from the world.

***

"That was one helluva shot," Frank said as Mac carried Em into the office. An ambulance had been called for Jake. "Someday, you're going to wonder what would have happened if you'd missed."

"I already am."

"You're a good shot," Frank added, "but I wish you hadn't taken it."

Mac's heart pounded like a set of bongo drums in his chest. Adrenalin pumped through his veins like a shot of morphine. "I saved her life."

"Yeah, but Emily saw the ugly side of you. I don't think seeing you in action is going to set well."

"I can't help that." Mac rubbed his neck and closed his eyes. "It's what I do."

With Em safely on the couch, Mac looked down and knew with a certainty that shattered his soul that he'd never see her again. Not unless Falcon business necessitated it.

"I'm going to the hospital to check on Jake. I'll be around."

Frank pointed to Em. "What about her?"

Mac looked away. "She's going to be okay." His voice cracked like a fresh egg. "Em's tough. She doesn't need someone like me."

"And you know that how?"

"Frank, none of us are marrying material."

"Who in the hell decided that?"

"Maybe it's an unspoken rule. You think she's going to want anything to do with me after seeing me drop a guy? No woman in her right mind would hitch up with a guy like me. Besides, next time I *might* miss. Or worse, lose my nerve and do nothing."

"Mac, she has to know you did what you had to do."

He walked what seemed like a mile to the door. "Yeah, when she comes to, tell her that and see if she believes you."

Out of the office, he took the stairs to the bottom floor. Cops and CSI were all over the place. He gave them a statement. When they learned Marino's Interpol status, there wasn't much left to say.

Mac got in his car and drove to the hospital and checked on Jake. That took about five minutes because he almost had a stroke cussing out Mac for taking such a tough shot with Em's life on the line.

Sadly, Mac went home, stood in the shower and let the warm water wash all the stress and anguish from his body. With his palms against the tile wall, he stood there mentally going over his shot. It *was* a good shot. Sadly, one he'd made all too often, but this one left him rattled and nauseous.

What if this once, he'd missed? Slowly, Marino's crumpled body morphed into Em's. Scalding tears blurred his vision. Intense pain knocked him to his knees. Hunkered in the shower, Mac buried his face in his palms and cried, until the shower ran cold and the tears no longer stung his eyes.

CHAPTER THIRTY

Belize
Two weeks later

Brenda stretched and sat up. She yawned then reached for a bottle of water in the ice bucket next to her beach chair.

"We having fun yet?" Emily asked.

"Oh God," Brenda groaned. "I'm ready to go home, except I don't think my stomach will let me fly."

"I warned you. But would you listen? No." Emily laughed. It sounded strange to her ears after so much sorrow. "Never party with the natives. They're better at it."

"Now I remember you saying that." Brenda squinted over at her. "About the time you finished off your third Margarita."

"The difference is I stopped there. Unlike someone I know. Someone who spent most of the night hugging the toilet."

Brenda put her sunglasses back on. "Shut up." She rolled over with a moan. "When did the sun get so frickin' bright?"

"Always has been."

Brenda sat up and gulped more water. Emily looked out at the Caribbean coast and smiled. The turquoise water, the warm sunlight, and the swaying palm trees were just what the broken-heart doctor ordered.

She'd finished a warm stone massage, a yoga class, and thirty minutes in the sauna. Her body felt relaxed and renewed, while her heart struggled to mend.

"I'm glad I punched your sister."

"I know you are."

"She deserved it."

"Definitely."

Brenda looked at her. "I wish I'd punched Stanley too. And choked those two dogs."

"No one has the right to hurt a dog."

"Okay, maybe just super glued their mouths shut."

Emily laughed. "Poor doggies. They don't know they sound so obnoxious."

Brenda rubbed her face. "I guess I should be glad she didn't sue me."

"I wouldn't let her do that."

"Did you get in touch with that guy? The one you did all the investigating on?"

"Yeah, I did, and I think Mac is going to be very happy."

"What about you? Are you ever going to be happy?"

"I'm working on it. I'm smart enough to know when to walk away. Mac's a great guy, but he can't be my guy."

"Love stinks."

"You're right. Love only wins the day in movies. In real life, love is elusive and damn hard on the heart."

"Maybe we expect too much from men?"

"As opposed to marrying the first guy wearing pants?"

"I agree. Let's keep our standards high."

Emily dropped her glass and rolled out of her chair, laughing. "What's the deal?"

"We have high standards? What about Howard?" Emily asked.

"Howard was a mistake."

"Howard was a thief."

"In my defense, I didn't know that until my brother ran a check on him."

"How smart can he be to date a detective's sister?"

"Duh." Brenda joined in the fun. "He looked so surprised when Kenny showed up at the door with an arrest warrant."

"You told me he peed his pants."

Brenda turned hysterical. "He did."

"And there is always me with Stanley. I can't believe I was that desperate."

"I don't think you were desperate. In a strange kind of weird way, Stanley isn't so bad."

"You're right."

"Until he took up with your bitch of a sister. That's so low, he's crawling on his belly."

"Poor Stanley wasn't the first man to fall for Victoria's charm. I think she's taken every guy I've ever dated."

"Then why didn't you smack her?"

"I guess because she's the only family I have."

"That's sad. Are you still going to their wedding?"

"I guess."

"I'm not."

"I don't think you are going to be invited."

"Good. I'd throw rocks at them."

Emily tried to put Mac behind her. She and Brenda had been in Belize for four days. Tomorrow, they'd fly back home and life would resume as normal. As if it could.

Emily picked up her cell phone and listened to Mac's voice mail again.

"Instead of playing with your phone, call the guy, for crying out loud." Brenda slipped on her sandals and walked toward the waves. "You have nothing to lose."

"Just my pride."

Brenda stopped and looked back at her. "How does that make you feel in the middle of the night?"

"He only wants to apologize, and I don't want to hear it. The man doesn't love me. He just wants to know I didn't commit suicide or something."

"The lies we tell ourselves."

Emily pushed the delete button and erased Mac's message asking her to call him back. It had been days. Time she got back to her life.

Frank had taken care of getting her another house and had put Mr. Dooley in charge of restoring everything back to normal. While Emily hadn't put out a dime, somehow whatever she needed or wanted magically appeared.

When her phone rang, Emily jumped. The caller ID was one of her clients in France. She'd been expecting the call. Next Monday, she had a corporate meeting in Paris.

***

Bedford, TX

Home from a recent assignment, Mac locked the door and looked around his silent apartment. After putting his gear away and showering, he'd flipped on the TV for another lonely night. A knock sounded at the door. In an instant, Mac's heart went from a normal beat into atrial fibrillation.

Em?

With her gone, his life had returned to normal on the outside. Inside, it was empty as a spent chamber. His emotions felt like they had been spit out of a blender. He wanted to go after her, but couldn't. Besides, she'd made her feelings known by not returning the one call that had taken him all day to gather the nerve to make.

Mac opened the door, and a tall man stood on his apartment landing. "Hi, you John McKinsey?"

"Yeah." This guy looked familiar in a bizarre kind of way. Mac wondered if he knew him from somewhere.

The guy took a deep breath. "I don't know how to say this, but I'm your brother James."

The air gushed from Mac's lungs as he stared into strangely familiar blue eyes. "I don't have a brother," he replied. Denial wasn't working. There was something so primal about this guy. Same height, eyes, built, and stubborn cowlick.

The guy shrugged his shoulders. "I didn't know I had a brother either until I received a call from a lawyer. Emily Richards."

"Em called you?"

The man calling himself Mac's brother put out his hand. "I'm James McKinsey."

Trembling, Mac stared at the offered palm. It represented a bridge to his past. One he feared crossing because he couldn't reverse this situation once the handshake put it in motion.

Fear turned to courage. Mac raised his eyes, clasped his brother's hand and pulled him to his chest. Tears gathered in the corners of his eyes.

When they separated, Mac invited him in and offered a beer. His brother took it and gulped down a mouthful before the questioning began.

"So, how do you know you're my brother?" Mac asked, silently praying this wasn't some cruel joke.

"I was born in '70. When I was a little guy, my aunt took me and raised me. I knew I had a mother, but I don't remember much about her."

"I was born six years later. Mom never mentioned I had a brother."

James rubbed the back of his neck. "Lucy, my…our aunt told me Mom was married to a jerk. Guess no one liked the old man."

"I didn't know him well. He took off when I was seven or eight." Mac finished off his Heineken. "Mom talked about him, but he never came around."

"I heard she was murdered during a drug deal gone bad."

"Worst day of my life," Mac said, his throat tight. "Everything changed after that." Memories rushed forward. Because he'd been a minor when it all happened, they had kept him out of the report and sent him into the foster system. "Mom was hooked pretty bad by the time she died."

"I read the report."

"They told me I didn't have any family."

"I don't know why they would say that. Then again, maybe they asked Lucy to take you, and she refused. I have no way of knowing. I didn't find out Mom was murdered until I became a cop and looked into the report."

"You're in law enforcement?"

"Yeah, I'm a Captain for the Dallas Police Department."

Pride filled Mac's chest and swirled around his heart as gently as a spring breeze. Considering their childhood, they could have become their parents all over again. Somewhere in the gene pool there had to be some decent people who were made of stronger stuff.

"Wonder what Mom would think about what we've become."

"I can't even imagine, since I barely knew her. You know, there are times I can't remember what she looked like," James said.

"I can see her as plain as day. I like to think of her straight, clean." Mac peeled the label from his bottle. "You know she tried a few times. Tried to get away from the dopers, pills, the booze…but she couldn't stay clean long."

"Aunt Lucy and her husband did a great job of raising me, but they had two kids of their own. And while they were really good to me, I never felt I belonged. Then I heard from this lawyer. She

201

came into the precinct several days back and asked me all these questions about my past." James shrugged "It made me wonder."

"I can't imagine how Em made the connection."

"Oh, you didn't hear?"

"Hear what?"

"Couple of weeks ago, Fort Worth PD picked up the old man on some outstanding warrants. Turns out this lawyer's friend, Brenda, has a brother in the department. I guess this Brenda mentioned you to him and started the wheels turning. Anyway, the detective said the guy told him he had two sons."

"Leave it to good old Rayland."

"So, Miss Richards started looking into some closed records and found you had a brother. She showed up at my house last week."

He chuckled. "That sounds like Em."

"You know her personally?"

"Yeah, I do."

James spread out his arms. "Bro, what have you been up to for the last thirty-two years?"

Mac laughed. "We can't cover it all in one visit." He pointed to his brother. "And you, a cop and all."

"And you." James leaned back and stretched his arms on the back of the coach. "Hell, nobody seems to know what you do."

Mac studied the family he'd missed all his life. How many times had he wanted to reach out to someone? How many times had he pulled away, frightened?

"Something I have to say," Mac said. "When Mom was murdered, I was there."

James sat up. "Oh, shit."

"Yeah, I hid in a closet. She'd shoved me in there. I stayed all curled up in a ball. Afraid to come out. Scared to save my own mother."

"You know, at seven you couldn't do much, don't you?"

"I do, but I fear one day on a job I'll turn back into that little kid. I won't be there when someone I love needs me."

"You're not that scared kid anymore, bro." James stood and put his arm around Mac. "You never will be again."

"How do I know that?"

"Because I'm your older brother and I say so," James said good naturedly. "And you need to stop blaming yourself for what happened to Mom. You couldn't save her. She couldn't save herself. From what I hear, you're pretty damn good at what you do."

"Yeah, but there is always a little bit of doubt."

"I know, John. And there always will be. I struggle every day to do the right thing. Just like every other person out there."

"The line of business we're in doesn't leave a lot of wiggle room," Mac said.

"This is how I deal with it. I am what I am. Yeah, I came from bad stock, but I learned a long time ago the difference between right and wrong. And I always try to do the very best I can at the time."

"Yeah, me too."

"Hey, I have another surprise."

"Really, I think you finding me is already a pretty big surprise."

"You have two nephews. Eight and ten."

"Well, holy shit. You're kidding, right?"

"Nope. I have the wife, two kids, a van, and a mortgage."

"Wow," Mac said. "I'm impressed as hell."

"What about you?"

Sadly, Mac hung his head. "Naw, nothing."

"You never married, had kids?"

Mac shook his head. "Work and all."

"That's bullshit, John. I walk around with a big assed target on my back. I worked SWAT for ten years. It never stopped me from being happy."

"Yeah, well, I never got around to it."

"You said you knew that lawyer gal."

"Em?"

James nodded. "She seemed pretty interested in you."

"She's sweet, but I'm no good for her."

James stared him hard in the eyes. "That's crap, John. You've got everything it takes to make someone happy. You got heart, you got honor, and you have a family. And nothing trumps family."

Tears filled Mac's eyes as he cried for the second time in the last couple of weeks. James pulled him against his chest. His eyes were misty too. "I think I've been a royal butthole."

James patted his back. "John, now that I've found you, I'll always be here for you. I'll back your play. I'll pick you up when you're down. And I'll always take your side. But *you* have to make the right moves. Find that girl and make a future. One we can all share for the rest of our lives."

They broke apart and James continued, "Listen, I'm going home, so my wife will know everything is okay. Diane has been a nervous wreck since finding out about you."

"Yeah, I want to meet her."

"You are. Next Saturday. She's got this big cookout planned. Our two cousins are coming and their kids, so be there at one." He turned to leave. "Oh, and bring Em with you."

"I will...if she'll come."

"Oh, that won't be a problem."

"Easy for you to say."

CHAPTER THIRTY-ONE

Paris

Emily dragged herself down the corridor toward her hotel room. She'd had a crappy job dealing with a French business venture gone horribly wrong. Her client wasn't happy and neither was she.

God, she needed a new line of work.

She removed her card key from the lock, shoved open the door to her room, and tossed the key into her bag.

Just as she dropped everything and started to remove her jacket, a rough hand grabbed her from behind and covered her mouth.

She screamed a muffled sound.

"Shh, I'm not here to hurt you."

Recognition plowed through her brain like women at a shoe sale. Her heart lurched, and her knees threatened to buckle.

The hand dropped and she slowly turned.

"Mac?"

He stood in front of her. She swallowed a lump the size of a donut. His reserved smile, those gorgeous blue eyes, and the funny cowlick made him welcome as rain in August. In the dim light, she shuddered at the sight of his tall muscular body.

When she pulled her gaze from him, she noticed yellow rose petals covering the carpeted floor from the door to the window. They blanketed the bed, the end tables and surrounded a bottle of champagne in a silver bucket.

Stunned, she waved her hand. "What's this all about?"

He stood completely still. "It's called an apology."

Looking back at him, everything inside her melted like chocolate in a microwave. "Where have you been?"

"Hiding."

"From me?"

"Oh, you bet." He jammed his fingers into the back pockets of his jeans.

"Because?"

"I couldn't face you."

"And now you can?"

"Now I have to."

Her brows lifted.

"I deliberately didn't tell you about my past. I have an ugly job. I do horrible things. But I do them for all the right reasons. I know you saw me kill a man, and that image will stay in your mind for a long time. I can't help that. But without men like me, there'd be a lot more bad guys around. I can't change what I do. It's who I am, and how I am."

"I don't know what's worse, Mac." To keep from grabbing him and holding on as if her life depended on it, she stepped back. "Being on the firing line or alone and miserable." She flicked tears from her cheek. "After Stanley, I gave up on relationships in general. I never meant to fall in love again."

"Not my plan either." He moved closer. "But I did." He touched her arm. "I met my brother, and I learned something."

Her eyes drank him up like margaritas during Happy Hour. "What?"

"That I could love someone. Let her into my life. Be happy and surrender everything, yet lose nothing."

She sniffed away the tears. "Look at you, all philosophical."

"Love makes a man do crazy things. It's time I stopped being an ass and reached out and touched someone." He took her hand. "I want that someone to be you."

She turned away, unable to think. "I've been hurt so many times before. I don't think I—"

"I give you my word of honor I will love you until the day I die. I'm not ever going to let you go. I'll protect you with my life and I'll always come back from a mission…to you."

"And if I object?"

He pulled her into his arms and kissed her as if his entire future depended on it. His lips against hers were warm, welcome, and wonderful. He tasted like forever. Once again, she found herself against his body. Her resistance shattered. She only wanted to remove their clothes and put that king-sized bed to good use.

Softly, he pulled back and smiled. "Overruled, Cupcake."

**Bonus: A sneak peek at the next Falcon Book:
Out of the Shadows**

CHAPTER ONE

Click.

The undeniable sound of a weapon being cocked sliced through the quiet Texas night. The cold, hard steel of a gun barrel touched Kate Stone's right temple. Inside her darkened bathroom, her breathing stilled, and so did her feet.

Before her next heartbeat, a strong arm coiled around her neck. A quick shot of adrenalin hurled her into action. She kicked and yelled while clawing viciously at the forearm across her jugular. The assailant jerked, and her back collided with a chest hard as the weapon.

With a flex of his biceps, the attacker tensed, and Kate stretched to her toes, hoping to relieve the pressure on her throat. Another move and her air supply would be severed completely. Not willing to let that happen, Kate struck back her elbows.

Afraid she'd pass out if he did something stupid, Kate locked her jaws, kicked backward and pushed with all her strength. A grunt slipped from her lips. Barefoot and taken by surprise, she couldn't break free.

An erratic heart tempo shook her chest as she fought. At the prospect of having only seconds to live, Kate looked around frantically to get a visual on the intruder who'd breached her security.

From the corner of her eye she spotted, reflected in the vanity mirror, a vague outline of a tall male dressed in black. She didn't need to look. Instincts told her a man held her hostage.

The pungent smell of his testosterone, and the feel of a body designed to fight told the story. By all indications, the situation wouldn't end well, and she wasn't foolish enough to expect a miracle.

Deep in the shadows, she sensed the ugly face of death sneak a peek at the situation and laugh. Ignoring defeat, her training kicked in, and a strained calm settled in place.

He hadn't covered her mouth. That meant he knew she slept alone and lived far enough from her neighbors that no one would hear a sound.

Tightening her jaw, Kate inhaled deeply, tensed her muscles then slammed back against the hardened body. On the silent count of three, using all her strength, she forcefully bent forward, trying to flip the man over her shoulder.

She grunted from the effort, but achieved no results. This guy had either nailed himself to the floor, or he worked as a sumo wrestler.

Slippery sweat covered her skin where their bodies met.

Not giving her opponent time to regroup from her last attempt, Kate swung her foot back behind his leg, hooked his calf and kicked out.

He didn't budge.

"Who do you work for?" she gasped, digging her nails into his leathery flesh. By God, she had the right to know who had put out the mark.

No reply.

Gritting her teeth, Kate tightened her fists and jabbed her elbows back. She landed a solid blow to his ribcage. A puff of air whizzed past her right ear. He staggered against the bathroom wall and sent a picture to the floor with a crash. Yet his confining hold remained firm.

"Cut the shit," he hissed against the side of her face. The warmth of his breath on her cheek sent a frosty warning down her spine, splashing through her body like a burst water balloon. The creepy rasp of his voice clawed at her flesh. "You want to die tonight?"

Kate shook her head, flinging strands of hair away from her face. "Maybe the cards will turn in my favor."

"Don't count on it."

"Oh, I'm counting on it, all right. Kicking your ass is my new goal."

"Lots have tried. Few succeeded."

"Good. I always like to be among the elite."

A harsh chuckle vibrated in his throat. "They were just lucky."

"Ha. Says the loser."

Whoever this guy was, he was broader than her back and a good seven inches taller than her five feet five. When he yanked her tighter, masculine heat slipped around her like a second skin.

Discomfort constricted her muscles and her jaw tightened in helplessness as his chest, stomach, and thighs pressed intimately against her body. The bulge between his legs rested near the waistband of her panties.

How could this happen? Yes, she was an agent for the CIA and considered good at what she did. Of course, she had enemies, but she'd made sure they couldn't find her. Her own home had always been a safe haven.

The assailant flexed the muscled forearm beneath her chin to get her attention, and Kate tensed.

How long had he been in her house? Long enough that his body had acclimated to the fact that her air conditioner had gone out and the house felt like a sauna. Even the whirling fan overhead did little to ease the discomfort.

"I'm not here to hurt you," said a voice hard as metal and rough as a nail file. "But if you get stupid on me, I'll waste you without a second thought."

Controlling her breathing, Kate sniffed. No cologne or deodorant. No garlic or liquor on his breath. No scents, no sounds, and no features. The man knew his business. He was a pro.

She licked lips dry as burnt toast. "What do you want?"

"You, Kate Stone."

"Why?" Hope that this might be a mistake evaporated. No mix-up or random act of violence. She *was* the intended target.

Sweat drenched his body. Thick, course hair covered an arm strong enough to snap her neck before she could scream. She had to do whatever necessary to keep that from happening.

It appeared he didn't intend to hurt her. Not yet anyway, but that could change at some point.

"I have a little score to settle. The bad news is you're the bait."

She tightened her grip on his arm. "I still don't know what you're talking about."

"If you're lucky, this will be over soon." The gun to her head, he ordered, "Move."

Her shoulders plastered against his chest, he loosened his grip and slowly slid along the wall. "Watch the broken glass." His arm skimmed to her waist, and he lifted her effortlessly. He stepped backwards and then lowered her feet to the bedroom carpet, so quickly she hadn't time to think. "Don't want you cutting your feet and leaving a trail of blood."

His familiarity with the surroundings proved he'd been here before, and that insulted her personally and professionally.

Kate's skin sizzled at the closeness of their damp clothes. She stumbled and brought her bare foot in contact with the toe of his boot. Were they military or covert?

Few could manage what he'd just pulled off. Anyone in her occupation knew the first line of defense was self-protection. Leave nothing to chance. She hadn't.

The sophisticated alarm system cost a fortune, but she'd considered the expense a wise investment, until now. Doors rigged, windows sealed, and the outer perimeter clean, clear, and unobstructed. She thought she'd created a safe environment...*evidently not.*

The invader paused. His scratchy jaw scrubbed against her cheek, setting her nerves ablaze. "I've warned you that I don't plan to hurt you. But, you cooperate or die."

Cautiously, she released one hand from his arm, leaned over and reached out.

Pulling her away from the bed , a chuckle rumbled from his chest. "The first thing I did was take the gun from beneath your pillow."

"I may not give you a reason to blow my head off," she gritted out. "But before this is all over, you may wish I had."

***

Brody Hawke blew off Kate Stone's threats as nothing more than talk. Okay, she was capable; he'd give her that. And the CIA considered her one of their best agents, but she was still a woman. A woman he outweighed by a good seventy-five pounds, and over whom he had eight years experience.

The bureaucratic CIA could take a flying flip and kiss his ass. Oscar Chavez and his drug cartel had his partner. People didn't last long in Chavez's custody, and A.J. had been there two weeks. Brody's buddy's chances were slim to none.

Brody had scoured beneath every rock, searching for a way to rescue his friend. Then out of the blue a source told him the drug dealer and Miss Stone had once been lovers.

The exact edge Brody needed.

When the heel of his boot landed on a wooden floor, Brody knew they were in the hall and heading in the right direction. The woman froze when his right elbow brushed the wall and the gun jammed against her temple.

Good. He wanted her scared. Otherwise, it could get ugly, and he didn't want this to blow up in his face. After ten years of covert action, he'd never hurt a woman, but desperation edged him on to do whatever necessary to bring A.J. home.

Brody had considered and reconsidered a hundred different scenarios before resorting to kidnapping a federal agent. He wasn't stupid enough to think he'd get away with this shit.

Hell fucking no.

The time would come when he'd pay for his actions, but the cost didn't matter.

Getting A.J. back on American soil was the only thing he cared about. When a man takes a bullet for you, there wasn't much you let stand between you and saving his ass.

His hostage deliberately took smaller steps. "Don't go limp on me, Stone. You won't like the results."

"I already don't like the results...or you."

For the last six days, she'd been his obsession. After he learned about her and Chavez, he wondered what her superiors would think if they knew. The things he'd found out about people thanks to good contacts continued to amaze him.

The scent of body lotion and freshly washed hair slapped Brody in the face like a wet rag, but he resisted the urge to dip his nose. The exotic aroma of a woman at nighttime couldn't tempt him.

If he had to harm her, he damn sure didn't want to remember her scent.

Walking backwards, Brody paused at the sliding glass door in the living room. He glanced left and saw the rear door still open.

Days earlier on recon, he'd memorized how many steps from the bathroom to the exit then deliberately broken her air conditioner, hoping she'd unlock a window, but she knew her business. So he'd spent ten minutes picking the high tech backdoor lock without a flashlight instead.

Talk about a challenge.

Desperate for time, Brody knew he had to get her outside, in his car, and tied up. The man inside Chavez's camp expected them by twelve thirty. He had to be on time. Late could mean death for A.J., and he'd already been held too long.

As they reached the door, a powerful elbow slammed into his sternum. With a strangled *whoosh*, his lungs emptied and his knees buckled. When he bent to gasp for air, Stone pulled loose, spun out of his grasp, and sprinted out the back door. She vanished in the blackness like a ghost.

"Son of a bitch!"

Though familiar with the yard, Brody had left nothing to chance. Reaching in his cargo pants pocket, he pulled out his night-vision goggles. Once in place, he caught sight of Stone pole-vaulting over the eight-foot privacy fence into her neighbor's yard.

Very good. He'd been careless to underestimate Stone and not to take care of her escape route. He had the same setup in his own yard.

Taking off at a full run, Brody catapulted over the fence, landed on all fours then caught sight of her slipping through the gate. Wasting no time, he followed her to the street. Once there, he took off in a dead run. Brody calculated he'd have her before the first intersection.

Sweat stung his eyes as he watched his prey practically fly. Damn, she ran like a guy. Her long strides, frantically pumping elbows, and high chest had her in the lead by a good margin.

The hot Texas wind carried the scent of cut grass and scorching asphalt. The humid air slammed against Brody, flew through his short hair, and plastered his black T-shirt to his chest.

Watching her sprint toward the main highway, Brody smiled as adrenaline surged through his body. Those bare feet would surely hamper her progress.

Swallowing great breaths of air, Brody struggled to catch up. He groaned when she moved further ahead of him. With or without shoes, the woman could move.

Then he remembered she ran marathons to keep in shape. She could run for miles.

Brody thought of A.J. and increased his speed. She could run, but so could he. Kicking it up a notch, he ripped off his night-vision goggles and stashed them in his pocket. Driven by desperation, he gained on her every time his foot hit the pavement.

Made in the USA
Lexington, KY
14 June 2015